Rapid City Summer

Connie Richardson

Black Rose Writing | Texas

ISBN: 978-1-68513-592-8
PUBLISHED BY BLACK ROSE WRITING
www.blackrosewriting.com

Printed in the United States of America
Suggested Retail Price (SRP) $20.95

Rapid City Summer is printed in Minion Pro

*As a planet-friendly publisher, Black Rose Writing does its best to eliminate unnecessary waste to reduce paper usage and energy costs, while never compromising the reading experience. As a result, the final word count vs. page count may not meet common expectations.

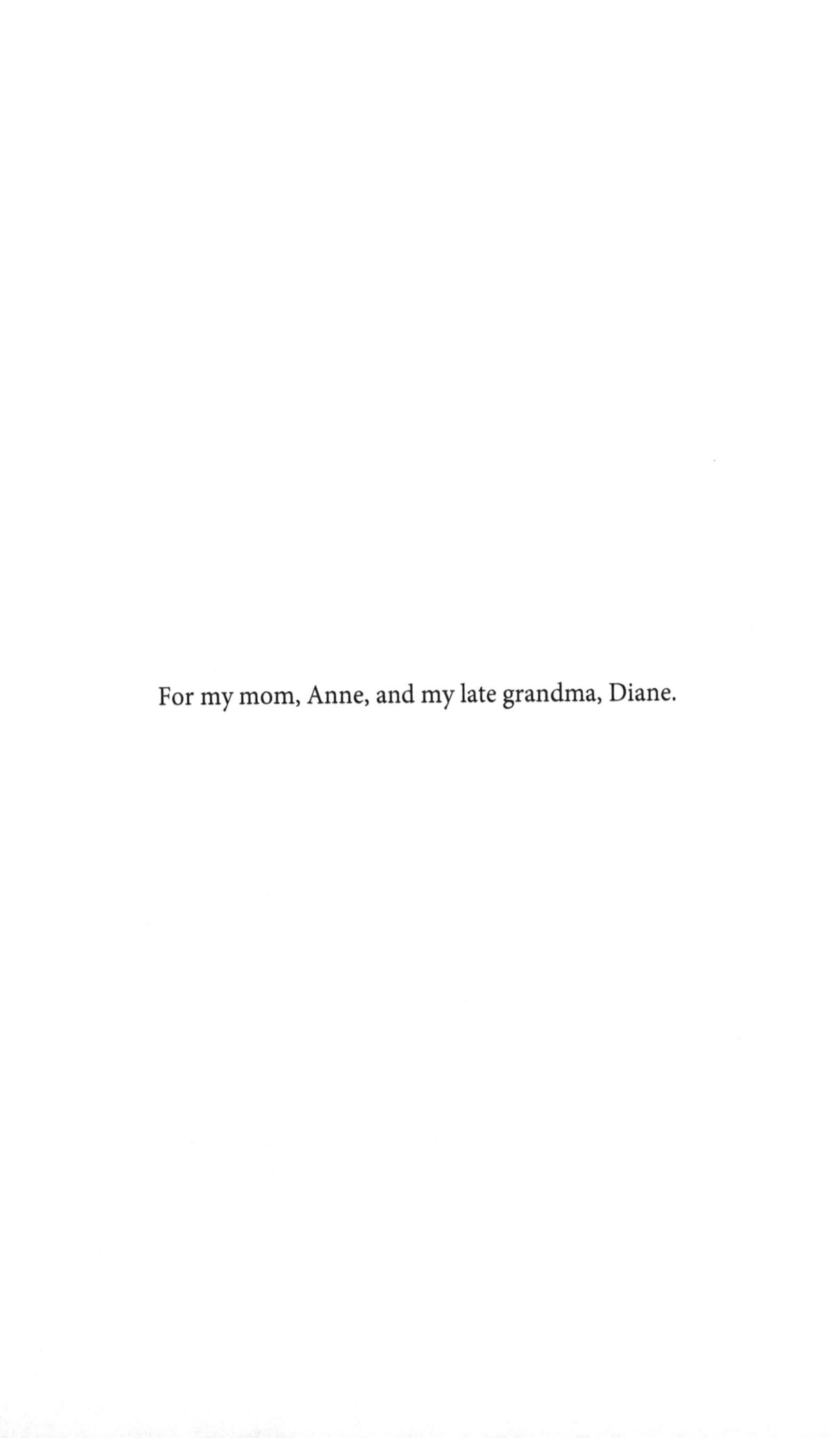

For my mom, Anne, and my late grandma, Diane.

Praise for

Rapid City Summer

"A touching exploration of change, courage, and the power of stepping beyond the familiar–a reminder that the biggest risks can lead to the greatest rewards."
–**Sublime Book Review**

"New friends, fly fishing, family struggles, and the great outdoors. Natalie learns what adventures South Dakota has to offer and will teach readers that change isn't necessarily a bad thing. A good bridge for those going from middle grade to young adult novels."
–**Kim Oclon, author of *Man Up* and *The War on All Fronts***

"Connie Richardson has crafted a heartfelt, coming-of-age story that tackles all the tough stuff of young adulthood: homesickness, first love, family conflict, belonging, and finding yourself. *Rapid City Summer* is sure to empower young readers to step outside their comfort zones and find the courage to believe in themselves."
–**E.C. Quinn, author of *Premonition: The Gift***

"A beautiful coming-of-age novel—like *A River Runs Through It* for middle schoolers or Sharon Creech's *Absolutely Normal Chaos*!"
–**Cam Torrens, author of the *Tyler Zahn* series**

Rapid
City
Summer

Chapter 1

Early June

"What's so great about South Dakota besides a mountain with some old guys' heads on it?" I asked.

"You'll find out soon," Dad replied.

"How soon? We've been in the car for over twelve hours already!"

Dad and I left our home for the past fifteen years, the Chicago suburbs, at 5 a.m. to get to our new home in Rapid City, South Dakota, before sunset. While all my friends were sleeping in and planning pool days to kick off their summer vacations, I was stuck in a car with my dad, staring at cornfields. I thought the burbs were boring, but nothing could prepare me for southern Minnesota. So when I saw the wooden "Welcome to Rapid City" sign, I felt a mix of dread (because we were officially in our new hometown–no turning back now) and joy (because I survived twelve hours of dad jokes and counting hundreds of Wall Drug billboards with my father).

Ping! I heard simultaneous notifications from my dad's phone and my own, which meant one thing: Mom texted the family group chat. I looked at her message—seven new pictures. She was standing in front of the new house, smiling with her arms in the air. She looked peppier than the cheerleaders at my old school.

Arrived at the new house! So did all our things! Can't wait for you both to get here. Natalie, you'll love the backyard!

She started her new job at Black Hills State University a few days ago, so she left the burbs before we did to attend orientation and get the keys to our new home.

We exited I-90 and drove into my new hometown. My first impression was that Rapid City reminded me of the Chicago suburbs because of all the stores and restaurants. I felt a sense of relief when I saw a Culvers AND Crumbl Cookies. Yet this familiar-looking place was unfamiliar in every other way. I noticed a creek that cut through part of town–it looked straight out of a Hallmark movie.

After several minutes of driving through town, Dad turned into our new subdivision. Soon I recognized a house I had only seen in pictures from online listings: on the corner lot was our new, blue house with the big yard. A large U-Haul truck filled the driveway, and Mom and a man I didn't recognize were unloading boxes.

"Looks like your mother made some new friends already," Dad said, suspicious of the strange man helping Mom. She smiled and waved at us, acting like she hadn't seen us in years.

"You made it!" she exclaimed as we exited Dad's car. "Isn't it so pretty here?" Mom wrapped me in a big, sweaty hug, and I quickly wrapped one arm around her before pulling away. I knew she was happy about getting this new job, but the rose-colored glasses wouldn't work on me. She clearly forgot how pissed I was about uprooting my life, or she was too busy with her new job to care.

I just finished my freshman year of high school, where I was a top distance runner on the cross country and track teams. All of my best friends were on the team with me, and we planned to run 5Ks this summer and train for the upcoming cross country season. Our goal was to qualify for the state meet as a team.

Now, my friends and my dreams were almost 900 miles away. My heart ached, realizing how lonely I already felt and all the things I will miss out on.

"How was the drive?" Mom asked while the strange man continued to bring boxes into our garage.

"Fine," I grumbled.

"Great!" Dad said. "We stopped at Wall Drug and counted over 100 Wall Drug billboards on the highway. They have five-cent coffee and free ice water!" Dad was a sucker for a good deal. "We also got to see some of the Black Hills. It's even more stunning in person compared to the pictures."

"Why are they called the Black Hills?" I asked.

"There are so many pine trees covering the hills that from a distance, it looks black," Dad explained. "You can start to see them here in Rapid City. We'll have to drive further west soon to see them even better."

I remembered seeing an abundance of pine trees scattering the hilly landscape as we approached Rapid City, but I didn't know what was so special about them. I still didn't get the appeal, but no majestic landscape, or even being reunited with my mom, would make me feel better right now.

The still-unnamed man walked up to us. "I wanted to give you all a moment before I introduced myself. I'm Mato." He reached out to shake Dad's hand, and then mine. "I'm your next-door neighbor."

"Mato introduced himself as soon as I pulled up with the U-Haul and offered to help unload until you got here. None of our neighbors back home were that friendly!" Mom said.

"And I'm happy to help in any way I can. My son should be out soon; he's finishing up some other chores in the house."

I looked around, taking in the sights of our new neighborhood. Mom was right (I hated admitting that): this neighborhood seemed way more inviting than our old neighborhood in Illinois. I never saw my old neighbors. I knew who they were, but had very few interactions with them. Within five minutes of being in our new neighborhood in South Dakota, I saw a group of six boys ride their bikes down the street, and a family of three walking their two golden retriever puppies. Everyone waved and smiled at us. Then I saw an older woman walking up our driveway, grinning from ear-to-ear and holding a casserole dish.

"You must be our new neighbors!" The lady gushed. "I'm Joanne, I live kitty-corner from y'all."

"I'm Jack," my dad introduced himself. "This is my wife Trish, and my daughter Natalie."

"What a beautiful family!" Joanne exclaimed. Was she always this cheerful? "Where y'all from?"

"Chicago," Mom answered. The actual answer was Arlington Heights, but it was easier just to say Chicago.

"That's such a big city! I used to live in Texas but moved to South Dakota ten years ago to be closer to family. I'll never leave."

Mom replied, "We didn't really want to leave, but I got a job at Black Hills State that was too good to pass up. And I also have family in the area. My mom lives ten minutes away."

"How wonderful! You must be so excited to be so close now."

We all looked at each other, collectively unsure how to respond. That was the reason we almost *didn't* move here.

"Anywho," Joanne drawled, "When I saw the moving truck pull up earlier, I thought I would whip you up a little something to eat. Just some chislic and potatoes."

"What's that?" I snapped, immediately regretting how rude I sounded.

"Seasoned lamb cut into bite-sized pieces. It's a South Dakota staple."

"Thank you," Dad said, smiling and taking the casserole dish from Joanne. "We should get back to unpacking."

"Of course. Holler if you need anything! Nice to meet you all!" Joanne gave each of us a hug before walking back to her house.

"Well, isn't she sweet!" Mom said. "I think I'm going to love it here."

Well, that would make one of us.

"Nat, can you help Mato unload the last boxes out of the truck?" Mom asked before she went inside with Dad. Left with no choice, I was stuck outside with this stranger.

"I'll come help in a second," I called to Mato as I pulled out my phone. I opened my text thread with my best friend, Syd.

`Just got here. Miss you already` I sent with a crying emoji.

Immediately, three dancing dots appeared, followed by Syd's message: `Dude come back!! Who am I gonna watch The Office with?` Followed by three crying emojis.

As I was typing, a deep voice startled my concentration. "Nat, I hear you like to run?" I looked up and saw Mato carrying a big box out of the moving truck. Feeling guilty for not helping, I shoved my phone in my pocket and hurried to help him.

"Yeah," I answered. "I ran cross country and track back home. Our team was pretty good."

"What's your favorite event?" Mato asked.

"The mile," I said, thinking about how close I was to qualifying for the state meet at sectionals only a few short weeks ago. It was devastating to fall short of my goal, but I was proud of running my personal best of the season at that meet.

"The cross country and track teams here are pretty good. I wish my son, Adam, would run."

As if on cue, a tan boy with dark hair and a royal blue t-shirt walked toward us. He looked around my age. He smiled and waved at me.

Maybe South Dakota wouldn't be so bad after all.

Chapter 2

"Welcome to Rapid City!" The tall, tan boy grinned. When he got to Mato and me, he extended a hand, and I noticed his toned biceps. "I'm Adam."

Adam. I didn't know any Adam's back home. I suddenly felt so self-conscious about my handshake. My hand felt like a dead fish compared to his strong, calloused grip. His dark blue eyes made me blush. After a few seconds, I realized I still hadn't said a word, which made the situation even more awkward. "I'm Natalie."

"Nice to meet you, Natalie." Adam turned to introduce himself to my parents, who somehow magically appeared back outside without me noticing. Out of the corner of my eye, I caught the glance Mom and Dad shared. Mom raised her eyebrows and grinned, and Dad looked oblivious, as always. Even though Dad had no clue, I knew exactly what Mom's look meant.

"Adam, can you grab some water bottles for our new neighbors?" Mato lifted a cardboard box with "silverware and placemats" scribbled in Sharpie on the side.

"I'll take that box," I said, giving myself something to do to avoid the awkwardness of my parents' looks. I also needed a moment to process the *literal* hot boy-next-door.

I weaved my way through a maze of boxes in the garage to reach the door, then stepped into the mudroom before walking down a short hallway that led to an open main floor. I could see the living room, dining room, and kitchen from where I stood. This house was so different from my home in Illinois. There was no island for me to sit down and snack after school while Mom cooked dinner. I noticed a fireplace in this living room. Did it actually work? Could we have wood-burning fires in the winter? I guess that would make up for no kitchen island. I ran my hands over the textured, white-painted brick of the fireplace. Mom would want to hang our stockings on the oak mantle over the fireplace instead of on the stair railing; I heard her talking about it when she and my dad did a Zoom house tour with the realtor.

"Want some water?" Adam's voice pulled me back to reality. I turned around, and Adam was leaning against the stainless-steel fridge, holding a water bottle. I nodded, walking over to him and taking it from his hand.

"Thanks," I said, feeling my cheeks blush.

"Must have been a long drive out here."

"Yep. Thirteen hours. What a great way to start summer break." My voice dripped with sarcasm, but I felt self-conscious for sounding so whiny. I was making a horrible first impression.

"My family drove to Chicago a couple of summers ago. No offense, but the drive got more boring the closer we got to Illinois. And don't get me started about the traffic in the city!"

Was he trying to convince me already that this place was better than my home? More importantly, why was someone this cute still talking to me?

"Yeah." How embarrassing–I couldn't come up with anything better to say than "yeah?"

"So, how old are you?" Adam asked. Either he didn't notice my nerves, or he was talking to me out of pity.

"Fifteen, going on sixteen in October. I'll be a sophomore at Rapid West."

"It's not a bad school. I'll be a junior this fall. Just turned sixteen last week and got my license."

Not only was he cute, but he could drive! My friends back home would die when I told them this. They may all have their pool parties and summer races, but I have a cute neighbor that can *drive*.

"Well, I'll let you get back to unpacking. I'm sure I'll see you around." Adam walked out the garage door.

My bedroom was on the second floor. The only furniture set up in my room was the bedframe and mattress. The neat freak in me couldn't stand the mess of boxes scattered around, so I had to start unpacking right away. I found my comforter and bedsheets and made my bed. In that weirdly normal moment, the reality of the move sank in. Right now, I'd probably be walking to The Freeze with my friends to get ice cream or starting a bonfire in our old backyard. Sounds from outside my window brought me back to the present moment–an electric guitar and other loud instruments. I opened the window that faced Adam's house, and the sounds grew louder. I looked down and saw Adam on the driveway, placing a wireless speaker on the ground.

"Do I hear Zeppelin?" Dad said as he walked past my room.

"Maybe?" I was horrible at identifying rock bands, and I knew my dad was ashamed of me because of it. I couldn't identify Led Zeppelin songs; he couldn't identify Billie Eilish songs. We're even.

"Our neighbors have great taste in music. Do you need any help in here?"

"No, I'm good." I fake-smiled at Dad and got back to adjusting the blue sheets on my bed.

"Ok. I'll heat up the chislic. I'll holler when it's ready."

When Dad walked down the hallway, I couldn't hear any floorboards creak. The upstairs hallway at our old house had lots of creaky spots that I knew to avoid, so I wouldn't wake my parents if I stayed up late or got home late from hanging out with friends. This house felt too perfect, too new. No quirks or oddities, like the squeaky floorboards, that made a house feel like a home.

After I unpacked a couple of boxes, I looked out the window again to see if Adam was still there. He was, but I noticed some long, skinny fishing pole laying on the driveway. Adam was sitting on a wooden stool, deep in concentration. He was trying to tie something, but I couldn't tell what. I also noticed a few open plastic containers, filled with dozens of furry, fake bug-looking things.

"Crap," Adam grumbled. He rolled his head to the right, and then to the left, before he resumed tying the miniscule object. It appeared to be some sort of bait for fishing, but I had never seen a fishing pole that long and skinny before, or bait that wasn't live worms.

How bizarre, I thought while moving onto the next unpacking project: running clothes. I had to get those unpacked tonight, even though I was exhausted. Exercise was our family's form of stress relief and bonding time, so tomorrow morning my parents were going to ride their bikes while I ran. Before we moved, Mom looked up trails and parks for running and biking. Luckily, there were a lot.

I pulled out a neon pink t-shirt from this past track season and was transported back to Illinois. This t-shirt was from the sectional meet where I just missed qualifying for the state meet in the mile by less than two seconds. I left it all out on the track, but 5:13 wasn't enough that day. The memory amplified the heavy mix of emotions I already felt.

I wondered what my friends were doing right now, so I took a Snapchat of myself with a forced smile unpacking my room. I sent it to Syd, and a group of girls from the track team.

Moments later, Syd replied. I recognized her basement, with the air hockey table and the soft blue sectional couch. The caption read, "Burbs are boring without u" and a crying emoji.

Normally, I would hop on my bike and ride the few blocks over to her house to hang out. Now, I have no one's house to ride my bike to, and no one to hang out with.

Mom knocked on my door before entering. Her eyes were wide with surprise. "Woah, you've done more unpacking than Dad and I have! Maybe we'll just leave all the unpacking for you!"

That gave me a much-needed laugh. "As much as I don't want to, I also don't trust Dad to unpack anything. Remember when Dad put the floss with the utensils because he said we could cut soft foods with it?"

Mom laughed. "That's why he's only allowed to put things away in the garage. You and I will take care of the rest." She changed the subject and asked, "You doing okay?"

"Yeah," I lied. I didn't need Mom worrying about me.

"Great," she said, believing me. "I think you will really like it here. Dinner is just about done. I had a bite of chislic, it's delicious! Come down in a minute to eat." She walked away, looking down at something on her phone.

The sight of my dusty running shoes on the floor made my eyes well up with tears. I could only hide my feelings for so long. I was optimistic about the move when I saw Adam, but even a cute boy could only cure my homesickness for so long.

Chapter 3

Although I set my alarm for 7:30 a.m., the sun woke me up an hour and a half before that. I hadn't thought through where my bed was facing in relation to my windows, but this east-facing window couldn't keep being my natural alarm clock. Note-to-self: order blackout curtains ASAP.

As much as I wanted to unpack everything last night, I only got through half my boxes. I rolled out of bed and walked over to a box marked "Notebooks & Books." On top was my freshman year journal. The cover had some pictures taped to the front of Syd and me, and some smiley face stickers. I liked how Ms. Laker, my freshman English teacher, let us decorate our notebook covers however we wanted. She was one of my favorite teachers I'd ever had.

I flipped through the journal, and the ache in my chest returned. This notebook encapsulated what I was like back at home. I wrote a lot about my friends, running, and the books I was reading. My journal entries were relatively positive, reflecting my glass-half-full mentality, which was how I viewed life back in Illinois. Besides Adam, Culvers, and Crumbl Cookies, I had yet to find other positives here.

During the last month of school, when I had just found out we were moving, Ms. Laker had this prompt on the board: *The transition from middle school to high school is a big life change. You have experienced a lot of change this year. People respond to change differently. How does change make you feel?*

I read my last journal entry, my response to that prompt, uncharacteristically scribbled in angry letters and red pen: *I was nervous about starting high school—who isn't? But I was lucky to have a couple of groups I already fit in with. I have my girlfriends from middle school, and my cross country and track teammates. It was a smoother transition than I expected. It seems like most of us have found where we fit in.*

For almost everyone, they'll come back to school in the fall knowing how to navigate the halls, which teachers give the least amount of homework, and planning spirit wear outfits for all the football games. But for me, everything is about to change. The house I live in, the state, the time zone, the people I go to school with. Nothing will be the same.

I think change is less scary when you kind of know what to expect. I had an above-average freshman year: my teachers don't suck, I was one of the top runners on the cross country and track teams, and I have a solid group of friends. Now I have to give all of that up for some dumb school in South Dakota.

Change is the worst when it's unknown and out of your control—and I don't like the unknown or being out of control. If it were up to me, I wouldn't go to South Dakota with my parents. I would stay right here in Illinois.

Well, that wasn't an option anymore. I glanced at my phone. 6:21a.m. Ugh. I put the journal down and went back to bed, but I heard Mom and Dad talking downstairs, and they sounded angry. Why were they up already? Another note-to-self: this house wasn't very soundproof. I tiptoed over to my door and cracked it open to hear better.

"I thought you were happy about the decision to move," Dad stated.

"Overall, yes. I finally have my dream job after not working for fifteen years. But when we said we were moving closer to my mom, I didn't think we would be ten minutes away."

"Would you rather we had moved to a cabin in the middle of a forest?"

"Of course not." Mom's voice was agitated.

"And we wanted a town Nat would like, right?"

"What kind of question is that?" Mom snapped.

"Well, you wanted to move to Rapid City. We could've moved to Pringle. The population is less than 200. I know you girls would love that."

"Knock it off, Jack. Rapid City is a big enough town, but now I'm second-guessing why we picked this neighborhood. I still don't know how I feel about being so close to my mom."

Dad spoke even more quietly than before, so I had to really strain my ears to hear the rest of the conversation. "This will be great for Nat. She has a right to know her grandma. Your mom isn't a bad person."

"Well, she's a crazy person."

"Bad and crazy aren't the same."

"Sometimes they are."

I couldn't hear the rest of the conversation after that. I saw my grandma a few times when I was really little, but I didn't have memories of those visits. So anything I knew about my grandma was based on what Mom and Dad had told me.

According to my dad, Grandma is fun, thoughtful, and adventurous. She was always up to try something new and always has an interesting story to tell. She's lived a lot of life in her years, and Dad admires that. But Mom didn't admire that about Grandma. According to Mom, Grandma would miss a lot of things she did growing up because she was traveling for her job as a flight attendant, but she always found a way to turn her work trips into a vacation. My Grandpa's job was more stable and required no traveling, so he was the one picking my mom up from school, taking her to her friends' houses, and spending time with her on the weekend. To me, that seemed like a petty reason to be mad at someone for so long. Was there more to Mom's resentment toward Grandma that she wasn't sharing? Would I learn more about their relationship now that we lived ten minutes away?

Considering this was my last living grandparent, I hope she wasn't crazy. I wanted the grandma that made cookies and gave cool gifts my parents wouldn't buy for me. More importantly, what if I actually liked her? Would Mom get mad at me if Grandma and I got along? I really didn't want to cause problems because of my relationship with my grandma–if Mom would even be okay with me getting to know her.

Most of the time, I was fine with being an only child. But I wish I had a sibling right now who would help me figure this out. Or at least a good friend close by. All of mine were 900 miles away.

6:32 a.m. I had been awake for less than an hour and was suddenly exhausted. I hoped we didn't make a mistake moving here.

Chapter 4

Beep-Beep-Beep!

I jolted awake, reflexively slapping my phone to turn off my blaring alarm. I threw on my running clothes and groggily went downstairs. My parents were ready for their bike ride, sipping their coffee in the kitchen, waiting for me.

"Good morning! How did you sleep?" Mom asked.

"I slept okay," I lied. I didn't need Mom to know I was up early and heard her conversation with Dad. "I can't believe how early sunrise is around here."

"We're on mountain time now, honey. The days get even longer here in the summer than at home. That means more time to be outside!"

Dad tossed me a banana and handed me a glass of water before going into the garage with Mom to finish getting their bikes ready. I devoured the banana, drank some water, and double-knotted my running shoes. Now that I was up and moving, it felt good to be in a familiar routine, even though everything was so different here.

"How does four or five miles sound to you? Mom found a park here in town with an eight-mile trail, but we can do as much or as little of it as we want."

"That's fine." It wasn't like I knew where else to go for a run.

"Great! Let's start on the outskirts of town, then make our way toward downtown. We need to pick up groceries afterward so that there's more to eat besides frozen pizza."

Mom and Dad strapped their bikes to the back of our car, and we drove a few miles to the trailhead at a dog park. Along the way, I noticed a big, brown brick building that looked like a school.

"That's your new high school," Mom said.

"How are their cross country and track teams?" I remember Mato saying the teams here were pretty good, but he was still essentially a stranger to me.

"Not bad, I think," Mom said. "I saw their girls' cross country team qualified for state 3 years ago." I was surprised Mom researched the teams. Based on that information, they didn't sound as good as my team back at home, but it was better than nothing. She continued, "You should join them for summer running. Might be a good way to meet some people before school starts."

We drove a few more minutes before getting to the dog park. As we got out of the car, some people turned to look at us, and then our Illinois license plate. They were used to seeing license plates with four presidents on them, not just Honest Abe. As these strangers smiled and waved at us, Mom and Dad waved back, but it felt uncomfortable to me. Why were these people being so friendly? I eventually gave an awkward smile and a quick wave, too.

This dog park reminded me of my favorite long run route near our old house. The path wasn't by a dog park, but people were always walking with their dogs on the trail. To pass the time on long runs, Syd and I would always count dogs. Our record was seventeen. Our coach would get annoyed because she would ask how our run was, and I knew she meant our effort level, but Syd and I would rate our runs by our total dog count. The more dogs we saw, the better the run was, even if we felt like crap that day. That memory made me homesick, wishing I was running with Syd and counting dogs together.

"Our first South Dakota workout!" Dad kissed Mom before they clicked on their helmets and got on their bikes. I set my Garmin to run mode and took off.

I started jogging at an easy pace, letting my legs get warmed up. The path had a gradual incline, so the first mile or so was slightly uphill. After that, the path leveled out and stayed flat for the next few miles. In Illinois, I was used to noisy runs: cars honking, tires squealing, music blaring. It was still noisy here, but in a different way. I heard the wind rustling through the trees. I listened to the speed of the water in the creek, picking up and slowing down alongside the path. As we ran past other people walking, running, and biking, every single person said hello to my parents and me. Mom and Dad stayed a little ahead of me the whole time, and I heard them laughing and talking about some new show they started watching on Netflix. I got so lost in my surroundings that four miles flew by, and I stopped counting dogs after the eighth one. The only part of that run that didn't feel effortless was my breathing. Even though I was running at an easier pace today, it felt like my lungs couldn't get enough air.

"We're barely in elevation, but I sure felt it today," Dad said as he got off his bike.

"There's an elevation change here?" I asked.

"Yep. We're a little over 3,000 feet."

"Do you know what the elevation was back home?"

"Somewhere between 600 and 700 feet."

Between the elevation change and my unsettled nerves, no wonder I had a hard time breathing today. I couldn't imagine what it felt like to run at really high elevation. I'd probably vomit or pass out. Or both.

"Will we get used to it?" I asked.

"Of course," Mom chimed in. "Just like anything new, it can take some time to get used to."

Chapter 5

It warmed up quickly during our run and bike ride. After picking up some groceries, all I wanted was to feel the blast of the AC back at the house. But when I opened the door, I was sucker punched in the face by the heavy, sticky heat.

"Why is it so hot in here?!" I exclaimed.

"The house was set at 72 this morning." Dad hurried to the thermostat to see the current temperature. Suddenly, he bellowed: "84 degrees!"

"I thought the inspector said the HVAC system looked fine?" Mom pointed out.

Dad ran his fingers through his sweaty hair. "Clearly it's not."

"I'll start looking up someone who can fix this as soon as possible." Mom pulled out her phone and began searching for names and phone numbers. Dad did the same, but stood with his head in the freezer to find some relief from the heat. We were all sweating just from standing in the house, and it was getting hotter by the minute.

Dad's voice echoed from the freezer. "These guys have great reviews. I'll give them a call."

"While you call, give me a turn in there," I begged. Dad grabbed an ice pack for his head, and I took his spot by the freezer. I had never been more thankful for the cold. A couple of minutes later, Dad hung up the phone.

"The soonest they can be here is tomorrow morning. They're booked today."

"At least they'll be here tomorrow." I understood Mom's calm, optimistic approach, but that didn't help us stop sweating like pigs. I needed to contribute to this adult conversation about broken air conditioners. There's no way in hell (and let's be real, the house was already hotter than hell) we could stay here until tomorrow morning.

"So what will we do until then? We're not staying here all day, are we?"

"Absolutely not. We can get a hotel room for the night," Dad suggested.

"Wait," Mom interjected. "I can ask my mom if we can stay with her tonight."

"Are you sure?" Dad asked.

"Listen, I'm not thrilled about the idea. But at least her house is free."

"You make a good point." Dad couldn't pass up a good deal, especially if it was free.

"I'll call her." Mom stepped into the living room. I heard muffled bits of their conversation.

"Hi, Mom. Are you busy?... Of course you are. Well, there's a bit of a problem here... No, not that kind of problem. Our air conditioner went out... yes! Thank you. We'll pack some bags and head over soon." As soon as Mom hung up, she groaned and shuffled her way back to the kitchen.

"She said we can come over, but she was going to bake cookies and organize her photo albums today. She would be 'delighted' for us to come over and do those things with her." Mom rolled her eyes.

"Remember, her house is free. Your words." Dad reminded Mom.

"Well," Mom looked at me, completely ignoring Dad. "You get to see your grandma a little sooner than planned. Go pack a bag for tonight and let's get out of here as soon as possible."

Less than ten minutes later, our bags were packed, and we were en route to Grandma's house. Dad cranked the AC in the car as high as it would go. On the drive over, I thought about how all my friends back home would talk about spending time with their grandparents over the weekend or during holidays. Syd's grandparents would even come to our cross country and track meets, ringing cowbells and bringing chocolate chip cookies to indulge in after each race. I had never experienced that with my grandma, and hoped I could, now that I lived so close to her.

We pulled into a neighborhood with houses that looked much older than our new house. The houses were spread out throughout the neighborhood, with lots of land separating each property. Dad's car slowed in front of a blue ranch with a rocking chair on the front porch. A mature oak tree was the focal point of the front yard. Before any of us got out of the car, a woman opened the front door. She had shoulder length silver hair and wore a lilac t-shirt and white, flowy linen pants.

"You're here!" the woman exclaimed. She walked with ease down the driveway to our car. My first thought was that she seemed so happy to see us, and I felt confused about what caused such animosity between her and my mom. Then I noticed how quick she could walk, and I immediately felt like a terrible person assuming she would be slow and frail.

"Hi Diane." Dad got out of the car and hugged Grandma. "Good to see you."

Mom took her time grabbing her bags, so I went to give Grandma a hug next. Her eyes doubled in size when she saw me. "Oh, Natalie! It's been years since I've seen you. Look at how tall you are!" Not that five-feet five-inches is tall, but I was taller than when I was at six-years-old. She gave me a strong, tight hug. Her hair smelled like lavender, and I immediately felt my body relax, despite how unnerving it was to see my grandma for the first time in nine years.

She pulled away and asked, "What's taking your mother so long?"

"Good question," I replied.

Mom finally got out of the car and forced a toothless grin. She extended only one arm for a hug, but Grandma didn't seem to notice or care. "Trish, I'm so happy you're only ten minutes away now."

"Yeah." Mom adjusted her purse strap and walked toward the house. Dad, Grandma, and I followed her. Pink and purple flowers lined the walkway, and scents of chocolate and sugar wafted from the front door.

"The first batch of cookies is almost done! I wanted to make these with you and Natalie, but I got bored waiting." Grandma held the door open as we walked in.

Grandma's house was unlike anything I had ever seen before. My first impression was that there was a lot of stuff. Everywhere. It was beyond overwhelming. Picture frames packed on shelves, trinkets displayed on the tables, throw pillows covered so much of the couch that I wondered if someone could even sit on it. A massive crocheted quilt covered the hallway wall leading from the front door, past the living room, and into the kitchen.

"I made it last summer. Took me a little over a week. It's too pretty to keep folded up!" Grandma led us into the kitchen—or what I thought was the kitchen, but it could easily be mistaken for the Nestle Toll House Factory. Pans, flour, sugar, eggshells, and chocolate chips covered the countertops. A turquoise KitchenAid mixer was blending the next batch of dough. The oven timer beeped, and Grandma scurried over to the oven. She put on pink and yellow floral oven mitts and pulled out the first batch of chewy chocolate chip cookies.

"Anyone want milk with these?" Grandma asked.

"Sure." I took up her offer to be polite, even though I didn't want milk. "I'm going to use the bathroom first." This was my chance to take a closer look at Grandma's stuff and get away from my cranky mother, who was sitting at the kitchen table on her phone. If homemade chocolate chip cookies couldn't cheer her up, nothing would.

I walked past the bathroom and went directly to the living room. I felt dizzy trying to process all the items in room, so I started with the dozens of pictures hanging above the couch. One image was larger than the rest, and the other photos surrounded it, smaller in size. The large image was a photo of a house I had seen in pictures before: a white house with black shutters, and a fire-engine red front door. A younger version of Grandma stood on the driveway. She was waving at the camera with one hand, and her other arm wrapped around her husband's waist. I looked at my grandpa, a man I had never met. He was almost a foot taller than Grandma, with broad shoulders and a radiant smile. Mom looked just like him. Standing in front of Grandma and Grandpa were two kids: a boy and a girl. The boy was sticking his tongue out at the camera, and the girl was smiling, but I can tell it was forced, like the Snapchat I sent to my friends the other night. The girl looked uncomfortable. Even a little annoyed.

I couldn't think of a more accurate representation of Mom and Uncle Dave.

I moved on to the other photos. One was of Grandma and Grandpa at the Grand Canyon, another was my mom after a cycling race. There were also pictures of Uncle Dave when he graduated from Notre Dame, one of Grandma standing in front of a yellow Volkswagen Beetle. Based on the few stories I had heard, I knew this was Grandma's favorite car she ever had. She cried for days when it finally stopped working. There was also a picture of Grandma holding me as a baby. I had seen this picture before in a photo album Mom made of my baby years. I wasn't sure how I felt about seeing it on Grandma's photo wall of fame.

On the far wall in the living room was a fireplace with little statues and figurines adorning the mantle. They had locations engraved on them, like Austin, Barcelona, and Sydney. Some of the other souvenirs didn't have a labeled location, like a glass jar filled with shark teeth, a dream catcher, and a snow globe with a moose and bear inside.

Across from the couch, in between the two front windows of the house, was a floor-to-ceiling bookshelf. Books, figurines, and pictures covered the shelves. Cookbooks, memoirs and autobiographies from actors, singers, and writers. A black-and-white picture of Grandma and Grandpa on their wedding day.

The living room alone made me realize how little I knew about my grandma. I had seen some pictures and Mom had told me some stories, but I felt like I was in a complete stranger's home.

"Nat, you okay?" Mom walked into the living room.

"Yeah, just looking around."

"There's a lot to look at in here," Mom commented. "Your grandma sure does like her things. Our house growing up was this cluttered, too. Total opposite of my style. Some of these things have been around since

I was a kid. Come over here." Mom walked over to the bookshelf. "See this wooden statue? Grandma got this from a friend who went to Hawaii. Her friend, I can't remember her name right now, knew Grandma loved little souvenirs like this. So she brought it back for her, and Grandma refuses to get rid of it."

"It seems like Grandma is always up to something, or always going somewhere."

"Always. Your Grandma *always* has to be doing something, going somewhere, seeing somebody...she doesn't slow down." Mom turns to look at the family portrait above the couch. She muttered, "And everyone has to be okay with it."

I followed Mom back into the kitchen. Grandma was scooping cookie dough onto baking sheets, and Dad was eating cookies and drinking milk without a care in the world. We sat down at the table with Dad, and I picked up a cookie. I took a bite, and the chocolate chips melted instantly. It was the perfect combination of chocolate, brown sugar, and–

"Natalie, can you guess the secret ingredient in my cookies?" Grandma asked.

"Um, extra chocolate?" There was a unique flavor, but I couldn't quite figure out what it was.

"Espresso powder! I started adding it to chocolate chip cookies a couple of years ago, and it's the only way I make them now."

"Mom, the last thing you need is more caffeine," Mom commented as she picked up a cookie. I'm glad to see she wasn't protesting the cookie-baking anymore.

"Oh Trish, I'm fine." Grandma waved her hand like she was shooing a fly away. But instead of a fly, it was my mom's concerns. "I was just at the doctor and she said I'm as healthy as a horse."

Grandma joined us at the table and shared what she had been up to the past few months: planting her garden, planning a trip to Florida in the winter, deciding which color to re-paint her bedroom, and training for a 5K in September.

"You run?" I was searching for ways to connect with my grandma's busy, vibrant life, and I finally found something we had in common.

"Here and there. I've never run a race before, so I thought 'What the heck?' and signed up! It's the Saturday of Labor Day Weekend. I hear you're a runner. Maybe you'll join me!"

"It's close to the start of cross country season," Mom interjected. "Is that really the best time to sign up for a road race?"

Mom clearly didn't get her cautious side from Grandma. I took a second to put together an answer that would make Mom and Grandma happy. "That sounds fun, Grandma! I'll look into signing up. I can run without going all-out. It would just be a workout day." Mom said nothing, but she slowly nodded her head, which I took as a good sign.

Grandma changed the subject. "I got some photos developed the other day. Do you all want to help me organize them?"

"Sure," Dad and I said. Mom glared at both of us. Even though we had been at Grandma's house for less than an hour, I could tell she had reached her limit of Grandma time for the day. Maybe even the week.

"They're in the basement. We can bring a plate of cookies and get started. Plus, it's nice and cool down there!"

If the main floor was an eclectic collection of knickknacks and keepsakes, Grandma's basement was a full-blown museum, curating as many memories from her life that might fit in this range of square-footage.

I tried not to pass out from sensory overload as I walked down the stairs. A green shag area rug covered most of the basement floor. Autographed portraits of people hung on the wall across from the stairs. Most of the images were black and white.

"These are signed pictures of some of my favorite singers. I've met them all, too."

"Is that Elvis?" I said, shocked.

"Yep. He was a cutie. Met him a year or two before he died. David Bowie was very nice, too. Oh! Do you know who Bono is?"

These were all names I had heard before, but was ashamed to think that I had never listened to their music. I bet Adam had. I would have to ask him next time I talk to him. Intrigued, I asked, "Wait, how did you meet these people?"

"At concerts and events. I'll tell you those stories another time."

The pictures Grandma wanted to organize were on the coffee table, but underneath them, sealed into the table, was some sort of design made of bottle caps. I couldn't figure out what it was with all the pictures strewn over the coffee table. There was a worn-in, dark brown leather couch against a bright white wall. Based on the texture of the wall, I could tell it was shiplap. Smart move to brighten up the space. It was very Chip-and-Joanna-Gaines of her. On the other walls were hanging shelves. I couldn't tell from far away what was on the shelves, so I walked over to one to get a closer look. There were small figurines and bigger figurines. The small figurines were always in a pair: two peas in a peapod, a dog peeing on a fire hydrant, a woman sitting at a slot machine. Then I looked at the larger figurines and noticed what they had in common. They were all pigs.

I had so many questions, but I started with an easy one: "Um, Grandma, are these all piggy banks and salt and pepper shakers?"

Grandma clapped her hands together and squealed, "Yes! I keep my collections down here. Aren't they delightful?"

"So delightful!" I lied. It was weird, but also seemed like a very "grandma" thing to collect. My next question was, "Where does one find this many piggy banks and salt and pepper shakers?"

"You can find them everywhere! Thrift shops, antique shops, souvenir stores, garage sales. You'd be surprised, too, what you can find on Amazon. Look at this shelf. These are my favorites."

On the middle shelf, Grandma had a whole assortment of items with her name on them: a coffee mug, shot glasses, keychains, a small teddy bear, and a pin. "I love going places and finding those souvenirs with my name on them. Surprisingly, I don't always find my name on these things, so it's fun when I do!" I picked up a "Diane" snow globe that had the Statue of Liberty inside of it.

"When did you go to New York?" I asked.

"Pretty recently. I would love your help putting my New York pictures in my photo albums, plus some pictures from other recent trips." I followed Grandma to the coffee table with all the pictures. Mom reluctantly joined us, and Dad sprawled out on the couch, playing some game on his phone. Since Grandma wasn't spending a lot of time with family, she had all the time in the world to travel. These pictures were from New York City, Seattle, Salt Lake City, Denver, New Orleans, and Boston. Those were just her big trips. There were pictures of her in Sioux Falls standing in front of the Falls, and at Devil's Tower in Wyoming. Then I came across a picture of Grandma at a very familiar location. I had been there with my friends, and my parents and I took pictures there after Christmas shopping last winter.

"When were you at the Bean?"

"Last fall," Grandma admitted. "I went to watch the Chicago Marathon."

"Wait." The pieces clicked together in my mind. "I didn't know you were in Chicago recently. Mom, did you know?" I looked at Mom, who was avoiding eye contact with me.

"You were busy that weekend," Mom answered, still avoiding eye contact.

I felt betrayed, like Mom had been keeping secrets from me. "So why didn't you tell me Grandma was in Chicago? I would've canceled my plans. She's my last living grandparent, in case you forgot." I could understand that there was tension in their relationship, but did that mean I didn't deserve a chance to form my own opinions about my family?

"I told you I was going to be nearby, but you never responded." Grandma looked at Mom. "I know you and I haven't been close for years, but there's no need to get Natalie involved in that."

"It's none of your business what I tell my daughter, or who's in her life," Mom snapped.

There was nothing I hated more than when adults talked to each other like kids weren't in the room. And I wasn't even a kid anymore. I could speak for myself. "I'm fifteen. Don't I get a say about who I want in my life?"

"Not when that person lives in her own little fantasy world and acts like nothing is wrong!" Mom yelled. Dad was trying his best to ignore this conversation, but he finally looked up from his phone at us.

"I always wanted you to travel with me and do things with me," Grandma shot back. "I miss spending time with you."

"Because those were the things YOU wanted to do." I never heard Mom get this angry before. "You never care about what I want or need. And you're still that way. Even today, all I wanted was an air-conditioned place to relax. We've been moving and unpacking, I'm starting my new job next week, which you know nothing about, by the way, because you only talk about yourself. And now you want us to help you organize all your crap."

"You don't have to stay here, you know. No one is forcing you," Grandma reminded Mom.

"Honey," Dad finally chimed in. "We have a free, air-conditioned place to stay. It's just one night."

Mom didn't respond. She got up and went upstairs, leaving the three of us in the basement. I didn't know whether to stay with Dad and Grandma, or go upstairs and check on Mom. I got up to go check on Mom, but Dad shook his head and motioned for me to sit back down.

"Let her be alone for a while. She'll calm down soon." Dad said.

"I'm sorry you had to hear all that," Grandma apologized. She did nothing wrong. I didn't understand what started that fight, or why Mom and Grandma didn't get along. "I'm very happy you're here, Natalie, and I hope we can keep getting to know each other better."

"Me, too," I agreed, which was the truth. I'm an only child, and so is my dad. My Uncle Dave lives in Iowa, and he and my Aunt Jackie don't have any kids, so I don't have a lot of family. I wanted the opportunity to get to know someone in this small family of mine, no matter how crazy Grandma might be. I gave her a hug. I could get used to lavender-scented Grandma hugs.

"Tell me more about David Bowie," I said.

Chapter 6

"Enough walking down memory lane. Time for dinner!" Grandma exclaimed. She'd told Dad and me about many of her celebrity encounters, memorialized by the pictures hanging on the walls. Her stories were interesting; I could've listened to them all day long. But I was disappointed that Mom never came back downstairs. She was sitting in the living room when we came up to eat. Although dinner was quiet and tense, I was still relieved to be in air conditioning, and that I could start getting to know my grandma, despite what Mom thought of her.

The next morning, we got up early to get home before the air conditioning guys showed up. When we arrived home at 8 a.m., Adam was in his driveway organizing his fishing gear. My curiosity got the best of me, since I had never seen this kind of fishing tackle before. One time when I was five, Dad tried taking me to a fishing derby. He bought me a pink Barbie fishing pole and everything. I caught one bluegill and wanted to go home after twenty minutes of being at the pond because I was hungry, or something silly like that. That was all the fishing experience I had. I walked over to Adam while Mom and Dad went into the house.

"Hey, Nat," Adam said while holding a box filled with some sort of fishing bait.

"Hey. This doesn't look like your usual fishing gear."

"I'm assuming no one fly fishes back in Illinois?" Adam laughed.

"Not really, no. So this is all for fly fishing? Like in that Brad Pitt movie?" I remembered seeing my dad watch a fishing movie a year or two ago. It caught my attention because of Brad Pitt. Dad enjoyed it because of the fishing and the scenery.

"Exactly like that. Here, check out this rod I just got." Adam picked up a long, green rod rigged with chartreuse fishing line. "I hope we catch a variety of trout today."

"There's more than one type of trout?" I asked, not realizing how dumb I sounded.

"Yes." Adam said as he took out his phone. He pulled up a picture of him holding a mostly silver fish with some speckles all over it, and a pink stripe through the middle of its side. "This is a rainbow trout." He swiped left and there was another picture of him. This time he was holding a fish with beautiful buttery brown scales and brown and pink dots. I noticed a flash of blue on its cheek, too. "That's a brown trout. They're my favorite."

I had to admit, I didn't know fish could be this pretty. "Why are they your favorite?"

"They look the coolest, act the most aggressive, and are the most difficult to catch," he answered immediately. "There's also brook trout and cutthroat trout, tiger trout, bull trout, and more than that, depending on where you're fishing."

"And you catch them using this?" I reached for the rod, and Adam handed it to me. It was lighter than I thought it would be–about as light as my track spikes, and almost twice my height.

"How long is this thing? Ten feet?"

"Close. Nine."

My brain couldn't process how people caught fish this way. "So you use this long rod, with this colorful fishing line, and then what do the fish actually eat?"

"Step right this way!" Adam motioned to an assortment of fishing tackle, Vanna White style. I looked down at dozens, if not hundreds, of objects that looked like bugs, flies, and who knows what else. There was even one that looked like a small mouse. "These are called flies. The goal is to mimic what fish would actually eat, whether it's small aquatic bugs, flies landing on the surface of the water, or bigger meals like grasshoppers or leeches."

"So you don't throw any actual live bugs?"

"Nope. But if they look realistic enough, and I present them naturally enough, then the fish will eat them. But that's if those bugs are what the fish are actually eating."

"What do you mean?" There was so much to learn! Fly fishing sounded so complicated.

"See this fly here?" Adam pointed to a two-to-three inch long fly with an orange belly and light brown back with six foam legs sticking out. "That's a salmon fly. You don't see them in South Dakota, but they hatch in other states like Montana for only a few weeks. If I threw one of those here, no trout would eat it. But if I threw it in Montana during the salmon fly hatch, I could catch fish all day."

"So you have to know a lot about what fish eat and where you're fishing to be good at fly fishing," I said, processing out loud.

"Yes, and no. Some fish aren't super picky. Like to practice casting, sometimes I'll put on a fly that looks like a worm and go to a pond and catch bluegills. They aren't picky. But trout and other fish are, which is part of the fun."

"Interesting."

Adam beamed. He was clearly proud to show off his fly fishing collection, and his knowledge of the sport. "It is! Maybe I can take you sometime so you can see for yourself how it's done."

I barely knew the guy, and now he was offering to take me fishing? I couldn't help but smile at his offer. My hands suddenly felt clammy. I hoped I looked more calm, cool, and collected than I felt.

"Let me know next time you're going and maybe I'll take you up on that offer." I mentally gave myself a high five for being flirty and not sounding like a total dweeb.

"Does tomorrow work?"

That was a little sooner than I was expecting. "I think so! I'll check with my parents, but I don't see why not."

"Great. Just let me know. You can text me. What's your number?"

He wanted my number? And he was so direct about it, too. I'd hung out with boys in groups with my friends back home, but none of them would talk to me one-on-one, let alone directly ask for my number. Adam seemed different than other boys I knew. I liked that a lot.

After we exchanged numbers, Adam walked into the garage and disappeared inside his house, but not before he turned back, smiled, and winked at me. I thought I would melt into a puddle in the middle of the driveway. I hoped he would text me as soon as possible.

Chapter 7

"Adam seems very nice and all, but you don't know him," Mom said.

"I thought you wanted me to make friends," I argued.

"Yes, but I was thinking with kids at your school through cross country and your classes. Not cute boys that live on our street and go fishing in the woods."

"I have an idea," Dad chimed in. "Maybe we can invite Adam and his dad over for dinner and get to know them better. Then we'll feel better about Nat and Adam going fishing together."

"Okay," Mom agreed. "And if Dad and I let you go, you both need to stay somewhere close to here. No wandering off super far yet. Wandering off in South Dakota isn't the same as wandering off in Illinois."

"Want me to go next door and see if they are available for dinner tonight?" Dad asked.

"I can text Adam." I unlocked my phone and sent him a text. Out of the corner of my eye, I saw Mom and Dad glance at each other.

Almost immediately, Adam responded. `Let me ask my dad.`

"He's asking his dad," I tell my parents.

Another text came in. `My dad said you can all come over here. How does 5:30 sound?`

"Adam invited us over for dinner at five thirty. Does that work?"

"Oh, how nice!" Mom gushed. It was a quick mood-swing from being worried for my safety, to swooning over the western hospitality. "Tell him we'll be there."

I confirmed our plans, and he sent a smiley face emoji in response.

I thought South Dakota would be boring, but the past few days have proved me wrong.

•   •   •   •   •

5:30 p.m. rolled around before I knew it. Well, more like 5:20 p.m., because my parents liked to be early to everything. "If you're on time, you're late," Dad reminded me as we walked next door with a large bowl of cut-up watermelon. For some reason, this dinner felt very high pressure. Our first official neighbor dinner…actually, ever. All this effort so I could go fly fishing tomorrow and reassure my parents that Adam wasn't a deranged serial killer.

Dad rang the doorbell. "It's open, come in!" Mato shouted. I opened the door; my eyes immediately focused on a large painting that took up a huge chunk of the wall in the living room. The canvas was painted with vibrant sunset hues–brilliant yellows, oranges, and pinks–in the foreground. There was a bison and a man kneeling on one knee quite a distance away from the bison. The man had shoulder-length brown hair with a feathered headpiece. His gaze toward the bison was a mixture of reverence, yet authoritative. The off-white walls and tan and brown furniture allowed the artwork to be the focal point of the space. I was so immersed in the painting that I didn't realize Adam and Mato joined us in the entryway.

"Welcome to our home. I see you noticed our artwork."

"It's beautiful," Mom complimented.

"My wife is an artist. She painted this," Mato explained.

"I can barely draw a stick person. This is amazing!" I said.

Mato grabbed the bowl from me. "Thank you for bringing watermelon. It's my wife's favorite. She's at an art show now, otherwise she would be here."

"Yeah, Mom spends a lot of her time on art," Adam affirmed. "She isn't home a lot."

Mom, Dad, and I all nodded. I heard the resentment in his voice, and I wondered if my parents did, too.

"Come in, I'll give you the tour," Adam said. "You can leave your shoes here by the door." As Adam showed us the first floor and the basement, I noticed some differences in the home decor compared to any other house I'd been to before. The tables, chairs, and sofas were all various shades of brown, but more beautiful artwork hung on the walls, along with dream catchers, and some mounts of deer and fish. Vases and bowls with intricate designs and hues of red, brown, and turquoise decorated the end tables. Did Adam's mom make all of those, too?

We made our way into the kitchen, where the smells of peppery burgers and salty fries filled the air. There was every condiment I could ever imagine for burgers on the counter. After touring Adam's house filled with indigenous decor and animal mounts, I was relieved to see a normal meal of burgers and fries waiting for us.

"Have any of you ever tried bison before?" Mato asked. We all shook our heads no. I didn't know people ate bison!

"You'll love it!" Adam chimed in. "Dad and I weren't sure how you would all feel about it, so these are a mix of beef and bison meat."

Wait. Did Mato or Adam *kill* the bison we were about to eat? It was an actual possibility, but I was too afraid to ask.

We grabbed plates from the counter and assembled our beef and bison burgers. I brought my plate into the dining room, where the table had extra condiments (Adam and Mato *really* like condiments, apparently. Or they were just that good of hosts), along with a platter of fries and a pitcher of lemonade. Adam sat to my left, Mom to my right, and Dad and Mato sat across the table from us.

Mom thanked Mato for the generous meal right away, and then Dad asked Mato about his deer mounts in the family room. Mato laughed and started telling hunting stories. Half listening, I took a bite of my burger, expecting it to taste a lot different because of the bison meat. To my surprise, it tasted exactly like a normal burger. If anything, it was even more tender and flavorful than a beef burger. Before I realized it, everyone was staring at me.

"Huh?" I mumbled, trying not to show that I wasn't listening.

"Mato asked you what you enjoy doing in your free time," Mom repeated.

"Oh, sorry. I love running. That's probably my favorite thing. And I listen to music, and journal sometimes."

"What kind of music are you into?" Adam asked.

"Um, right now I'm into Olivia Rodrigo and Billie Eilish." I was going to name more people, but Adam interrupted with a chuckle. "What?" I snapped, suddenly feeling defensive of my music choices.

"That's not real music," Adam said. "That's mass-produced radio garbage."

"Alright then, so tell me what real music is," I retorted.

"I listen to a lot of rock, like Led Zeppelin and Metallica, but I also appreciate the Beatles and Queen. Chris Stapleton is my favorite modern artist."

"You have great taste," Dad chimed in.

"Thanks. My first concert was Eric Church. Dad and I drove out to Sioux Falls to see him. It was epic."

"Sure was," Mato agreed.

"All the music I like, everyone has their own sound. And they aren't afraid of being original. Now everyone looks and sounds the same, and that gets boring." Adam grabbed a handful of fries.

I nodded, thinking about what Adam said. Everyone back home listened to what's on the radio, and I never thought about how similar those songs sounded. They were catchy, but maybe Adam had a point.

"Is everyone ready for watermelon?" Mato asked.

"I think so," Adam answered. "I'll go grab the bowl from the fridge."

"I'll help you." I joined Adam in the kitchen, welcoming a needed break from the adults as they talked about inflation and rising gas prices.

"You excited to go fly fishing tomorrow?"

"I'm just happy to spend time with anyone but my parents. I've been with them twenty-four seven since we got here." Setting the cups down next to the ledge of the sink, I leaned against the edge of the counter while Adam took the watermelon out of the fridge.

"You'll love it. In my opinion, it's pretty easy to learn. There's an awesome stretch of creek close to here that I want to take you to tomorrow. There's lots of great water to fish within an hour or so of here, but I won't take you to those places until you've gotten some more practice. And possibly some waders."

"Wait, I have to get in the water?" I did not sign up for this!

Adam laughed. "No, not tomorrow. But eventually, if you want to keep fishing with me."

He was thinking about hanging out with me more, and not afraid to tell me. I wanted to be half as bold and assertive as Adam one day. This–South Dakota, Adam's confidence, bison burgers–was all uncharted territory.

I wanted to keep flirting with him, but knowing our parents were in the next room quickly killed the mood. "So, what time are we going tomorrow?"

"I'll come over in the morning, around eight?"

I would wake up at 2 a.m. if that was what he told me. "Sounds good."

After enjoying our watermelon, we all brought the dirty dishes into the kitchen. Adam and Mato insisted we didn't help clean up, so we thanked them again for their hospitality and walked back to our house. No one said anything on the short walk, but once we were inside, Mom proclaimed her love for our new neighbors.

"Aren't they the best? They're great neighbors. Nat, you can hang out with Adam any time you want."

"I definitely need to talk to Mato about hunting this fall," Dad said.

"Adam is going to pick me up tomorrow at eight," I told my parents. "He's taking me somewhere in town to fly fish."

"Sounds fun!" Mom said. I could've told her we were going to go hang gliding off of Mount Rushmore and she would've been all for it.

"Maybe I'll tag along next time," Dad said. "I've always wanted to learn how to fly fish."

"Dad!"

"What?" Dad said innocently.

The last thing I wanted was Dad tagging along to hang out with the boy I had a crush on.

Chapter 8

I had been awake since 6 a.m., excited to hang out with someone who wasn't my parents, especially since that person was Adam. Even though my friends back home were still sleeping, I was texting them since I couldn't fall back asleep.

Hanging out with the cute neighbor today, I texted Syd. Can't stop smiling. He's taking me fishing.

A few minutes later, I sent a follow-up text: Miss you! Will tell you all about it later. I knew it was early, so I wasn't expecting a response right away. But I didn't have time to think much more about it because I heard the doorbell. Adam was here.

I hurried downstairs before my parents could get to it. When I opened the door, Adam was in front of me with his hands in his pockets. "Hi," he said.

"Hey," I smiled back.

"Good morning, Adam!" Mom's cheery greeting filled the entryway.

"Hi, Mrs. Ryba." Adam looked from my mom to me. "You ready?"

"You can call me Trish," Mom said. I looked at her, having a silent conversation through eye contact, telling her to be cool and not ruin this for me.

"I'm ready." I grabbed a small backpack that I threw together last night with a bottle of water, a chocolate chip granola bar, and a banana. At the last minute, I put my portable charger in there, just in case. "See you later, Mom!"

"Where are you kids going this morning?" I glared at Mom again. "Nat, we're new to the area. I have a right to know where you're going." Even though I understood why my mom was being protective, I was hoping she would give me more independence. I would be sixteen in a few months, not six.

"We're heading to Founders Park," Adam happily answered.

"Sounds great, thank you, Adam." Mom said. "You two have fun!" We walked to Adam's driveway, where his car was packed up and ready for a morning of fishing. I opened the passenger door of his blue Subaru Outback and was engulfed by the aroma of coffee.

"I wasn't sure if you drank coffee or not, so I made you a small one. If you don't drink it, no worries." My mom said I shouldn't drink coffee until I'm an adult, but what damage will one cup do?

"Thanks." I lifted the Styrofoam cup and took a small sip of the scalding beverage. I was prepared to taste liquified dirt, but the vanilla creamer that cut the bitterness of the coffee was a pleasant surprise. "This is good," I commented.

"It's my go-to." Adam started driving to our destination, which was only ten minutes away. Upon arrival, I noticed there was a trail running through the park and a creek behind the trail. There were lots of trees, and I welcomed the shade on this sunny morning.

"This is a great place to learn how to fly fish," Adam explained. "You don't have to get in the water if you don't want to. I don't recommend that today, anyway. Let's get you comfortable casting, and maybe you'll catch a fish, if you're lucky."

Was he doubting me? Adam would learn very quickly that when I did anything, I gave it 100% effort, every single time. "Or maybe I'll be a natural. Don't count me out yet."

"We'll see about that." Adam winked at me and opened the trunk. He pulled out two fly rods. Adam handed me a forest green rod, and he used a charcoal gray rod. I looked closely at my fly rod and noticed a worm hooked on the end of my fly line. Upon closer inspection, I realized it was a fake worm.

"Did you think that was real?" Adam must have caught me making a face. The worm looked so realistic; I definitely freaked out for a second. One element of fly fishing that appealed to me (so far) was that I didn't have to handle live bait, but Adam's fly choice had me wondering if I would, indeed, have to touch worms and bugs. I was still mustering up the courage to hold a slimy fish sometime today, let alone put worms on a hook.

"Um…" I was about to say no, but something tugged at me not to play tough. "Yeah, for a second."

"If that worm can fool you, then it should be able to fool some trout today, too." We approached the edge of the creek. The water was clearer than I expected, and I could see rocks of all shapes and sizes below the surface of the water. Out of the corner of my eye, I saw something dart off through the creek and disappear again. "Trout are moving," Adam commented. "Let's get ready to fish. Watch me take the first few casts, and then I'll get you set up. Watching someone fly fish helps a lot when you're learning. Besides actually doing it, of course."

I stood next to Adam as he unhooked his minuscule fly from a tiny notch in his fly rod. Then he looked over at me. "Unless you want to get whacked in the face, move a little further away." I took a few steps back and gave him some space, even though I wanted to be as close to him as possible.

Adam let out some fly line. A lot of motion came from his arm and wrist, almost like he was casting a spell using a wand. The tip of the fly rod started straight up and then moved a little behind him. He flicked his wrist and brought the fly rod forward, but the line didn't hit the water yet. It whipped through the air, and Adam's other hand pulled more line out from the reel. He flicked his wrist back again, and then forward. This time, he let the line hit the water.

"That's called false-casting," Adam explained. "Gotta make sure my cast is perfect before it hits the water. You only get so many chances with trout."

I could barely see his fly, which looked like a piece of blue fuzz floating on the water. A couple of seconds after Adam's line hit the water, he pulled his line out and took another cast. The fly landed on the water, drifted downstream for a few seconds, and then he took another cast. Cast, drift, repeat. After repeated casting for a few minutes, things finally got interesting. I watched Adam's fly soar through the air and land delicately on the water. Almost immediately after the fly hit the water, there was a quick splash. A fish pulled the fly underwater.

"Got one!" Adam exclaimed. His rod bent as he fought in the fish. It pulled his line to the left, and then to the right. Instead of reeling in the line, Adam used one hand to pull the line and bring the fish closer to land. "Nat, grab the net!"

I ran over to Adam and grabbed the net lying next to him. The fish was a lot closer to us, and I could probably net it without getting in the water. I knelt on the ground and just as I thought I could get the net under the trout, it splashed its tail at me and swam away from us. Adam kept pressure on the line and tried to bring the trout back to me.

"Crap," Adam muttered. "Get ready Nat, I'll try to bring her toward you," he took a big breath, "but you might need to get in the water for this one."

At that moment, the trout calmed down, and Adam pulled it closer to me. I could see the fly hooked in the top of its jaw. Reaching out as far as I could, I felt like I would belly-flop into the water at any second. Right when I thought I was going to fall in the creek, I scooped the net under the fish.

"Yes!" Adam let out a sigh of relief, and his shoulders relaxed. "That's a nice rainbow. About thirteen or fourteen inches, I would estimate." Now that I got a good look at the fish, I noticed how surprisingly beautiful it was, for a fish. A bright pink stripe went horizontally across its middle. The rest of its body was flashy silver.

Above its pink stripe were dark speckles, and below the pink stripe was a solid chrome belly. "Let's get her back." Adam knelt next to me. He took small pliers and used them to unhook the fish from the tiny fly it tried to eat. "Here, I'll take the net." He grabbed the handle of the net with one hand and wet his other hand before touching the trout. He carefully lifted the trout out of the net and held it in the water until it swam off. "Pretty cool, huh?"

"Actually, yeah," I agreed. "I didn't know fishing could be that cool. Or fish could be that pretty."

"So that was a rainbow trout I caught," Adam explained. "There's also brook trout. Those have super cool colors and patterns. And then there's brown trout. Those can be tricky to catch, but they're awesome, too. Why don't you grab your rod and try casting?"

I picked up my rod and took a few steps away from Adam, giving myself plenty of room to cast. I unhooked the worm from the hook keeper, and suddenly, my fly line came falling through the eyes of the rod until the worm was sitting on the tip-top of the rod. Adam chuckled at my mishap. My face was on fire. Could I look like any more of a pathetic rookie?

"Lots of little things I forget to mention until I see someone learning how to fly fish. My bad." As Adam walked closer to me, my heart started racing–from embarrassment, from nerves, from the stress of learning so many new things, all at once. "First, make sure you always have control of your line. Don't let your line and leader, that's this clear stuff at the end of your line, fall through the eyes of the rod like that. Always keep your leader and a little line all the way outside the rod. It's just easier to cast that way." Adam pulled the leader and line through the eyes of the rod again, until a few feet of fly line were out, along with all the leader. "This is an eight-foot rod, so you have about seven feet of leader and line out now." I stared at him, processing all this new information and fishing jargon. "Keep the rod in your right hand and hold the excess line in your left hand. You'll control how much line you let out using that hand. You use your hand as a reel more than the actual reel."

I did as Adam instructed, beginning to understand the intricate mechanics of what he was explaining. "Anything else I should do before I cast?"

"Double check your surroundings–look out for people and vegetation. You're guaranteed to get caught in a tree at some point, but let's make sure that doesn't happen on your first few casts. Then you can cast. Use your left hand to pull out a little line, while bringing the rod slightly behind you with your right hand. Use your wrist more than anything. Then, bring the rod forward again and let your fly hit the water."

"Got it." Looking around, the closest thing I saw behind me was Adam's car, at least 100 yards away. I visualized Adam casting and tried to remember all those directions. I took a cast, and my worm fly landed at the edge of the water. Better than not making it into the water at all!

"Not a bad first cast. Try again, but let out even more line. And take your time. You don't need to move fast. But not too slow either."

I tried again, and this time, my worm landed closer to the middle of the creek.

"Good! Let your line drift a little and then take another cast. Try to land it in the same spot."

I followed Adam's instructions and slowly caught on. I didn't see any signs of fish yet, but I could see why people enjoyed fly fishing. It seemed way less boring than regular fishing. I took another cast and let my worm drift down-river. After a couple of seconds, I felt something tug at the end of my line. I saw a bright flash in the water and realized it must be a fish.

"Set the hook! Keep your line tight!" Adam commanded. I didn't understand what that meant, so I yanked the rod and line quickly, and then watched the trout go airborne. It landed back in the water, staying deep where I couldn't see it. "Keep the line tight, but don't be afraid to let out line if you need to! I'll net it as soon as I can." My heart started pounding. I couldn't believe that fish just ate a rubber worm, and now it was doing everything it could to swim away. But I wouldn't let it.

What did Adam mean by not being afraid to let out line? There was so much to think about at once!

At that moment, the trout nearly pulled the rod out of my hand. That seemed like a good time to let out some line. I used my left hand to let out some line from the reel, and my rod sprang back upright, still maintaining plenty of tension. Adam splashed through the creek, trying to net my fish as soon as he could. Just like earlier, the fish took a break from its fight, and Adam seized that moment to net it. As soon as it was in the net, it started flopping around, and the worm flew out of its mouth.

"You got lucky! Must not have been hooked well. We'll work on your hook sets." Adam waded over to me with the fish in the net. After all of that fighting and jumping, it wasn't a big fish. It was another rainbow, like the one Adam caught. Upon further inspection, it was definitely less than twelve inches long.

"I'd say that's about a nine-incher," Adam read my mind. "Want to hold it?"

I suddenly felt nervous to hold my first trout, especially having minimal fishing experience. "Um, sure."

"Okay. Set your rod down and wet your hands first. Trout are super delicate, so you want to handle them the best you can. Grab it out of the net when you're ready."

I wet my hands in the creek. The water was ice cold, yet it felt refreshing. I reached into the net to grab the trout, and its slimy body slipped away from me as soon as I touched it. I tried again, being a little less gentle this time, and I got a grip on it. Holding a trout wasn't as gross as I thought it would be.

"Good, now lift it out of the net and I'll get a quick pic before releasing it." Following Adam's coaching, I lifted it up and admired the brilliant coloring of the fish. The pink stripe of this fish was lighter than the one Adam caught, but it was just as beautiful as the first fish.

As soon as I held the trout up, it flopped out of my hands and plopped back into the water. We watched it dart to the deeper part of the creek and disappear. Adam looked down at his phone and started laughing.

"What?" I asked.

"These pictures. Look." Adam couldn't stop laughing as he got out of the water. He handed me his phone, and I swiped through the photos. The first picture was the best one–I was smiling, and the fish was behaving. But it went downhill quickly after that. There was a blast of photos where my face transformed from happy to shocked, and the trout startled in my hands, and flopped back into the water. I couldn't help but laugh, too.

"These are great. Send them to me!"

"Will do. Want to keep fishing?"

"Absolutely." We continued to cast for another hour. With each cast, I grew more comfortable with the motions. I felt relaxed by the sounds of the creek, the sun's gentle heat, and Adam's presence. It was the best morning I'd had in a long time.

Chapter 9

That night, I watched TV with my parents. My phone buzzed on the couch next to me. It was a text from Syd. She finally responded to my messages from almost twelve hours ago.

`Hey girl. How was this morning?` 😊

Although it was hours later, I was happy that Syd checked in to hear how my morning with Adam went. It made me feel better about our long-distance friendship.

I texted back: `Facetime?`

`yeah now's a good time`

I went up to my room and sat on the floor, leaning against my bed. I started the Facetime call. Syd answered right away.

"Look at you, stranger! Glad you aren't dead."

"Haha, very funny. Adam's not a serial killer."

"It's too soon to tell," Syd joked. "Just don't be too busy with the hot next-door-neighbor to forget about your friends here." I noticed the background of Syd's call, and I didn't recognize where she was.

"Where are you?" I asked.

"At Kennedy's house. She had a bunch of people over for a bonfire tonight."

"But I thought you didn't–"

"Hi, Nat! Miss you!" Kennedy shouted from the background. I could see her holding a bag of marshmallows and her Stanley water bottle.

"Hi, Kennedy." I faked a smile and waved back. "Let's talk later, Syd. I'll text you tomorrow."

"Sounds good. Miss you! Byeee." Before I could say another word, Syd ended the call. I thought it was weird that she said it was a good time to talk, but she was at Kennedy's house hanging out with people. It didn't seem like a good time to talk to me, so I didn't take it personally that the call was cut short.

The next morning, I texted Syd as promised.

How was the rest of the bonfire?

Throughout the day, I kept checking my phone, thinking I missed her message. By dinner, still no response. I even checked my phone at the beginning of dinner, breaking a cardinal rule in the Ryba household: no phones at the dinner table. I felt disappointed, and a little angry, that Syd still hadn't responded.

"What's so important on your phone?" Dad asked. I could tell by the tone in his voice that he was upset with my untimely phone use. "Are you talking to Adam?"

"No, Dad!" I groaned and rolled my eyes. I looked over at Mom. "It's Syd."

"What's going on?" Mom was way better at this stuff than Dad.

"So yesterday I called her and she was at Kennedy's house," I started.

"I thought we didn't like Kennedy."

"We don't," I confirmed.

"Wait, we don't like Kennedy?" Dad chimed in.

"No," Mom and I said in unison.

"Got it. Who's Kennedy?"

"Anyway," I continued, "Syd was at Kennedy's house last night for a bonfire with some other girls. As soon as Kennedy saw Syd was talking to me, I told Syd I would text her later. And Syd kind of looked relieved. So I texted Syd today like I said I would, and she left me on read."

Mom grabbed my hand and gave it a squeeze. "Try not to take it personal, Nat. But I know that's not what you want to hear."

"Nope, not really. It definitely seems personal. Like I get if she's annoyed because I haven't texted her much these past couple of weeks, but then she wants me to reach out more. So I do, and now I get ignored? And on top of that, I'm being replaced by Kennedy?" I stab at a piece of lettuce on my plate with my fork.

"Your salad did nothing to you, just Syd." Dad grinned, trying to be funny.

"Jack, honey, just listen for now, okay?" Mom turned back and looked me in the eyes. I hated when she forced eye contact. "Nat, this unfortunately is part of growing up. Again, I know you don't want to hear that either, but it's true. When I was younger, I had this friend, Julie. She was my best friend from second grade all the way through middle school. She moved an hour away when we started high school. We promised we would stay in touch and see each other once a month, but after she moved, we only talked a handful of times and saw each other once. It was no one's fault, it just happens sometimes. Some friendships last a lifetime, some don't. And that's okay."

"Yeah, but you also had those old phones with the twirly cord that only one person could use at a time. What were those called?"

"A landline? Don't make me feel older than I am."

"Sorry. But my point is, it's easier to stay connected now than when you were growing up."

Mom gently said, "Both people have to choose to stay connected. If one person wants to and the other doesn't, it won't work."

I sat in silence for a minute, looking down at the salad I attacked moments before. Staring at a tomato, I asked, "But Syd and I have been best friends since preschool. And I still want to be best friends. What if she doesn't feel the same way?" I thought I sounded like a little kid asking that question, but it was a fear I had deep down that I was too afraid to admit.

"All you can do is put forth your effort in the friendship. Text her and call her when you can, and hopefully she does the same. And if not, then you find people here that want to be your friend. Which you already are, and I'm proud of you for that."

I forced a smile. "It helps that everyone talks to everyone around here. I can barely grab the mail without one of the neighbors starting a conversation with me."

Mom laughed. "Sometimes, I wish these people would keep to themselves. If Mary-Jo from down the street tells me about the radishes in her garden one more time, I don't know what I'll do!"

Chapter 10

Even though Adam was consuming more of my thoughts and free time, I wouldn't let a boy deter my summer running plans. Cross country camp started right after Father's Day, and I couldn't wait to have a team to run with again. After missing the qualifying standards for state cross country and track by only a few seconds, I was even more determined to push myself this year. Although I was competing in a new state, the goal was still the same–qualify and be competitive at the state meets.

On Monday morning at 7 a.m., I met my future teammates in front of the school's athletic entrance. Back home, our team of fifty girls would gather all over town: at the school, at different forest preserves, and our favorite spot: the park next to the ice cream shop (because who doesn't want ice cream after a run?). But here, I saw at a group of sixteen girls. This was a much smaller group than I expected to see. Everyone was stretching and synching their smart watches, ready to go. The girls all turned toward me when I approached, eager to see who the new kid was.

"Hi! I'm Savannah," a tall, blonde girl introduced herself. "I'm one of the cross country captains."

"I'm Natalie," I replied. Savannah didn't seem judgmental or annoyed by my presence. She seemed genuinely happy to have me there. Her friendliness was refreshing and immediately put me at ease.

"We're happy you're joining us," a skinny woman with thick, dark hair pulled into a tight ponytail walked toward me. "I'm Coach June. Set your stuff down here; we're heading out on our long run soon."

"Want to run with us today?" A red-headed girl asked. "I'm Ali."

I smiled as I synced my watch. "Thanks, that would be great." Running by myself was one thing, but going for a long run by myself was a whole other level of excruciating torture. The time went by so much faster running in a group.

Coach June led the team through dynamic stretches and an overview of the week's schedule, which was like training with my team back in Illinois. Coach gave us the choice of two groups to run in today: a fifty minute long run group, and a sixty-five minute long run group. I immediately knew what group I wanted to be in and hoped Ali was also planning to run that long.

"You good with sixty-five minutes?" Ali asked. I nodded, and then we were off. Even though I knew nothing about Ali but her name, running with her felt comfortable. Our stride was in sync within seconds.

"We don't get new people here often," Ali said once we settled into our pace. "Where are you from?"

"Illinois, near Chicago."

"I've been to Chicago once. They have good pizza."

"Yes! Deep dish is my favorite," I agreed. And just like that, our shared love for food solidified our friendship. An hour and five minutes flew by as we chatted while running through the hilly and sleepy neighborhoods. When we were stretching back at school, another girl on the team, Sarah, asked me a seemingly innocent question.

"Have you met any other kids here yet? Or just us so far?"

"My next-door neighbor, Adam. He goes to school here, I think."

"Adam Smith?" Ali sounded concerned.

"Yeah," I confirmed hesitantly. No one responded, but they all looked at one another. I broke the awkward silence. "We've hung out a few times. He seems nice."

"There are some things you should know about Adam," Ali says.

•   •   •   •   •

After practice (and after my parents met Ali's parents and my new teammates), I joined Ali, Sarah, and another new teammate, Becca, at Ali's house for breakfast. Ali's parents were out doing yard work, so we had the kitchen to ourselves. Ali poured everyone glasses of chocolate milk and got out ingredients to make pancakes.

"So Adam's your next-door neighbor?" Ali wasted no time starting the interrogation.

"Yeah. He's taken me fly fishing."

"No hunting offers yet?" Sarah asked. "Do people even hunt in Illinois?"

I had to think about that for a minute because it was such a rare occurrence in my circle of friends. "I don't know if people actually hunt in Illinois, but some kids' dads would go deer hunting around Thanksgiving. Usually in Wisconsin."

"We've all been hunting before. Deer, pheasant, duck, stuff like that," Becca explained. Ali and Sarah agreed.

"Wait, like gun hunting?"

"Yep. And bow hunting."

"You're not scared of guns?" This was not where I was expecting this conversation to go.

"We learned as kids how to use them and how to be responsible with them," Sarah chimed in. "It's pretty common around here that kids know how to hunt, or that someone owns some sort of firearm."

My brain spiraled out of control with questions. This was so different from how people viewed guns back home. Would I learn how to use a gun one day? Did I even need to know how to use one?

"I can tell you more about that later. Let's get back to Adam," Ali redirected the conversation. "Here's the tea. Has he told you about his mom yet?"

"Just that she spends a lot of time on her artwork."

"Yeah, 'artwork.'" Ali threw up some air quotes and rolled her eyes. "She's never home. Rapid City seems like a big town, but everyone still knows everyone's business. My parents used to be friends with Adam's parents when we were little kids."

"Why aren't they friends anymore?"

Ali took a sip from her glass of chocolate milk, then continued. "Adam's mom always loved art. Painting and sculpting are her passions. I overheard my parents talking one time, and I guess Adam wasn't planned, if you know what I mean. So once Adam was born, his mom's artwork took a backseat. And once he started school, his mom started spending more time on her art again, and less time with Adam and his dad."

"My older brother and Adam played baseball together for four or five years," Sarah added. "I would go to a lot of his games with my parents, and everyone's families were at the games. I always saw Adam's dad, but I never saw Adam's mom at a game."

"I didn't know Adam played baseball," I said. I thought fly fishing was his only hobby.

Ali answered, "He doesn't anymore. He quit a couple of years ago because he wanted to spend more time learning how to fish and hunt, according to him. But I think there's more to it than that. It doesn't add up."

"What do you mean?" I asked.

Sarah explained, "He was so good at baseball. Like, he could've made varsity as a freshman. But my brother and his friends had to join these expensive travel teams to even have a chance at a spot on the high school team."

I nodded, understanding what Sarah was getting at. It sounded like Mato couldn't afford the travel team on one salary, or having to take Adam to all the games and practices by himself.

"Supposedly, Adam's mom started drinking a lot, too," Becca said. "I'm surprised his parents are still married."

Sarah added, "A couple times back in like kindergarten or first grade, I remember seeing Adam sitting in the front office, waiting to get picked up from school. My brother told me that there were days Adam's mom was supposed to come pick him up from school, but she forgot because she either was too busy with her artwork, or she was taking a nap and forgot to wake up and get him."

"Maybe she was too drunk to get him," Becca gossiped.

"So he had to give up on baseball and his mom sucks." What was I missing? I couldn't see the red flags they all saw. "No one's family is perfect."

Ali said, "I agree; no one's family is perfect. My parents can be weird and annoying and overprotective, but at least they're around. They come to my cross country meets. They like to spend time with me. All our parents do." Ali looked at Becca and Sarah, then back at me. "Imagine how it would feel if one of your parents, the person who is supposed to care about you and have your back no matter what, decides over and over again that they would rather do literally anything else than spend time with you. That could mess a person up."

I didn't have to imagine it. I knew. That was probably how Mom felt about Grandma.

Resentment. Hurt feelings. Lack of trust. Betrayal. Mom hadn't processed it, even into adulthood. Who knew how Adam felt?

"I would be pissed, and that's an understatement," Becca said. "Especially if I had no outlet for that anger and hurt." I thought about my mom again. Her behavior since we moved here was making a lot more sense.

"All that to say, he's a great guy. Super cute, too. None of us deny that. I think we all have had crushes on Adam at some point. But just be careful. You seem cool and we don't want Adam to hurt the new girl," Sarah said as she put some pancakes on her plate. "Like Ali said earlier, this place has that small-town feel where everyone knows everyone, you know? And you're part of that now, so we want to look out for you."

"Thanks," I said. I knew these girls had my best interest in mind by sharing all this with me. Back home, there were girls in my grade who would purposefully withhold information like this, just to watch you get hurt and then laugh about it. I avoided them like the plague. I didn't sense any of that mean girl drama here.

Based on first impressions, Ali, Becca, and Sarah were welcoming, honest, and liked food as much as me. The perfect foundation for a strong friendship. But should I be concerned about Adam, especially if the problems had more to do with his mom than with him? I appreciated the tea, but I still wanted to figure things out for myself.

Chapter 11

Later that week, Grandma came over for dinner. Dad insisted we couldn't avoid Grandma forever, and after some fighting over the phone (I listened to what I could from my bedroom. It was loud), Mom reluctantly agreed. Dad was prepping chicken in the kitchen, and I was rolling out from this week's runs when I saw Grandma's car pull into the driveway. Mom was outside doing yard work. Mom and Grandma didn't come into the house for a few minutes. I used this moment to ask Dad something I had been wondering for a while.

"Dad, why do Mom and Grandma still not get along after all these years?"

"What makes you think that?"

"Dad, I'm almost sixteen. I'm not an idiot."

"I know you're not an idiot," Dad said while rinsing potatoes. "It's been a busy month. We're finally unpacked, you started cross country, and you've been spending a lot of time with Adam and your new running friends. Which is all great, but that hasn't left a lot of time for other things. You know, you can reach out to your grandma, too. She would love that."

"I barely know her. That feels weird. And you didn't answer my question."

"Well," Dad hesitated before continuing, "All I'll say is your mom and grandma love each other, but they don't see eye-to-eye on most things." Dad couldn't say more than that because Mom and Grandma walked into the house at that moment.

"Hi Natalie," Grandma came over and gave me a hug. "Smells good in here, Jack. What's for dinner?"

"Grilled Greek chicken, potatoes, and vegetables. We might even test out the new outdoor furniture and firepit if the weather holds out."

"Sounds wonderful! I'd love to see the furniture in the backyard." Mom, Grandma, and I went in the backyard while Dad finished prepping everything for the grill. I would never understand why my dad doesn't enjoy cooking inside, but as soon as it got warm enough to grill, it was all he wanted to do. It was only a matter of time before he started grilling breakfast.

"Oh, these new chairs are very nice," Grandma told Mom. Although Grandma's words were complimentary, her tone sounded judgmental. "I just hope they are durable. I read some bad reviews about these wicker chairs, so I went with a sturdier, wrought iron outdoor set for my patio."

Without looking at Grandma, Mom snapped back, "I read a lot of reviews, and one of my co-workers recommended them to me."

Grandma tsked. "Time will tell. Can I get a glass of lemonade?"

"I'll get it," I eagerly offered. I went back in the kitchen and poured lemonade for everyone.

"How's it going out there?" Dad asked.

"Let's just say I'm going to take my time pouring lemonade for everyone."

"Listen," Dad advised. Any time he started a sentence with "Listen," he was about to tell me something he thought was important, whether it was advice or a dad joke. "Don't let your mom's relationship with Grandma affect your relationship with her. I think you're quickly seeing that they are both set in their ways. Sometimes, there's not much you can do about that, but people's ways aren't always right or wrong. I agree with your mom often. And not just because I'm married to her.

But I also agree with a lot of things your grandma has said or done. They're both amazing women, even though they're very different women."

"Easier said than done, but I'll try." I carried Mom's and Grandma's lemonade outside. They were sitting in the chairs Grandma didn't like, now smiling and laughing about something instead of preparing for battle over who owned more durable outdoor furniture.

"And that's why I have a trail cam in my backyard. Otherwise, I would've never seen those deer! You got that lawn treatment I told you about, right? The one that doesn't make deer sick?"

"I will, Mom." Mom responded to Grandma the way I do to Mom sometimes—I could almost see the annoyance seeping out of her mouth as she spoke.

"If you get anything else, your grass won't be as green and any deer coming through to graze could get sick. You don't want deer diarrhea in your yard, right?"

"I'm going to see if Jack needs help with dinner." Mom went back inside, leaving Grandma and me on the back deck.

"Tell me about your running, dear," Grandma said.

"Running has been going surprisingly well," I answered. "I like my new teammates so far. They were friendly when I started camp with them, and they are, um, interesting."

"What do you mean by interesting?"

I sipped my lemonade before answering. "They have unique hobbies and interests. Like some of them actually go hunting. We're all similar but really different, if that makes sense."

"That's good company to keep," Grandma said. "Life is boring when you surround yourself with people that are just like you. You don't learn to think differently or be open to new ideas. I'm glad you found these girls."

"Me, too." We talked more about running, and I helped Grandma tweak her training calendar leading up to the 5K race. I even planned to go for some easy runs in the evenings with her.

"How's it going out here?" Dad came out carrying a tray full of chicken and vegetables to grill.

"Natalie is going to help me win the master's division of this 5K! This lady would make a great coach one day." Grandma winked at me. Her hazel eyes sparkled in the sun, and her smile radiated joy. As wild as she was, I couldn't help but be happy around her. Nothing, and no one, could tame her.

Chapter 12

Over the weekend, Adam and I were hanging out at my house, watching TV in the basement. After finishing our fourth rerun of *The Office,* Adam had an idea.

"Pull up YouTube," he suggested. He grabbed the remote and started typing in the search bar: *Black Hills Fly Fishing.* The thumbnails of the videos that popped up showed picturesque landscapes, beautiful trout, and joyful people. Adam clicked on a video called "Rapid Creek Slay Fest," and we watched a five-minute video of some guy catching brown trout on a different stretch of Rapid Creek than where Adam took me to fish. Every trout the guy caught was on a nymph, which is a super small, subsurface fly. But toward the end, the guy's GoPro caught footage of a rainbow trout going full airborne out of the water to eat.

"Did you see that?" I exclaimed.

"Yeah! That was sick," Adam said.

"Let's watch another one!" I felt the adrenaline pumping through my veins, and I wasn't even on the water. Adam went back to the search results, and he clicked on a video that was filmed somewhere called Spearfish Creek. According to the guy in the video, Spearfish Creek was in a canyon. Spearfish Canyon, fitting enough. The scenery was breathtaking. He also included footage of a tall waterfall called Bridal Veil Falls, and a trailhead for a hike called the Devil's Bathtub.

"This place doesn't look real," I commented.

"Oh, it's real. I've been there a few times. You and I should go sometime."

"Is it far?" I asked. I wanted to visit Spearfish Canyon with Adam. Honestly, I would travel anywhere with Adam if he asked me to.

"About forty-five minutes."

"I might take you up on that offer, then. Any other cool places that are great for fishing and sight-seeing?"

"Custer State Park," Adam answered immediately. "The wildlife drive is epic. Especially if you go to Custer for the Buffalo round-up. The number of bison you see is unreal."

"What's the most you've seen at one time?"

"Over 100, easily. It's natural to want to see them up close, but they get mean and territorial. Have you heard stories of people who try to get too close to bison?"

"No, but I'm guessing it's not good?"

"Let's just say there are idiots every year that think it's a good idea to stand right next to a bison for a picture, like they're at a freaking petting zoo. If the person walks away alive, they're lucky. But I'm getting off-topic here, back to fishing. There are some breathtaking places to fish in, and near Custer State Park. Honestly, there's a lot of good fishing spots within an hour of here."

"We should check them out sometime soon," I suggested. Look at me making plans!

Adam raised his eyebrows at me and smiled. "You went from not knowing what fly fishing was about a month ago to wanting to plan fly fishing trips. I'm impressed. And a little shocked."

"Those YouTube videos sold me. If there are places that cool within an hour of here, I have to see them for myself."

"And chase some chunky South Dakota trout," Adam added.

I opened the Notes app on my phone and created a shared list of places we wanted to go fishing in the Black Hills. We started with the places in the YouTube videos, and Adam added some other creeks he had fished already, or that he'd heard about but hadn't fished yet.

"So where to start?" Adam asked.

"I think I want to go to Custer first," I suggested. "If the fishing is tough, at least we get to see some animals. I'm picturing it like a zoo, but without the cages and stuff."

Adam laughed. "Good job. You just described the wilderness."

"Shut up," I playfully punched his arm. "But for real, when are we going?"

"Friday?"

"That should work, after my run in the morning." As the cross country season got closer, I couldn't sacrifice my training for time with a boy. I had to keep my priorities in check.

"It's a date," Adam said.

"Huh?" The word "date" caught me off guard.

"Like, Friday's the date we'll go to Custer." Adam's cheeks turned bright red.

"Of course," I grinned. Was I looking to date anyone right now? Not necessarily. But did I hate the idea of going on a date with Adam? Absolutely not.

·　　·　　·　　·　　·

Friday morning started with an easy run around the neighborhood while Mom rode her bike with me. The whole time, Mom asked questions about my plans with Adam today.

"What time are you leaving?"

"When will you be back?"

"You'll have cell service there, right?"

"Can you text me when you get there and when you're coming home?"

"You know to stay away from bison, right? They're not fluffy cows!"

Luckily, she only grilled me with logistical questions. Mom had gotten to know Adam and Mato, so she didn't worry (as much) whenever we hung out. Before Adam picked me up, I made sure my backpack had my essentials for the day: water, snacks, my portable charger, sunglasses, and the box of flies Adam gave me from his collection of extras in the garage. Around 10:30 a.m., Adam knocked on the door to pick me up. Dad answered the door, and he chatted with Adam for a few minutes. They were in the middle of talking about Metallica when I came downstairs and interrupted.

"Dad, Adam and I have to get going." I tried my best to be polite. I was excited to do some fishing today, and of course, to hang out with Adam. Earlier, I looked up Custer State Park, and after seeing they have fields full of prairie dogs, I really wanted to get going.

"Alright. You kids have fun."

"Text me when you get there!" Mom shouted down the hallway.

"Will do," I agreed.

Adam and I made the drive to Custer State Park. The park felt peaceful. Pine trees and spruce trees towered over us at the beginning of our drive, and then the park opened to acres of wide, open fields. The green rolling hills looked like they went on forever. On top of one hill, I saw an animal that looked like a deer, but had tall antlers.

"What's that?" I pointed at the mysterious animal.

"Antelope." Adam answered. "Let's keep track of how many different animals we see here today."

There were a few more antelope grazing the hills. The road took a sharp turn, and then we were facing another field filled with bison. There were at least a dozen lying in the grass, enjoying a lazy day. Two of them walked closer to the road. Adam pulled the car over so we could get a better look and take some pictures.

"Wow," was all I could say. I didn't realize how massive a bison's head was. Their small but sharp horns made them even more powerful and intimidating. Chocolate brown fur covered their massive bodies. Some of them had a hump on top of their backs, making them look more intimidating, like they could charge at us at any moment. As they continued walking closer to the road, I tried to wrap my mind around how those short, skinny legs could carry that massive of a head and body.

"Are they going to cross the road?" I wondered out loud. Soon enough, I found out the answer to my question. The two bison walked across the road, and people had gotten out of their cars to take pictures. Some people used their phones, but others had professional cameras. Adam rolled down the window and snapped a few pictures on his phone. I was too awestruck to grab mine. I wanted to be fully present in the moment.

The bison safely crossed the road and continued walking through the field. "Should we continue driving? There's a few more miles to go before our first stretch of water." I nodded, and we continued along, finding a few more bison and antelope before spotting the one animal I wanted to see. Outside my passenger window, I noticed a field scattered with small holes like Swiss cheese. I had my window rolled down, and suddenly I heard a squeaking sound. It came from a prairie dog sitting on its hind legs. Then more appeared! Some of them were running from one hole to another, joining in a chorus of squeaking barks.

"They're so cute! Stop the car!" I started taking pictures and videos on my phone. I immediately sent a video to my cross country group chat and Syd. If I was going to put effort into my friendship with Syd, I had to show her more of my new life here. She would probably leave me on read again, but at least I could say I tried. After sending the video to Mom as proof of life (my own and the prairie dogs), I put my phone down and kept watching the prairie dogs run around.

Adam snapped me out of my trance when he asked, "Can I keep driving?"

"I mean, I could watch them all day. They're so cute. But let's keep going."

We drove along, noticing a few more antelope and a bald eagle. The road climbed and continued to twist and turn throughout the park. We saw some rock structures among the fields and trees before driving up to a sizeable lake surrounded by gray, rugged cliffs.

"This is Sylvan Lake," Adam said. "Want to check it out?"

"Sure! Should we grab our rods?"

"It's like you read my mind." Adam drove into a parking area, which connected to a trail that led to the lake. We hiked down with all our gear in tow. The gravel path brought us to a glass-calm lake, with only one other family hiking around. This place was so majestic and serene—I couldn't believe no one else was here.

"Pretty cool, huh?" Adam asked.

"Yeah, this is incredible." If I wasn't carrying a fly rod in one hand and a net in the other, I'd reach out and grab Adam's hand. This place had the vibes to make a move.

"Let's take a few casts. There's trout in here, and some other fish, too." Naturally, Adam would focus more on fishing than flirting.

Boulders and cliffs surrounded most of the lake, but we found a grassy edge for us to cast. My rod still had the worm tied on. I kept it on for now, hoping the fish in this lake would eat worms. Adam and I gave each other space and began casting. This was different than fishing in the creek closer to home. The water had no current, so I had to be smart about where I was casting. Adam must have thought the same thing because he continued to cast on one spot.

"Hey, Nat," Adam called.

"Yeah?"

"If you cast toward where I am, there's trout here. I can see a couple. It's more shallow over here. Don't come too much closer, though, or you'll spook them. Take one or two steps closer to me, and then try to bomb a cast this way. I bet one of these trout will eat that worm."

How did Adam see trout in this water? I took two steps closer to Adam and looked in the water again. My sunglasses helped a lot. They were a polarized pair, and polarized sunglasses (Adam taught me this) helped with seeing below the surface of the water. A dark outline in the water caught my attention, and it was moving ever so slightly. At first I thought that was a rock, but Adam was right. It was a fish.

I was getting more comfortable casting, especially with having a lot of line out. I pulled out some fly line with my left hand, and then brought my rod back and took a cast. My line didn't go very far, and a lot of the line was crumpled near the bank of the lake.

"Try false casting," Adam suggested. "Just before your fly and your line hit the water, bring your rod back to wind up again. Do that two or three times until you think your fly will land right where you want it. It's easy to practice here, since there's not a lot of trees or stuff around you."

I took his advice, bringing my rod back to begin my cast. I flicked my rod forward, and just like Adam said, I brought my rod back again to wind up, letting out more line as I did so. After two more false casts, I finally let my fly hit the water. The worm sank right into the strike zone. After a few seconds, I felt a slight tug at the end of my line, and I could see my leader straighten and pull in the water. I had a feeling it was a fish, so I set the hook. My rod bent, and I saw a flash of a trout darting around at the end of my line.

"Good work! I got the net." Adam kept his eyes on the fish while I fought it in. Like last time, I paid attention to the fish's movements. I pulled line in when I could, and if I felt the fish darting out, I let out a bit of line so it wouldn't break off. After some back and forth, I eventually brought the fish close enough to shore for Adam to net it. It didn't look like the trout Adam I caught in Rapid Creek. I had no idea what I just caught.

"Nice! It's a brookie," Adam said. "Brook trout, to be exact." I set my rod down and looked in the net. This fish was stunning, just like the rainbow and brown trout. The brook trout had a darker body than a rainbow trout, but also had speckles kind of like a brown trout. Its back had a yellow swirl pattern, and some speckles had a blue halo around them. I don't think I would ever stop being in awe of the intricate variations in colors and patterns on trout.

"Can I get a quick picture before we release it?"

"Of course. Wet your hands first, and let's release it soon. It's warm out, so it's important to keep the fish out of the water as little as possible. I'll unhook it for you."

After Adam unhooked the fish, he gave me the net so he could get out his phone. I wet my hands and reached into the net to grab the trout. It was much calmer than the rainbow trout I caught. I lifted it up for Adam to get a picture. Adam gave me a thumbs up, so I knew he got a picture—a good one, I hope. Then, with the calm trout still in my hand, I put it back in the water. Almost immediately, the trout swam off.

"That was a great cast," Adam said.

"You're a good teacher. Couldn't have caught it without your help, and your good eye."

"Let's fish here a little longer, and then we can keep driving. There's another creek I want us to check out."

Before I took another cast, I sent that picture to my parents so they wouldn't worry that I died in the wilderness. Mom replied right away. `It's so cute! Great catch!`

I saw some messages from my cross country group chat, but I could respond to those in the car. Even though Syd never responded to my first video, I still sent her a picture of the trout I just caught, remembering my conversation I had with Mom. Friendships took effort, and if my friendship with Syd ever fizzled out, I could confidently say I put in the effort on my end.

Adam and I fished for another half hour before continuing our drive along the Wildlife Loop toward the next creek. We didn't see many more animals, but the scenery was just as breathtaking. Pristine fields and mountains as far as the eye could see.

While I was lost in my thoughts, Adam pulled the car over by another trailhead. "Hidden Creek Natural Area" read the sign.

"Let's check it out. I've heard it's a crazy hike, but worth it." Without waiting for my reply, Adam jumped out of the car and grabbed his stuff from the back. Following reluctantly, I slung my backpack over my shoulder and looked at the trail. I couldn't see too far ahead because of the amount of trees and vegetation. This trail was more overgrown and rugged than anywhere Adam had taken me yet. I felt unequipped in my leggings, tank top, and old running shoes. What had I gotten myself into? I didn't want to admit that I was in over my head, but I feared this would be a big test, and even worse, that I would fail.

Adam began the hike and I followed, watching his steps. I had to remind myself to look up every once in a while, because there was a gorgeous canyon wall to our right. The mesmerizing brick red rock distracted me from the hike ahead. This trail had some semblance of a path to it, but this was the most untouched wilderness I had come across since I arrived in South Dakota.

"Watch your step!"

Adam's voice refocused my wandering mind. I looked down again and saw the tail of a snake slither into the tall grass.

"I doubt it was poisonous," Adam commented, "but you always have to be careful out here. We'll need to keep an eye out for poison ivy, too. And when you're stepping on bigger rocks, double check that it's a rock and not a snapping turtle." Adam turned around and kept going, as if what he just said to me were normal topics of conversation. Did he forget I moved here from a place that had more houses and buildings than trees?

We kept hiking, and eventually the creek was in sight. This stretch of it was shallow, and crossing it was required in order to continue along the trail. Without hesitating, Adam walked through the creek. Once he was across, he turned around to wait for me. Not wanting to seem like a coward, or show how uncomfortable I was with this hike, I followed him. The first step in the creek was as cold as snow. I let out a small yelp and took quick steps to get across. On my last step before getting back on the trail, my foot slipped and I almost fell. But I have excellent balance, so I regained my footing and got across the creek.

"You good?" Adam asked.

"Never been better," I lied. Clearly, Adam believed me because he turned around and kept hiking. At this point, I was frustrated. My shoes, socks, and bottoms of my leggings were soaked. The trail became more uneven, and Adam wasn't staying with me. It was like he forgot I was even there. Did he assume I embarked on treacherous hikes through the suburbs of Chicago? I was an expert at looking out for distracted drivers, not poisonous plants or snapping turtles disguised as rocks. It was easy for me to navigate my way around a new neighborhood with the help of GPS, so why couldn't I do that here? I pulled my phone out of my backpack to look at a map and get a better idea of our location, but nothing wanted to load. There was no service out here.

I wanted to turn back. But I didn't want Adam to think I was scared.

I would consider myself tough. I run long distances for fun. If I could handle a move halfway across the country, then I could certainly handle a hike. Why was this hike getting to me so easily? The fact that I couldn't quite pinpoint my frustrations made me even more frustrated.

Then I saw the trees getting thicker up ahead. And Adam ducking to walk under the branches of the trees. I heard more water up ahead, too.

The unknown was exciting at first, until it wasn't. This was too much, all at once.

I told myself the same thing I tell myself during hard workouts and tiring races: one foot in front of the other. And that's what I did, until I got to the low-hanging trees. Adam was no longer in sight.

"Adam?" I called out. No response. "Adam?" I tried again, and finally got a response.

"Nat? Where are you?" I heard his footsteps coming closer to me. "Sorry, I didn't realize you fell that far behind. Do you want to keep going?"

I hesitated, not sure how to answer. Was I physically capable of continuing? Sure. Did I want to continue? Not really. My silence answered that question.

"This was probably too intense of a hike for right now," Adam admitted. "Let's turn around. The water looked low up ahead, so fishing wouldn't even be good."

I felt relieved that we would turn around and head somewhere closer to cell service. Part of me still felt bad for giving up on that hike. I felt like I failed. Adam and I were silent most of the walk back, but after a few minutes we both broke the silence at the same time.

"Sorry."

Then again, "Why are you sorry?" We both laughed, then I spoke first. "I'm sorry for giving up."

"That's nothing to be sorry about. That hike is nuts. I'm surprised you didn't question me before we started. It's badass that you tried. We can always go back another time if you want to try again."

"Okay. And what are you sorry about?"

"For assuming you were ready for that hike. You know what they say when you assume." Adam and I laughed, bringing some much needed joy back to the day.

The drive back home was quiet, but my thoughts were loud. The lingering dampness in my socks was a constant reminder of the highs and lows of our Custer State Park adventure. I went from feeling more confident as an angler to being almost abandoned on a remote hike with no cell service. Knowing Adam almost left me behind didn't sit right with me. Like, he actually hiked a ways out before realizing I wasn't with him. He needed to remember I didn't have the same skill set as him, at least not yet.

I opened my phone, looking for a distraction. My new cross country teammates couldn't get enough of the brook trout or the prairie dogs. But all their words and emojis of encouragement didn't take away from the fact that Syd ignored me. Again.

Mom said I needed to put effort into friendships to make them work, but it really sucked when the effort wasn't reciprocated.

Chapter 13

A warm shower and good night's sleep put things in perspective. Yeah, Adam almost abandoned me in the middle of nowhere, but he helped me catch fish and made the day fun. And even though Syd forgot I existed, my new friends were already acting like better friends than the ones I had back home, Syd included.

Ms. Laker used to say that it's important to cut ourselves some slack from time to time (another one of her wise journal prompts inspired by a book we read in class). Be as kind to the person looking back at you in the mirror as you would to the people around you. It wasn't easy, but I decided to not let Adam, or even Syd, ruin a good day. I could only control my thoughts and actions, as much as I wished I could control other people.

At the end of our tempo run at cross country camp, we went to the weight room to finish our workout. Ali, Sarah, Becca, and I talked about our plans for the rest of the week while starting our circuit with squats.

"We're taking our pontoon out on Pactola," Ali said. "It's so relaxing."

"I love Pactola!" Becca chimed in. "My dad took me ice fishing out there last year, and it was a blast. We caught a bunch of trout."

Sarah added, "I heard Crazy Horse Lake has good ice fishing, too. My brother went with one of his friends and his dad last winter, and my brother caught a lake trout. He said it fought like crazy. I would go with, but don't you get cold being out there all day?"

"Not with an ice shack!" Becca said. "We have a heater and everything. We bring hot chocolate and snacks and hang out until we catch a fish or flags go up."

"Huh?" It sounded like they were speaking a foreign language to me.

"I'll take you all ice fishing this winter if you want to go," Becca said. "You would love it."

"Aren't you afraid of falling through the ice?" I asked.

"There's always that risk, but we wait until there's a few inches of ice and it's been solid for a while."

"Sounds cool. I would give it a try." I genuinely meant that. Most of the new things I've tried here, except for my hike with Adam, have been fun so far. Why would ice fishing be any different?

"Sweet. I like how you're down for an adventure," Becca said.

"Speaking of that," Ali said, "are you going fishing with Adam this week?"

"Maybe," I said. "No set plans yet, but I am going on my easy run tomorrow morning with my grandma."

"Wait, you're running with your grandma?" Sarah asked.

"Like, are you pushing her in a wheelchair? Or is she going to walk while you're running?" Ali asked.

I laughed. "No, my grandma actually signed up for a 5K in September. I told her I would train with her when I could, so I've been running with her on Fridays and occasionally on the weekends."

"That's so cool!" Sarah exclaimed. "I wish my grandma could still do stuff like that. She has Alzheimer's and barely remembers my name anymore."

"Both of my grandmas have passed away," Becca added.

"My grandma loves to go for walks, but her knees are hurting her, so walking is even tougher now," Ali said. "Your grandma sounds like a badass."

"She kind of is," I explained. "She has all these crazy things in her house from places she's traveled. There's even an entire wall of autographed pictures of musicians she's met."

Everyone laughed as I told my stories about Grandma's random knick-knacks and celebrity encounters. Weightlifting and core work were a lot less painful in the company of good friends.

•　　　•　　　•　　　•　　　•

The next morning, Grandma picked me up from my house and we drove to a park to run and walk together. It was a sunny morning, but Grandma's outfit was brighter: she wore an orange tank top with turquoise capri tights and turquoise sunglasses to match. We warmed up by walking for a half mile. Grandma asked how I became interested in running, and I explained how I started running because of Syd, and ended up loving it.

We transitioned from a walk to an easy jog, going at an easy enough pace for us to keep talking. I needed a good recovery day; Coach gave us some hard workouts this week. Plus, I didn't know how fast someone in their early 70s could run. I was about to find out.

"What else did you do for fun back home?"

"Well, I run with Mom and Dad when they go biking. I also hung out a lot with Syd outside of track. Sometimes I would go shopping with other girls from school or hang out at a friend's house and watch movies or learn dances."

"What kind of dances?"

"TikTok dances. I can teach you one if you want!"

"Only if I teach you some real dance moves after that. I used to go line dancing all the time with your grandpa, and we had a blast! That man could dance, too."

"Deal!" Ali was right; Grandma was a badass. How many other teens were teaching their grandparents TikTok dances?

We continued jogging in silence, punctuated by our steady breathing and our feet hitting the limestone path. I looked over at

Grandma, checking her form. Honestly, she looked more relaxed than I did half the time. She was smiling, her arms were at perfect ninety-degree angles, her hands and shoulders weren't tense, and her posture was nice and tall. I self-evaluated my form, realizing my shoulders were creeping up by my ears. I reminded myself to relax, and I felt my shoulders drop what felt like several inches.

"Why were you so tense?" Grandma asked. "Your shoulders went from being up by your ears, back to where they belong."

"I don't know." But that was it–I truly didn't know why I was so tense. And not knowing made me want to tense back up. What a vicious cycle!

"How do you feel about being in South Dakota? You've been here a few weeks now. Are you liking it?"

"Yeah," I said. It was mostly the truth.

"Are you sure?"

I paused, thoughtfully crafting my response. "Ok, at first, I didn't want to like it. Too many things were different compared to life back home."

"Like what?" This time, Grandma picked up the pace. It was still an easy pace, but my breathing required a little more effort.

"Everyone was so friendly here. It was weird. People don't talk to you like that back home."

"Ok, what else?"

"The scenery, obviously. Like, there are actual mountains here."

"What's wrong with mountains?" Grandma asked.

"Nothing. It's so pretty here."

"Were you expecting South Dakota to be this ugly, boring dump of a state?"

"You said it, not me." We both laughed. I added, "It was just a lot of change in a short amount of time. I had my assumptions about what South Dakota would be like, and I'm still trying to process all the changes here. Including some new things I wasn't expecting."

I waited for Grandma to say something, but she didn't. I hated awkward silences, so I told her what was on my mind.

"I'm mad that Syd hasn't been talking to me much since I moved, even though she insisted our friendship wouldn't change. And my next-door-neighbor, Adam–"

"Oh! He's a cutie!" Grandma interrupted.

"And that's the problem. I wasn't expecting to have a crush on the first guy I met here. I'm still trying to play it cool, but I don't know how long I can keep that act going." Although that was true, I also wanted to say that meeting her was unexpected, and I was clueless about how to navigate her's and Mom's estranged relationship, while finally get to know my grandma after almost sixteen years and not pissing off Mom in the process. But I kept that one to myself.

"Sometimes you have to lean into the unknown." She picked up the pace again.

"Am I going too slow for you?"

"Kind of," she said. "Let's push here these last few minutes." We were jogging a little slower than nine-minute mile pace, and Grandma had already pushed us near eight minutes and thirty seconds per mile pace. She had better running form than most of my teammates, yet she still looked relaxed, so I brought us below eight-minute mile pace for the last 3 minutes. Although Grandma wasn't right next to me for those last three minutes, she remained only a few strides behind. My workout was to run for thirty minutes. Once I hit that time, I stopped my watch. We ran almost four miles. So much for an easy run today.

After cooling down, Grandma drove us back to my house. We poured ourselves tall, icy glasses of water and sat out on the back porch.

"You did a great job pushing the pace at the end there," Grandma said.

"I should be the one saying that to you! I'm impressed. You're a natural."

"I know you said today was supposed to be an easy run, but sometimes it's good to push yourself at the end. See what your limits are and even go beyond them. That's why I keep running as much as I can at my age. It isn't supposed to be comfortable. It's good to be uncomfortable sometimes."

"Are we still talking about running?" I had a feeling we weren't.

"Yes and no," Grandma chuckled. "You said you were afraid of how different things were here when you moved. It's normal for that to feel scary. But I don't want fear stopping you from taking chances."

"But what about things that are truly scary? Like skydiving or swimming with sharks?"

"I've done both. And I would do them again!"

Why was I not surprised?

"The point is," Grandma continued, "how many times did you *really* take a risk or embrace change up to this point?"

I thought about it for a minute and could only come up with one time.

"When I joined track," I answered. "I was so used to riding my bike with Mom and Dad all the time, but I was ready for something different."

"And was it worth it?"

"For sure. I don't know what I would do if I didn't run."

"Exactly. And that time you were ready for a change, ready for something new. Look at how well it turned out. I know you weren't ready for this move, but look at all the good that has come of it so far. Don't be afraid of changes, Nat. And don't be afraid of being uncomfortable. One of the worst things you can do is stay in your comfort zone."

Mom opened the back door to check on us. "How was your run this morning?"

"Great!" we said simultaneously.

"Good," Mom said. "I'm heading over to the university soon. I'll be back this afternoon. Love you both."

"Love you," we said as Mom closed the door.

Once the door was closed, Grandma said, "This move is one of the best things your mom ever did for herself. Besides having you, of course."

"Why's that?"

"Your mother is the queen of comfort. And not just those soft, fuzzy blankets you all have. Growing up, she knew what she liked and never wanted to do anything other than that. She wasn't one to try new things or take chances. I think that's part of why she and I don't always get along. We're the complete opposite in that way." I nod, suddenly realizing how right Grandma is. I couldn't pinpoint it until now. Grandma added, "That doesn't make her a bad person, you know."

"I know," I said. I thought about the past few weeks and how much I've experienced since I've been here. How many new people I've met, how many new experiences I've had, and how much I've learned. I don't know if I lived as much in the past fifteen years of my life as I have in the past four weeks in South Dakota. I didn't like it at first, but moving to South Dakota was something I was becoming happier about more and more each day.

Chapter 14

Remember how I said people were extremely friendly in South Dakota?

Well, not everyone was.

After a tough mile repeat workout with the cross country team, Adam and I went to a stretch of the Rapid Creek right in town. This morning's workout was beyond frustrating. Coach June had set paces for all of us, and I struggled to hit those times. I was even more annoyed because my teammates had no problem keeping up with the workout. Disappointment and jealousy could only be cured with one thing: an afternoon on the water.

Adam and I picked a stretch of water just past a bridge and started casting. We wanted to stay mobile and not tied down to one stretch of the creek if fish weren't biting. So, after a few minutes with no signs of fish, we walked upstream.

"All I want right now is a peaceful afternoon of fishing," I said.

Adam laughed. "Pretty sure no one ever said fishing was easy. It isn't helping that we have bluebird skies right now."

"Great weather for tanning, but not for fishing," I sighed. Not too far up ahead, I saw two men fishing with three boys, maybe middle school aged. One boy put his fishing rod on the ground and started skipping rocks across the creek.

"Are you kidding me?" Adam said.

"What's wrong?"

"That kid is literally ruining this stretch of water. He's spooking any fish that are here. Fishing definitely won't be easy now." At first I didn't agree with Adam–it was nice to see these kids out here having fun, but I got where he was coming from. Both things could be true.

We kept fishing the stretch of water we had claimed, even though there were no signs of hungry fish. Adam had been teaching me about fishing etiquette, such as: don't get too close to someone else's fishing spot, and don't steal a fishing spot until the other person is done fishing there. So we had to wait until the other group had moved on so we could fish their spot. A few minutes later, the group of men and boys walked back toward us.

"Any luck?" one man asked us.

"Not yet," Adam answered. "We haven't been out here that long, though."

"Hopefully your girlfriend won't slow you down too much," the other man chuckled. I saw Adam blush out of the corner of my eye. I felt my own cheeks flush with embarrassment.

"Hey dad!" one of the boys shouted. "What's that girl doing out here?"

"I'm fishing," I said, feeling an unnecessary need to defend myself.

"Girls can't fish. Mom doesn't even like to touch worms."

I looked at Adam, hoping he would help me out here. He just continued talking to the group of men, oblivious to the boy's comments.

The men turned toward Adam, their body language excluding me from the conversation. "The bite here has been slow the past few days, but hopefully it picks up soon. Good luck."

"Thanks, you too," Adam said.

"Boys, let's go!" The three kids ran to keep up with the men, but one boy stayed back.

"Hey," he said, looking at me. "If you catch a fish, will you touch it?"

I was about to make a snarky reply when one man shouted, "Jackson, stop talkin' to that girl and get in the car!" Jackson sprinted away.

Just as my frustration at the failed workout was subsiding, those feelings reappeared. "They were jerks," I said to Adam. He ignored me and started walking upstream. His silence aggravated me.

"This spot looks good. Let's try here."

"Are you seriously going to ignore what just happened?"

"What? Guys joke around like that all the time. They weren't being serious."

"It's not funny."

Adam thought otherwise. "I'm surprised they didn't make a comment about you not having a pink fishing rod."

"Adam! I'm serious. You didn't even stand up for me back there."

"What was I supposed to say?"

"Oh, I don't know, something about how I'm not slowing you down, or literally anything to shut them up. Or even including me in the conversation. You acted like I wasn't even there."

"Relax, Natalie."

Oh, no he didn't. I didn't care at the moment that his mom probably wasn't around to teach Adam this lesson, but he should know better than to tell a girl to relax.

"Fine. You fish here, I'm going upstream." I hiked ahead of Adam. I'd rather fish alone than with someone who treated me like I was invisible. He didn't argue or follow me. I walked far enough upstream where we would have to shout to talk to each other, but not far enough where he was out of sight. Even though I wanted to keep my distance from Adam, I wasn't ready for a solo adventure yet. I still felt better having Adam in my line of sight.

We fished for the next hour separately. As I took cast after cast, I caught myself becoming overly critical of every move. Was I making good casts? Did I even have a fly tied on that would catch fish? Then my thoughts spiraled around those sexist comments.

Hopefully your girlfriend won't hold you back.

Do girls even fish?

Would you touch a fish or a worm?

Why did those men think it was okay to say any of those things to me? And especially around what I was assuming were their kids, who asked me equally stupid and sexist questions.

I tumbled further into my own mental demise by telling myself degrading, damaging lies.

I don't fit in here.

I'm a phony.

If those guys think it's dumb that I'm out here, everyone probably thinks that. Even Adam.

I don't even know why Adam brings me with. Probably because no one else will go fishing with him.

I heard Adam holler it was time to head back to the car, and his voice broke me out of my trance. I trudged back to the car, feeling physically and mentally drained from the day.

I wouldn't let Adam off the hook, though. As we got in the car, I brought it up again. "So, when are we going to talk about what those guys said?"

"Jeez, chill. You aren't over it yet?"

"No, I'm not over it yet. What's wrong with a girl going fishing? You're the one who encouraged it, and now you won't stand up for me?"

Adam ignored my question, and neither of us spoke the entire drive home. Adam pulled into the driveway, still without saying a word to me. I couldn't wait to get away from him. I was so angry, my hands were shaking, and it was like I was seeing red. Screw Ms. Laker's advice about cutting people some slack. I wanted to wallow in my self-pity and be mad. The behavior I witnessed–from those men, from their sons, and from Adam–was maddening.

Before I slammed the car door, I had the last word. "You're such a jerk. Even more than those guys were."

Chapter 15

Back in Illinois, the Fourth of July was a pretty chill holiday. My friends and I would walk to the local fest, ride the Tilt-A-Whirl and Ferris wheel, eat funnel cakes bigger than our faces, and make sparkler art during the firework show. Always a good time with little drama.

My first Fourth of July in South Dakota was the opposite of a good time with little drama.

I had plans to join Becca's family for a boat day on Pactola Lake, and then my parents let me invite some of my new friends over to watch the Rapid City fireworks from our backyard. Adam wouldn't be on the boat, but he and his parents were probably going to be at our house for the fireworks. We hadn't talked since the incident.

Many people had the same idea for the holiday, but luckily the lake was big enough where we could all cruise around safely. The sunny skies, slight breeze, echo of country music from all the boats on the lake and screams of joy from water-skiers made me feel like I was in paradise. A pontoon cruise with my girls and a cold lemonade in my hand were exactly what I needed to take my mind off my fight with Adam. Even though Adam was the last thing I wanted to talk about, he was the only thing everyone else wanted to talk about.

"So what's new with Adam?" Ali asked, tanning in the back of the pontoon.

I hadn't told the girls the details of what happened a few nights ago, so I filled them in. By the time I was done, everyone had an opinion to share.

"I can't believe those guys said those things to you. And in front of their kids!" Becca said.

Becca's eleven-year-old sister, Jackie, agreed. "They're losers. I think it's cool that you're getting out there and having fun."

Sarah added, "And Adam is a real loser. He should've stood up for you."

"I agree," I added. "But I wonder if he was embarrassed to say something. Like, some unwritten bro code."

Becca's dad spoke up. "Sorry to eavesdrop, but I have to jump in here. You're all correct. Natalie, good for you for learning how to fly-fish. I wish Becca and Jackie would come with me more." He gave both of his daughters a look, then turned back to me. "Those guys were wrong to say those things about you. But I also get why Adam didn't stand up for you. It's way easier to stand up for people when you're older. But don't forget, you're all teenagers. You want to look cool all the time, right?"

"Yeah," we said in unison.

"And how many times do you step in to stop someone from doing something they shouldn't be doing, especially if you're around other people? Don't they talk about peer pressure at school?"

I hate when the adults are right.

"All you can control are your thoughts and your actions. What's done is done. Now, all you can do is move forward. If you didn't like how those guys treated you, and you shouldn't, what can you do about it?"

I took another sip of my lemonade, which tasted warmer and more watered down since the ice cubes had melted. Becca's dad's advice really resonated with me. I thought about what he said—what could I do about it? I was a fifteen-year-old fly fishing wannabe. What impact could I possibly make? How could I possibly prove anyone wrong, being so new to fly fishing myself?

●　　●　　●　　●　　●

After a fun morning cruising around Lake Pactola, we were ready to head back to my house and devour all the Fourth of July foods. Upon arrival, I could smell every grilled meat imaginable. Dad was in the backyard, thriving at his happy place at the grill, while my mom and grandma sat on the porch drinking lemonades. My parents set up a bags set and a volleyball net, and most importantly, a snack table.

The conversations on the boat this morning had me feeling more confused than ever. I was still mad at Adam for a lot of reasons. First, for how he acted at the creek. And now, for ghosting me for as long as he had. If he came over today, it would be SO awkward.

Since the girls knew everything that had happened, I knew I would have to ask them to do something I would normally ask Syd to do. But Syd knew nothing about the situation, and she was barely acting like a friend, so I would rather ask Ali, Becca, and Sarah.

"I need you all to do me a favor," I said as we grazed at the snack table. "I need a buffer if Adam comes over."

"Operation Avoid?" Ali suggested. "I'm a pro at that. We got you covered."

I smiled, relieved that I had friends to count on. But there wasn't much time to plan our operation because it began almost immediately.

Adam and Mato walked into the backyard, along with a woman I had never seen before. She had long, dark hair, and her big tortoise-shell sunglasses covered most of her face. Not only was I feeling annoyed and awkward, now I had to figure out who the mystery woman was.

Adam walked toward my friends and me, but Ali took the lead. "I got this. Natalie, go inside. You're getting more chips."

"I am?"

"Operation Avoid! Play along." Ali and Becca walked over to Adam, distracting him while I went inside. Not long after, Sarah joined me.

"We need to watch and observe for a bit before you go back out there," Sarah directed. I appreciated her cues to execute the operation as smooth as possible. I was too flustered to think for myself. "You also need to figure out what you're going to say to him. Or even if you want to say anything to him."

As I pondered whether or not to give Adam the silent treatment all night, I watched Mystery Woman go straight to the alcohol cooler. My parents didn't drink often, but they would knock back a few for the holidays, including the Fourth. She closed the cooler and walked toward the house.

"Hey, is there any wine?" Mystery Woman asked when she opened the back door. No introduction, and honestly, no manners, period. Sarah and I looked at each other, totally thrown off our strategy. This was not on our bingo card for today.

"Um, I don't think so. Just what's outside." I knew my mom had wine downstairs, but I figured if it wasn't out, she didn't want people to drink it.

"Cool." She closed the door and beelined for the cooler, grabbed a beer, and chugged it quickly. In less than five minutes, she was going back to the cooler for a second one. Ali and Becca joined me inside the house, their eyes as wide as could be.

"Time to debrief." Becca declared. "Adam acted like nothing ever happened between the two of you. He asked where you were. I just said you were moving laundry around."

"Why would I be doing laundry?" I asked.

"That's what I said!" Ali exclaimed. "Not our best lie. But then we saw Adam's mom talk to you guys, and then chug that beer faster than anyone in my brother's frat."

So that's who the Mystery Woman was. That tracked, based on the little bit I knew about her. "For what it's worth, this is the first time I've ever seen or talked to Adam's mom. She didn't even introduce herself, she just asked where the wine was."

"That's so weird," Becca said.

"I KNOW," Sarah and I said at the same time.

"Do you know how you're gonna handle the Adam situation?" Ali asked.

"I can't avoid him forever," I said. "But I'm not starting this conversation. I shouldn't have to." My friends nodded in approval. "Let's go back outside. I'll wait until he comes over to me, and then I'll figure it out from there."

Just as we stepped onto the back deck, Adam made his way over to us.

"Nat, can I talk to you for a minute?"

Chapter 16

We all stared at Adam, not saying a word. You know you have good friends because when one person was mad at someone, you were all mad at that person, no questions asked.

"Sure." He and I walked to the bags set.

"I wanted to talk to you as soon as I got here, but you were inside doing laundry." Adam's comment confused me at first, and then remembered that was my cover. Operation Avoid.

"Oh yeah," I lied. "My grandma got ketchup on my tank top. I didn't want it to stain!" I was getting better at fishing, but I would always be bad at lying.

Adam smirked. I couldn't tell if he believed me or not, but it didn't really matter. "Look, I'm sorry about the other day. You're right, I should've said something to those guys."

"Yeah, you should have." I stood with my arms crossed, waiting for him to continue.

"You've learned a lot in the few weeks we've been fishing together, and I'm glad this is something we can do together. I also know people have dumb stereotypes about girls fishing. It's so cool that you're into fly fishing; I just didn't know what to say to those guys in that moment."

"You didn't know what to say? Or were you too worried about a stranger's opinion?"

Silence.

I thought about Grandma and how she never cared what people thought of her, and how happy that made her–as far as I knew. That was also how I wanted to live my life.

I sighed. "Look, you can care what other people think of you and let it hold you back from living your best life, or you can stop caring what people think. Especially the wrong people. You cared more about the opinions of two strangers in the woods than you did about me."

Adam sighed. "You're right. I'm going to work on it."

I had to make a choice, too. Either stay mad at him for this or forgive and move on. I chose the latter. He had to swallow his pride in order to apologize, so I opened my arms for a hug. He accepted, and when he wrapped his arms around me, I felt the stress of the last few days melt away. Adam and I would be okay.

"Now that we got that out of the way, I'm assuming the mystery woman with you and Mato is your mom?" I asked.

"Yeah. She actually came with us today." Adam rolled his eyes. "Did you meet her yet? I'm being really rude–"

"Yeah, you are," I smirked, hoping he could pick up on my sarcasm.

"Come on, I said I was sorry."

I took a step closer to him. "I know. I was kidding. But if your mom asking me for wine is considered an introduction, then yes, I've met her."

"Typical. Let's go say hi, so she doesn't yell at me for being a rude boy."

"Boy?" I laughed.

"For real. I'm sixteen and she still calls me a boy."

I was going to have to tease him for that another time. Adam's mom was talking to my grandma on the deck, so we walked in their direction.

I heard Grandma say, "And that's how you make bourbon." Of course, Grandma knew how to make bourbon, and I was also grateful that she could hold a conversation with Adam's mom. Maybe that would prevent her from causing any more embarrassing moments at this party.

"Mom," Adam interrupted their conversation, "I want you to meet Natalie."

Adam's mom turned to look at me. "We met already. You said there wasn't any wine here. But there's plenty of beer, so that will have to do. You can call me Jasmine."

She turned back to Grandma to continue their conversation, clearly more interested in how to make bourbon than talking to Adam and me. We stood there awkwardly, not knowing what to do next.

"Do either of you need anything?" I asked.

"I'm going to go inside for a bit to cool off," Grandma said. She squeezed my hand before going inside.

Jasmine said, "I'll have another beer." I thought she would go get it herself, but she stared at us like we were her servants. Adam reluctantly went to the cooler, knowing he would lose the silent stand-off. I tried to think of ways to break the awkward silence with Adam's mom.

"So, Adam told me you're an artist?"

"Yes. Are you dating my son?"

I was not expecting that question at all. I felt my cheeks turn red, partly because that was such a blunt question from a woman I didn't know, and partly because of what I wanted the answer to be, even though it wasn't true. "No, we're just friends."

"Good, dating the new girl is so cliche. I mean, you're cute, but he hardly knows you."

"Mom!" Adam shoved the beer into his mom's hands, grabbed my arm, and pulled me toward my friends playing bags on the other side of the yard. I was too stunned to even process what had happened.

"Nat, you okay?" Becca asked.

"Honestly, I'm not sure," I answered. I didn't want to lie and say everything was okay, because it wasn't.

"My dumb, drunk mom said some idiotic things to Natalie. I'm sorry about that," Adam said. I nodded, accepting his apology.

I didn't care as much about what Jasmine said, but I worried that was really how Adam felt. Was he just hanging out with me because I was the new girl? Like he felt sorry for me? I shoved that thought into the back of my mind. I didn't want to let that moment ruin an already dramatic afternoon.

We continued to enjoy the party, including a bags tournament and a kid vs. adult volleyball game. No surprise to anyone, but Grandma had a killer serve no one could return. As it got closer to sunset, we prepped for the fireworks show by lighting sparklers, swirling them around, and taking too many pictures and videos. As Adam and I were writing "USA" with our sparklers, Jasmine walked toward us. At least, she tried to. She couldn't walk in a straight line, and tripped every other step she took.

"Woah there!" she slurred her words. "Are there some sparklers for me?"

"Jasmine," Mato walked over. "I don't think you need sparklers right now."

"Don't tell me what I need!" Everyone got quiet and stared at Jasmine and Mato. I looked at Adam. His face was red, and he looked furious. Jasmine walked over to my dad, who was holding the bag of sparklers, and she tried to take them out of his hand.

"Mom, stop!" Adam yelled. He went over to his mom and grabbed her hand. "I think you need to go home."

"It's time to party! Happy birthday, America!" Jasmine started clapping her hands and cheering, even though the fireworks hadn't started and nothing was happening. Just as suddenly as she was ready to party, Jasmine yawned and walked over to the blanket laid out on the grass. She laid down, stared at me, and said, "I want to hang out more with your grandma! She's way more fun than your mom." And then she fell asleep. Within minutes, she was snoring.

I had no idea what to do. Luckily, Adam and Mato came over and grabbed Jasmine. Adam grabbed her legs, and Mato lifted her up by the arms.

"So frickin' embarrassing," Adam muttered. They carried her back home. A few minutes later, the first fireworks exploded in the sky. Would Adam and Mato come back? At the very least, I hoped Adam would. I envisioned this fairytale moment in my head where Adam and

I watched the fireworks together, and maybe he would kiss me (bonus points if my parents weren't secretly spying on us). I kept checking my phone to see how much time had passed, and after twenty minutes, I assumed he wasn't coming back.

"Hey," I heard behind me. I turned around and saw Adam. "Is it too late to join you?"

"Not at all," I replied as he sat down next to me. He grabbed my hand, and even though I didn't let go, the fireworks weren't there between us like they were in the sky. I couldn't stop thinking about Jasmine's behavior and what she said about my mom. How dare she come over and insult my family, especially when she barely knew us? But she was drunk, so did she really mean it? I felt confused and my wandering thoughts distracted me from the finale of the fireworks show.

"Nat?" Adam said my name, sounding worried.

"Huh?" I snapped back to reality.

"You were zoning out. I asked if you wanted to grab dinner tomorrow. I'll take you wherever you want to go."

I hoped we had the same idea in mind. "Like a date?"

"Yeah, like a date," Adam confirmed. "I owe you one after today."

"That sounds great." I squeezed his hand as the last fireworks exploded in the sky.

Chapter 17

The next day, Adam and I planned to go out to dinner in downtown Rapid City, then go watch a movie. Clearly, there was potential for something more than friendship between us, and tonight would allow us to test those unchartered waters. As I was getting ready that afternoon, Mom came into my room.

"Do you know what you're going to wear?" Mom asked. We didn't always talk about girly things like this, but when we did, I absolutely loved it. I could enjoy fly fishing, going for ninety-minute runs, and doing my hair and make-up. All those things could exist together.

"I was thinking those light wash jeans with the frayed hem, and that golden yellow tank top," I said, pointing to the clothes hanging on the closet door.

"You're wearing jeans! You must like Adam even more than I realized," Mom teased. She was right about the jeans; I only wore jeans on special occasions. But I still was unsure about how much I liked Adam, and if our friendship was meant to be something more. Was I attracted to him? Yes. But I thought about what my friends told me about Adam, and last night's chaos with Adam's mom. If I was going to get any clarity about my relationship with Adam tonight, I had to do my best to ignore outside opinions from my friends and family.

"We'll see," I said. "That's what dates are for, right?" Mom sat on my bed and we chatted and listened to Taylor Swift while I finished getting ready. Just before 5 p.m., the doorbell rang. Suddenly, I felt nervous. Why was I nervous? Adam and I hung out alone all the time. I didn't realize until now that labeling tonight as a date would make things feel so…different.

"Just have fun. You and Adam are already great friends, and I hope that never changes. And if your friendship turns into something more, remember that a lot of relationships start out as strong friendships." Mom rubbed my back, I took a deep breath, checked my hair one more time, then skipped downstairs. I could see Adam through the front door window, running his fingers through his hair. That was his nervous twitch. It was reassuring to know he was nervous, too.

"Hey," I said as I opened the door.

"Hey." He even sounded nervous. "You look great."

"So do you." I felt like we were being watched, and sure enough, my mom and dad were standing on the stairs, watching our every awkward move.

"You kids have fun!" Dad waved at us, acting a little too eager about my date.

"Thanks, Mr. Ryba," Adam said, handling my embarrassing parents with dignity, while I rolled my eyes and waved back as I walked toward Adam's car.

The drive from our block to downtown Rapid City took ten minutes, but it felt like ten hours. Neither of us said a word in the car. I obviously knew how I was feeling, but I couldn't stop wondering what Adam was thinking and feeling. Was this weird for him, too? Were we better off as friends after all? We would never find out if no one talked all night.

"Is the food good here?" Really, Nat? Why would Adam take me to a place where the food is bad? I tucked my hair behind my ear and stared out the window, hoping Adam wouldn't think anything of that painfully stupid question.

"It's incredible," he responded. "Lots of options. I think you'll love it." When we got to the restaurant, we sat outside. It was a perfect summer evening with low humidity and barely any wind.

The awkward small talk continued, ranging in topics from the weather to my thoughts on the Cubs, who were back to being a terrible team. Once we placed our orders (chislic as an appetizer, chicken sliders for me, and a bison burger for Adam), the actual conversation began.

"So," Adam started, "I hope you're not mad about the Fourth of July."

"I'm not," I answered honestly. "I know you apologized for how you acted on the river, but I'm worried that will happen again."

"It won't."

"How do I know that? I didn't think you would act the way you did the first time."

Adam didn't answer right away. As each second of silence passed, my anxiety levels rose. My palms were sweaty, and I feared that the rest of our night would be full of conflict and tension before the appetizer arrived.

"You don't."

Huh?

"Look, I'm not perfect, as I've made very obvious in the past few days. But I know I was wrong, and I will work on being more supportive. That's what good friends do."

Now it was my turn to process before answering. First, that was a very mature response for a teenage boy. Maybe he learned that from his dad? Or he had a weird social media algorithm where he watched a lot of self-help videos? Either way, it worked for me. Second, he said *friends,* which we were, but someone had to make a move at some point. And if I'd learned anything in South Dakota so far, it's that you can't let the unknown stop you from living life.

I reached my hand across the table, and Adam held my hand. With our sweaty fingers intertwined, I said, "Thank you. I trust you, and I'm ready to put this behind us and move forward."

As if on cue, the server brought us our chislic and grinned at us holding hands. Adam and I frantically unlaced our hands and placed them in our laps like we got in trouble. Honestly, I felt more comfortable once I let go.

The chislic helped ease our nerves and hanger. After Adam got the check, we drove to the movie theater. I didn't know my way around Rapid City too well yet, but I knew the direction Adam was driving wasn't toward the movie theater.

Oh no. This was what they always warned you about. I was getting kidnapped.

"Aren't we going to the movies?" I tried to hide the panic in my voice, but epically failed.

"It's too nice of a night to sit inside. What do you think about ice cream and a walk?"

I exhaled and felt my shoulders drop. "That sounds great." Partly because I love ice cream, and partly because I realized I wouldn't die that night.

Adam bought our scoops of ice cream (cookies and cream for me, vanilla for him) and we walked to a nearby park to eat our ice cream. The tension weighed heavier and heavier on me as our silence grew. It felt weird to hold hands earlier, and the thought of any more hand-holding, or even kissing, made me nervous. Not because I didn't like Adam, but because I realized I wanted to continue being friends, and not have any romance interfere with that.

"Let's sit here for a bit," Adam gestured to a nearby bench. When we sat down, I stared down at the melted remains of my ice cream, and Adam put his arm around me. Yep, this felt awkward, too. Adam's arm felt stiff around my shoulders, and I wondered if he felt the same way.

I looked at Adam, and before I could realize what was happening, he moved in to kiss me. I'd seen enough movies and read enough books to know this moment should feel like fireworks or melting into a cozy blanket, but there was none of that. In eighth grade, I had my first kiss with this boy in most of my classes, Blake. He kissed me at the end of the eighth-grade dance, as we finished an awkward dance to Green

Day's "Good Riddance (Time of Your Life)". There weren't any fireworks with my kiss with Blake, and there weren't any fireworks with Adam, either. It wasn't a bad kiss, I just felt…nothing.

Adam and I pulled away after the quick kiss and stared at each other. What was I supposed to say? What if he felt something that I didn't?

Simultaneously, we both blurted, "I think we should just be friends." Then we laughed, relieved the feeling was mutual.

"I knew kissing you would help me figure out how I felt once and for all," Adam explained. "And I don't want to mess up our friendship."

"I feel the same way!" That agreement sounded too eager, so I explained myself more. "I mean, I was excited to go on this date with you, but as the night went on, I realized I don't want to be more than friends. At least right now."

Adam smiled, taking his hand away from around my shoulders. "I agree. You're quickly becoming one of my best friends, but I definitely needed to see if there was anything more there. Maybe one day, but not right now."

"Look at us, being mature!" We high-fived and laughed.

"Want to watch *A River Runs Through It* at my house?" Adam asked.

"That sounds perfect."

Chapter 18

My date with Adam left me feeling at peace. I had no regrets about any of it: the conversations, the hand-holding, or the kiss, even though some of those moments were so cringey. Those risks confirmed we were better off as friends (for now), and it was a relief to know Adam was on the same page. Our foundation was solid. So solid that it was about to be put to the test once again.

A few days after our date, my family hosted dinner for Grandma, Adam, and Mato. My parents kindly invited Jasmine, despite how rude she was on the Fourth of July, but she said she had to finish some artwork for an upcoming show. Dad and Mato grilled bison burgers, and the six of us ate dinner on our back deck. All week it had been hot and dry, but I could feel the heavy humidity in the air.

"Storms must be rolling in tonight or tomorrow," Mato commented as we sat down to eat. Then he looked at me and said, "Natalie, Adam and I have a question to ask you."

I wondered what they were going to ask, especially since it was a team question. "Shoot."

"My dad and I planned a weekend trip to go hiking and fly fishing in Montana," Adam said. "We'll fish the Gallatin, near Bozeman and Big Sky. It feels like you're in a movie. We go there a few times a year to either fish in the summer, or go skiing in the winter. We're going in a week and a half, and we want you to come with, if you want to and you're available." Adam looked nervous, but also relieved after he asked. I thought I knew nothing about South Dakota, but I knew even less about Montana, besides that it existed. Sadly, I unlocked my phone to look at a map of where Montana was in relation to South Dakota, and how big of a state it was.

"What are you doing?" Mom asked, embarrassed by how rude it appeared I was being.

"I didn't know how far Montana was from here."

"The Bozeman and Big Sky area is about seven hours from here. We would leave Thursday afternoon and have all day Friday and Saturday to fish and hike, and then part of Sunday before driving home Sunday," Mato explained, mostly to Mom and Dad.

"That sounds awesome," Dad said.

"Where would you be staying?" Mom asked right away.

"In an RV that I'm borrowing from a friend," Mato said. "It's in great shape and we've used it for the past two summers. We stay at a campsite. Sometimes we'll sleep in the RV, and if the weather is perfect, sometimes we'll sleep in a tent. There's enough space, so we're all spread out." Oh no, did the parents think Adam and I would try to hook up on this trip? That *definitely* wouldn't happen on a remote fly fishing trip, and Adam and I already kissed and had no interest in kissing again anytime soon.

Mom's next question was, "Is there cell service?"

"Depends on where you are," Mato answered honestly. "It's not the best at the campsite that we're at, but we'll stop in town for food and gas, and there's service in town. If Natalie goes, we'll let you know exactly where we'll stay, and provide any other information you need."

Mom nodded and then looked at me. "What do you think, Natalie?"

"I agree with Dad. It sounds awesome."

"Really? You've never been camping. And you didn't even know where Montana was."

"Trish, she said it sounds fun," Grandma chimed in. "And Adam and Mato seem like very safe people to be in the Montana wilderness with."

"We always keep bear spray on us at a minimum, but Dad usually carries a pistol just in case, too," Adam said casually, like he told someone he has pencils and notebooks in his backpack for school.

"A pistol?" Mom sounded worried, like this information might cause her to not let me go on this trip.

"I think that's smart and responsible," Dad said. "In case there are bears or moose that get too close." I was thankful for Dad's voice of reason to ease Mom's anxiety.

"Me too," Grandma added. "Montana is beautiful, Nat. I think you'll love it."

"When have you been to Montana?" I asked.

"Years ago, your grandpa and I went to Glacier National Park. Beautiful beyond words. I've also been to Big Sky. Justin Timberlake has a house there."

Does Justin Timberlake fly-fish? I would never guess Montana would be the place for celebrity sightings, but apparently I was wrong. "How do you know?"

"I Googled it." Grandma said, sounding proud of her research skills. "If you go, you'll see what I mean about how beautiful it is. But you have to see it for yourself."

Now I was intrigued. I could see where Justin Timberlake lived, travel to another new state, and spend an entire weekend with Adam.

"What's the fishing like?" I asked.

"Think about how fun fishing here has been," Adam said. "Now multiply that times 100."

"That's a lot of fun," I laughed. "I'm in," I declared.

"Yes!" Adam high-fived me, and then fist-pumped the air. "This is going to be the best weekend." We spent the rest of dinner talking about the trip—Adam and Mato shared some of their best Montana memories, Grandma told us more about Glacier National Park, and

Mom asked a thousand questions about bears, moose, and sleeping arrangements.

After dinner, Grandma pulled me aside. "You must be so excited about this trip! A weekend away with a cute boy," Grandma winked.

I blushed. "Yes, a weekend away with a cute boy and a great friend," I said, trying to play it cool. Even though Adam and I agreed to remain friends, I could still think he was attractive.

"This will be your biggest adventure yet. Enjoy every second, and you better tell me about everything when you get back."

"Of course I will! You'll be the first person I tell, along with Mom and Dad, of course."

After everyone left, my parents and I made a bonfire in the backyard. Mom and Dad started brainstorming home improvement projects for the weekend I'll be in Montana.

"Maybe while you're gone, we'll put together that bookshelf in the office," Dad suggested.

"And pick out new handles for the kitchen cabinets," Mom added.

"You know I'm only going to be gone for three days, right?"

"I know," Mom said, "But we'll miss you! I'll need to stay busy." While they kept talking about home improvement projects, I journaled about my upcoming Montana trip. I wrote a list of what I was excited for and what I was nervous about:

Excited about:
- Going to another new state
- Learning more about fly fishing
- Getting to know Mato better
- Seeing more mountains
- Camping for the first time
- Beautiful hikes
- Catching my biggest trout (hopefully!)
- Spending more time with Adam

Nervous about:
- Seeing a grizzly bear
- Getting hurt
- Bad weather
- Spotty cell service
- Spending more time with Adam

I glanced down at my list—more to be excited about than nervous about. Just as it should be.

Chapter 19

In a few days, I would head to the wilderness of Montana with two men. Or, with a sixteen-year-old boy and his dad, anyway. Totally unfamiliar territory for me, both literally and figuratively. There were a million things I should have been doing to prepare for this trip, but all I wanted was girl time, pizza, and a bonfire. I felt like most people would be embarrassed to hang out with their friends and their grandma simultaneously, but my teammates were excited to see my grandma again, since the last time was on the Fourth of July.

Ali, Sara, and Becca came over, and we were snacking on raspberries in the kitchen when Grandma walked in with a small duffel bag on her shoulder.

"Hi Grandma," I greeted. "What's in the bag?"

"Some things for your big Montana weekend!" she exclaimed.

"We definitely need to talk about your weekend getaway with Adam," Sarah said. "Camping and hiking in Montana? How romantic."

"His dad will be there, so definitely not romantic," I said. "And we agreed to just be friends."

"It better not be romantic!" Mom shouted from the living room.

"It won't!" I shouted back. "Really, it won't be," I said again, this time to my friends.

"Yeah, yeah, we'll see." Sarah teased, rolling her eyes.

Although Adam and I decided to just be friends, I wondered in the back of my mind if a weekend away would change anything. We agreed to be friends…for now. I wanted to hear what my friends thought, but at another time. I didn't want to discuss the possible romantic implications of this trip around my grandmother. She was cool, but she was still my grandma.

I approached the duffel bag on the table. "Let's see what's in here." I unzipped the bag and found a random assortment of survival and outdoor items: bear spray, a new hat, socks, a windbreaker, a long sleeve top, and a pink funnel. I took all the items and laid them out on the kitchen table. Ali, Becca, Sarah, and Mom joined me to look at what Grandma had brought.

"The duffel bag is yours, too," Grandma added.

"These are great things to have for your trip!" Mom said. "You didn't have to do this, Mom. That was very nice of you." I watched Mom and Grandma hug. Even though they had their differences, I loved when they got along–and meant it. Mom picked up the pink funnel. "What exactly is this for?" Mom asked.

"Oh! I read about it online. And you haven't been camping before, Natalie, so you probably haven't thought about this yet. Do you know where you're going to pee if you're not near a toilet all day?"

Grandma's question stunned me. I stared at the pink funnel, then at Grandma, and back at the funnel again. I hadn't thought about the bathroom at all. What else hadn't I thought of yet? I needed to say something before my brain spiraled out of control.

"Um, that's a fantastic question." I thought about it for a minute because I still didn't know what I would do. "I mean, I could hold it as long as possible, but that would get uncomfortable."

"This is why guys have it made," Ali said. "They can pee wherever, and whenever, they want."

"And now you can, too," Grandma interjected, "with this funnel!"

"Wait." I picked up the pink funnel. It was a little bigger than my hand and made of silicone. If this was supposed to be used for peeing, then…

"So it basically helps girls pee like guys do?" Sarah said exactly what I was thinking.

"Exactly!" Grandma shouted. "And you don't even need to pull your pants down all the way. This won't help with solid waste, if you know what I mean. Do that at camp, or you might need to go squat behind a tree if it's an emergency."

"Fantastic," I deadpanned.

Mom giggled. "Do you want to test it out?"

"Yes!" All my friends exclaimed.

I had been chugging water all day, and immediately felt the need to pee. "Fine," I grumbled, walking to the bathroom.

"No!" Grandma said. "Go test it outside!"

"In the backyard?"

"Yes!" Becca laughed. "You need to try this out in a natural habitat." Everyone was laughing now.

I turned around and walked to the backyard. Is this how dogs felt when they had to go pee? Thank God our backyard was fenced in. I went to the side of the house so my family and friends couldn't watch me test out the funnel. I was wearing running shorts, so I didn't need to unzip anything. This should be pretty easy, in theory. I adjusted my shorts, put the top opening of the funnel where it needed to go, and then there was only one thing left to do.

I started peeing through the funnel.

I've never been more jealous of boys before in my entire life. This was amazing! Grandma was a genius!

Just as I was finishing, I heard a familiar voice shout, "What the hell are you doing?" My face turned bright red, and I splashed a couple of pee drops on my leg. I removed the funnel and quickly adjusted my shorts before looking to see where the voice came from. I had to look up to find it.

"Did you just pee out of that thing?" Adam laughed. He poked his head out of an upstairs window.

"Did you just watch me pee?" I shrieked. This was mortifying.

"I did." Adam couldn't stop laughing. "Where did you get a pee funnel?"

I sighed, embarrassed about the whole situation. Adam just watched me pee. Outside. Out of a funnel. "My grandma actually gave it to me. She got me some things to bring on our trip, including the funnel. I didn't even think about not having access to a toilet most of the weekend."

"Me either. That was really smart of her." He was still laughing. "What a funny, but amazing invention. And I promise I won't watch you pee when we're in Montana. Okay, maybe once. Not in a creepy way–it's just hilarious to watch a girl pee like a guy."

"Shut up," I laughed back. "I'm not letting you watch me pee! I didn't even know you were up there!"

"I was putting laundry away and just so happened to look out my window. There you were, testing out your new survival goods." Adam said. "Tell you what. I'll help you think of other things you might need, and I'll text you a list of stuff later."

"Sounds good," I shouted back.

"Later," Adam said before he closed his window.

I walked back inside, and everyone was awaiting my return.

"What took you so long?" Becca asked. I explained what happened, and we all burst out laughing.

"That's the funniest thing ever!" Sarah was laughing so hard tears rolled from the corners of her eyes. Even Mom couldn't stop laughing, and she didn't freak out that my best guy friend had just watched her daughter pee through a funnel.

After testing out the funnel, Mom ordered pizzas for dinner. She and Grandma made a salad in the kitchen (using fresh vegetables from Grandma's garden, of course), and my friends and I hung out in the basement. We were watching YouTube videos when I got a text from Adam. He sent me a list of other items I might want to bring on our trip to Montana.

```
Waders, or shoes you can wear in the water,
sunscreen,  bug  spray,  nail  clippers,  water
```

bladder, sunglasses. We'll need more flies for where we're fishing, but we can stop in the local fly shops for those.

Another text came through. It said, Don't forget the funnel! I swiped out of my texts and went back to laughing at videos of dogs riding on Roomba vacuums. Eventually, the smell of cheese and pepperoni filled the air.

"Pizza's here!" Mom called down to us.

We went upstairs and sat down with Mom and Grandma. "Grandma, how did you know what stuff I would need for Montana?" I asked.

"I know you've been more interested in fishing lately—or Adam, more so than fishing—either way, I looked up some things you would need for a weekend of fishing and camping. And like I told you before, I've been to Montana, so I know what you might experience out there."

"You and Dad went to Glacier for your twenty-fifth anniversary, right?"

"That's right," Grandma smiled. "And we went several times after that, too. It's unbelievably beautiful out there. When you drive into the park, there are mountains everywhere. There's a river that cuts through the park called the Flathead River. People say the water in the Caribbean is pristine turquoise water. I would argue the color of the Flathead River, and the lakes in Glacier, is even prettier."

"Really?" Sarah asked. "I went to Hawaii a couple summers ago, and I remember the water was so clear. It's hard to imagine water even prettier than that."

"Oh yes, Hawaii is beautiful," Grandma agreed. "But I would pick Montana over Hawaii if someone made me choose. Anyway, back to Glacier. There are some different hikes you can do, and plenty of campsites. One of my favorite hikes was around these two waterfalls. Oh, they were magnificent. You girls could look it up on your phones, but pictures don't do any of it justice."

Challenge accepted. We grabbed our phones and searched Glacier National Park. Grandma wasn't kidding. The water was bright turquoise, pine and fir trees towered over the lakes, and snow-capped mountains surrounded the parks. I also read there were over 700 miles of trails to hike. Custer State Park seemed big to me; I couldn't fathom over 700 miles of trails and over one million acres of wide, open spaces.

"There's a lot of beautiful country out there to see," Grandma said after taking a few bites of salad. "You all should see as much as you can in your lifetime. And actually SEE it, don't just take pictures and videos on your phone without appreciating where you are. These cell phones are nice, but part of me is glad I didn't have them when I was growing up."

"Agreed," Mom said. "I worry sometimes that your generation depends on your phones too much. They're great and all, but can you go all day without it?"

"I'm about to find out," I joked. "I'll let you know."

Mom, Grandma, and my friends talked more about some places they've traveled to. Grandma had the most to share, and her captivating stories kept all of us laughing and listening the entire evening. Mom even shared a couple of stories about trips she went on with Grandma when she was growing up. I had nothing to contribute to this conversation, and felt like a sad, uncultured hermit. I'd been to four states: Illinois, Wisconsin, Iowa, and now South Dakota. It was no secret that Mom didn't like to travel, and Dad would do whatever Mom wanted to do, which resulted in our lack of family vacations. But tonight showed me I had a lot in common with grandma's adventurous spirit, and I was even more excited now about this next adventure.

Chapter 20

The day before leaving for Montana, Adam and I went to Crazy Horse Lake, located a little over an hour away from Rapid City, in the heart of the Black Hills. Crazy Horse Lake was going to be good fly fishing practice for Montana. Adam packed the car with our fly fishing gear, turkey and bacon wraps, Chex Mix, and beef jerky. Between cross country training and fishing days, I'd never eaten more in my life!

"Did you buy some of the things I suggested for this weekend?" Adam asked on the drive over.

"Most things," I said. "Mom found a pair of cheap waders on Amazon. She insists waders are safer than water shoes. They should be delivered tonight."

"She isn't wrong. You'll stay protected from poison ivy and thorny branches and stuff like that. The water can be ice cold in some of these creeks, so waders keep you warm."

"Good to know." Every time I felt like I was grasping an understanding of the great outdoors, I learned something new. "My parents and I went out and bought the other things you mentioned, and a lot of other stuff my mom insists I bring."

"She worries about you a lot, doesn't she?" Adam asked.

"Sometimes. It's about the most random things, too. She won't stop asking questions about this trip, but it didn't bother her at all that you saw me pee through a funnel in the backyard."

Adam laughed. "It's probably because this is all new for her, too. New state, new job. Not to mention, you're picking up reckless hobbies. I don't blame her for being worried."

"How is fly fishing reckless?"

"A teenage boy you just met takes a pretty girl into the remote wilderness to catch trout, with the potential of encountering untamed wildlife, and all the other potential things that can go wrong in a rural environment."

I couldn't help but smile and do my best to focus on the point he was trying to make. "You're right. It's a lot for her to adjust to. And you're also right that I'm pretty."

Where did that confidence come from? I needed to do that more often—not overthink everything I said and did.

"I bet your mom doesn't worry about you the way my mom worries about me." I went from overthinking to not thinking at all, and I immediately regretted my choice of words. My cheeks burned as I tried to take back my awful word vomit. "I'm so sorry. That's not what I meant at all."

Adam shook his head and smiled, then he finally responded. "No, but there's nothing I can do about the way she is. At least I have one good parent. My dad trusts me, because I learned everything I know about the outdoors from him. And some YouTube hacks here and there. Even though my dad's pretty chill, it's the things he can't control that worry him."

"Like what?"

"Weather, animals, other people, stuff like that. Last year I went out fly fishing with a buddy. It was the perfect day. Mid seventies, not too windy, sunny, but with a little cloud cover. Couldn't ask for better weather. All of a sudden, a storm appeared out of nowhere. That happens here sometimes. I wasn't close to his car, either."

"So, what did you do?"

Adam laughed. "I ran back as fast as I could, but I couldn't outrun the rain. I was soaked by the time I got to the car. The worst part was, my friend wasn't at the car yet, and he had the keys. I had nowhere to take shelter, so I covered my head with my backpack. But my backpack was soaked, so that didn't help at all. A minute later, I saw him running from the other direction. He was soaked, too. He unlocked his car, and we threw our things in the trunk and drove off, just as lightning struck a tree maybe 100 yards from us."

"No way! That close?"

"Yeah! It was so loud. The drive home was nuts, too. We were about an hour away, but it took way longer than that. He had to drive so slow for the first part of it because it was raining so much. My buddy had the wipers going as fast as they could, and that still didn't help. About ten miles from home, the rain cleared up, and the sun came out like nothing had happened. I'm glad Mom wasn't around for that one; she would've freaked out."

"Sounds crazy." I could only imagine how my mom would freak out if I was stuck in the woods an hour away from home during a torrential thunderstorm.

"It was. Even I got a little scared. But sometimes things like that happen. At the end of the day, we made it back safe. The worst thing that happened was getting cold and wet. You just have to roll with the punches sometimes, you know? You can't always predict what's gonna happen."

Adam winked at me, and then I busted out the snacks as he continued driving. The drive to Crazy Horse Lake was beautiful, just like the rest of the drives we've been on together. As we got closer to the lake, we drove through some small towns connected by rural, winding roads. Cell service disappeared as we got closer to the lake. I didn't mind, though, because I was taking in the scenery. There were houses few and far between, sitting on acres of land. Some of them had horses, and I saw a couple of people on riding lawn mowers. Every person waved to us. I wondered if we were one of the first people to drive through this area today, or how many people drove this way.

Crazy Horse Lake wasn't as vast and beautiful as Pactola, but it was still beautiful in its own way. The road curved around the lake, and then I noticed a creek jutting out from the lake. The road followed down the creek, and Adam parked near a spot that has a makeshift bridge to cross the creek and access a public campground.

"This is it," Adam proclaimed. "Let's scope it out before grabbing our things." The grass here was tall, and I was glad I had pants on. I didn't want to scratch my legs on something thorny or accidentally touch something poisonous. I followed Adam down a makeshift path to the creek. He was a few steps ahead of me, but he turned around, put his hand out to tell me to slow down, and then put his index finger to his lips to tell me to be quiet. I approached the creek cautiously, and when I got closer, Adam pointed to the water. This creek ran crystal clear, and I couldn't believe what I saw in the water. As clear as day, I saw dozens of large trout. They weren't swimming around much, but if they moved, it was to eat something off the bottom of the creek. No fish were rising.

"We're going to have to be quiet and stay out of sight," Adam whispered. "Let's grab our rods, and then approach slowly again. Make sure you walk upstream so you don't spook any fish." I nodded, still in awe of the jumbo trout I saw. They were all over twelve inches long, maybe even closer to eighteen or twenty inches. Some of them looked fat, too, almost like they had shoulders or a hunched back. If that's what they looked like in the water, I couldn't imagine what they looked like out of the water.

We grabbed our gear from the car, and Adam took the lead walking back to the creek. He avoided loud, tall grass, and followed worn-down paths toward the water. I walked a few feet behind, trying my best to stay as quiet as possible. Once Adam got closer to the creek, he positioned himself a few feet back from the edge to stay out of sight from the trout. I looked at my fly rod and noticed Adam had tied on the smallest fly I had ever seen. It had a copper bead-head, and the tiniest brown body. I had seen Adam throw nymphs before, but I had mostly thrown flies that looked like worms up to this point. I knew if I was going to fly fish in Montana, I had to learn new fishing techniques. Luckily, with the clear water, I could see exactly where my casts landed, and try to follow the nymph's drift the best I could.

I unhooked the nymph from the hook keeper and prepared to take my first cast. In my mind, I visualized my cast just like I visualized my track races: my fly line floated through the air effortlessly, the line and leader landed in the water naturally, and the nymph drifted right in front of a large, hungry rainbow trout. My perfect cast fooled the trout, and it ate the nymph. I set the hook, fought in the fish, and even netted it myself. I executed the catch perfectly, applying all the techniques and strategies Adam taught me so far this summer.

If only it were that easy. Instead, here's what really happened.

I unhooked my nymph from the hook keeper, but the wind took my fly line and whipped it around. The nymph got hooked on a plant full of burrs a few feet behind me. I slowly turned around and unhooked the nymph from the plant, only getting three burrs stuck on my hand. I quickly brushed them off and got ready to cast again. This time, the wind died down, and I had more control over my cast. I took two false casts so I could make sure my fly landed exactly where I wanted it to. On my third cast, I watched my line soar through the air, carrying the distance I needed it to. However, my cast traveled a little too far, and my fly landed on the other side of the creek. I yanked my fly rod back, hoping the nymph would pop right out of the grass on the other side—it did, but then it hooked into a yellow flowery plant on the far edge of the creek.

I didn't catch a monster rainbow like I envisioned. I caught a stupid yellow flower.

Adam looked at my line, and then at me. He held his hand straight out in a "stop" gesture. I didn't think he wanted me to spook the fish, mainly so he could try to catch one. I felt so stupid, standing there with my fly rod, unable to fish. My only job was to cast my fly into the water. And I couldn't even do that. How was I going to hold my own in Montana when I couldn't handle casting here? I waited for Adam to take some more casts before we did whatever was necessary to unhook my fly from the other side of the creek.

It was torture. I watched Adam effortlessly cast a similar nymph like the one I had tied on, wishing that were me casting at the hungry trout. The nymph drifted past the fish, and none of them swiped at it. They all ignored it, and a couple of trout even moved out of the way when the nymph drifted past. Adam took a couple of steps back, so he was closer to me. I thought he was ready to help me out of my snagged mess, but he wasn't ready yet. He took another cast, and I had to duck so the fly wouldn't hook me.

That was the one to do it. Adam's cast was just how I visualized mine would go–a perfect, natural cast, a drift right in the strike zone, and a tricked trout. As soon as Adam set the hook and fought the fish in, the remaining trout darted away quickly. They all swam under the edges of the bank of the creek. Adam grabbed his net from his waistband and kneeled to scoop up the trout with his net. It looked even bigger out of the water than I had imagined. I wasn't sure how a trout could grow to this size from eating a bunch of microscopic bugs, but it was definitely possible. I would never get tired of looking at the vibrant pink stripe across a rainbow trout's belly. This fish's pink stripe was darker than others I've seen; it almost looked more red than pink. I also noticed its jaw was more pointed and pronounced than other rainbow trout I've seen.

"This is a nice, healthy male," Adam announced.

"How can you tell it's a male?" I genuinely was curious, but I was also hoping I wasn't about to receive a trout anatomy lesson.

I was relieved when Adam said, "By looking at its jaw. Males have a longer snout than the females do. When males get older, their jaws get kyped out. It makes them look intimidating, almost in a prehistoric way."

"What's a kyped jaw?"

"I'll show you pictures when we get home. This trout doesn't have a pronounced kype yet, but it's definitely a male. I'll release him, and then let's look at your prized catch."

"You're so funny," I said sarcastically. After Adam released the fish, he took the rod from my hand.

"Go cross the bridge, walk along the edge of the creek, and you should be able to unhook your fly from that plant." So I did. The other side of the creek had taller grass and more vegetation, and the ground felt very uneven. I felt like I was walking on a tightrope. Prickly grasses tickled my legs, even with pants on. Burrs stuck to my clothes, but I made it to the plant where my fly was stuck. I could barely see my fly— it was caught underneath a yellow flower. I finally unhooked it, and Adam reeled my line back in for me. Once I hiked back to Adam, I took my rod back, feeling less ashamed. He didn't make me feel bad about my mishap, so I shouldn't beat myself up over it, either.

"Good work," he complimented. "That wasn't easy hiking."

"No, it wasn't," I agreed. "Sorry for spooking any fish and ruining this spot."

"It happens. That's part of fishing. No one's perfect." Adam was far from perfect. But ever since our talk on the Fourth of July, he's been a much better fishing partner.

Adam drove us to another part of the creek down the road since we spooked the fish at our first spot. We fished there for a bit with no luck. Before heading home, Adam drove us back up to the lake so we could hike one of the trails. We talked about everything from fishing to high school to my improved taste in music. The afternoon flew by.

On the drive home, the sunset painted the sky brilliant shades of orange, blue, and pink. There was less out here in the Black Hills—less people, less hustle, less cell service. But somehow, South Dakota still had more to offer than Illinois. If this was what South Dakota sunsets looked like, I couldn't wait to see what Montana had in store.

Chapter 21

Montana camping and fishing weekend was finally here! I went for a run in the morning before I finished packing. It wasn't the best run–I couldn't get my breathing under control, and my easy pace felt like a labored effort. Although I was excited to leave for Montana, I couldn't deny feeling some nerves about the trip. But a bad run was better than no run at all. I could clear my head and get in some much-needed movement before sitting in an RV for seven hours.

Mom went to campus for the morning, and Dad was out running errands, so I was home alone most of the day. Around lunchtime, Grandma's car pulled into the driveway. She walked to the door, carrying a small gift bag. I heard her come in as I was making a sandwich for lunch.

"Today's the big day! Are you excited?" Grandma set the bag on the counter and gave me a hug.

"Yes, a little nervous, but excited."

"You'll have the best time. What's the weather going to be like while you're there?"

I opened the weather app on my phone to check. "It looks good now. No rain, highs in the upper seventies and lows in the fifties at night. Maybe upper forties Friday night."

"That will be perfect. Make sure you pay attention to the stars at night. You think you see a lot here? They don't call Montana Big Sky Country for nothing."

"I'll look at the stars, promise." Then I asked, "Do you want anything for lunch?"

"No thanks, I just ate," she said. "I just wanted to see you before you left. And give you one more thing for your trip."

"But you already got me so much!" What else could I possibly need? I already felt like I had so many things packed for this trip.

"It's not enough. I'm making up for years of gifts I owe you." She grabbed the bag from the counter and handed it to me. I pulled out the blue tissue paper and found a brown leather-bound journal. On the cover was an embossed quote that read, "The journey is more important than the destination." There was also a small jewelry box. Inside was a gold necklace with a delicate mountain pendant. Three mountain peaks were all connected, with detailing to look like the mountains were snow-capped.

"I know you told me you like to write, so I thought a new journal would be perfect to bring this weekend. You can write all about what you see and experience in Montana. And now that you're a mountain girl, I thought this necklace would be perfect for you."

Grandma already went above and beyond with the duffel bag full of gear, especially the thoughtfulness (and ingenuity) of the pee funnel. But these gifts were special. They were keepsakes. "Thank you." I gave her a hug. "Could you help me put the necklace on?" I held up my hair, and Grandma clasped the necklace around my neck. When she was done, I put my hand on the cool metal mountain pendant.

"It's perfect," I said.

"Just like you." It was the cheesiest response, but I didn't care in that moment. Even though Grandma had been in my life for less than two months, I couldn't imagine life without her now. "Send me pictures and texts, only if you have time. You can fill me in on everything when you get back."

"I'll definitely send updates if I have service."

"Great. I'm going to head out, I'm stopping at the craft store to get some paint, and then I need a new pair of running shoes. Mine are getting worn out, and I have my eye on a pair of blue and rose gold Brooks."

"I'm pretty sure one of my teammates has that same pair. They're super cute! Go get them before your size is gone. We'll go for a run when I get home, and then maybe we can get breakfast or lunch after?"

"Sounds like a plan." Grandma gave me one more hug, and I walked her to the door. "I love you, Nat. Have the best time in Montana. And with Adam." She winked at me and laughed.

I rolled my eyes and said, "We're just friends! Love you too." I watched her walk to her car. I always forgot that she's in her early 70's. It was amazing to see how youthful she was in mind, body, and spirit. I waved as she drove off, and I watched her wave back. Once her car was out of sight, I walked back to the kitchen and picked up the notebook. I couldn't wait to fill it with memories from Montana.

My most exciting journey was just beginning.

•　　　•　　　•　　　•　　　•

Mom and Dad got home around 2 p.m. In our final preparations for my trip, Mom triple-checked that I packed everything, and Dad looked up fishing reports.

"This report from a fly shop in Bozeman says a Rusty Spinner has been catching a lot of fish. And what the heck is a Chubby Chernobyl?"

"I'm pretty sure those are types of flies," I explained. "Adam's been trying to teach me, and it's impossible to remember the names of all the flies and what to throw when."

"Regardless, it's great that you're stepping out of your comfort zone and learning something new. I'm proud of you, kid."

A few minutes later, Dad and I started carrying my bags next door. Adam and Mato were on the driveway loading up the RV. Mato had his Jeep hitched behind the RV.

"You don't think I'm going to drive this RV around town this weekend, do you?" Mato laughed. He must have noticed me giving the car and RV weird looks. "Here, let me take your bags." I saw Adam walk out of the house, carrying a backpack and a fly rod case.

"Today's the big day!" He grinned and gave me a high five. He glanced down and noticed my new jewelry. "Cool necklace. Where'd you get it?"

"My grandma gave it to me earlier today. Another gift for this trip."

"Speaking of that, did you pack the funnel?"

"It was the first thing I packed!" I laughed.

Mato stepped out of the RV. "I triple-checked, everything we need is in this RV. I'm ready whenever you kids are." I turned back to look at my parents. Mom's eyes were watery, and Dad put his arm around Mom's shoulder.

"I just worry about you," Mom's voice shook. "But you're in good hands, and I can't protect you forever."

"Mom," I groaned. "I'm going to Montana for the weekend, not Pluto."

"I know," she said. She gave me a tight hug, and then she whispered in my ear, "We're proud of who you're becoming. And I know your grandma is, too."

After what felt like an eternity, Mom pulled away, and I could finally hug Dad. Just as I thought I was free to go, Mom reminded Mato (again) to send updates, locations, and pictures whenever we had time and cell service. Dad had to remind Mom (again) that we had a long drive ahead, and literally pulled her away.

I walked up the steps of the RV. I'd never been in one, so I didn't know what to expect. My first impression was that it was nicer on the inside than I thought it would be, and it smelled like lemons. Mato got in the driver's seat. It was one long bench seat, and there was a bed lofted above him. There was a small kitchen area, a booth-style table, another bed in the back of the RV, and a bathroom. It was a relief to see the RV bathroom had a toilet *and* a shower. Maybe I wouldn't have to use the funnel as much as I thought I would.

"You kids ready?" Mato turned around and asked.

"Yeah!" Adam and I shouted. There was something about being in an RV and ripping open a bag of Bugles that made us feel like little kids again.

The beginning of the drive was pretty uneventful. Adam and I ate some snacks, played cards, and sang along to the road trip playlist we had collectively put together over the past few days. There were only two songs both of us could sing along to. While belting the chorus to "Don't Stop Believing," the reality of the moment, and my new life, hit me all at once. I was traveling to Montana with my new friend and his dad on a fly fishing trip. None of those things were on my bingo card for this summer. But I wouldn't want to be anywhere else at that moment.

The scenery changed while driving through Wyoming. There were less tall pine and fir trees, and more mountains looming over the farmland. As our RV winded through the mountains during sunset, I saw the Montana welcome sign.

Even though the only thing different at this point were the state lines, somehow, Montana felt like a magical land straight out of a fairytale. I immediately knew this place was special. I was waiting for it to get completely dark out, but I was surprised how long it took before the sun completely set.

Mato was focused on driving, and Adam had fallen asleep, so I pulled out my new journal from Grandma and took some time to write.

July 23

At this moment, I am in an RV with my hot next-door-neighbor and his dad, driving through Montana, heading to a campsite, and preparing to fly-fish in the remote wilderness all weekend.

If someone told me 4 months ago that I would be doing this, I wouldn't have believed it. Neither would my parents and my friends. Speaking of which, I haven't heard from Syd since that night I found out she was hanging out with Kennedy and her crew. I've tried texting her here and there, but she never responds. I haven't heard from anyone else back home, now that I really think about it. There's a lot of time to think when you're driving through the middle of nowhere.

It makes me realize how much life has changed in such a short time. I'm finding out what's important, and who's important. My love for running has only grown stronger since I moved. Seriously, how could I NOT love running somewhere so beautiful? That's always been important to me, but now, so is spending more time outside, and less time on my phone. Although Syd and I hardly talk, I have made some great new friends here. It feels like I've known Ali, Sarah, and Becca forever.

Getting to know my grandma has been a lot of fun, too. I only wish that I'd known her sooner. I understand that she and Mom haven't always been close, even though I'll never exactly understand why. But better late than never, right? And how badass she is? She has cooler hobbies than most people my age, and she's in her early 70s. I can only hope I'm that cool when I get older.

And then there's Adam. I can't deny that he's cute. I thought the hot next-door-neighbor only existed in movies, but he's here, in the flesh. Along with that, he's smart, adventurous, thoughtful, funny, fun to be around, and easy to talk to. He made me feel less nervous about going on this trip.

We DID agree to just be friends, which I know is the right move. Why ruin a good thing? But sometimes I still wonder—

"Whatcha writing?" I snapped back to reality at the sound of Adam's voice, and his body hovering over my shoulder.

"Nothing," I said as I slammed the notebook closed. That wasn't suspicious at all.

"Smart idea to bring a notebook on this trip," Adam said. "You can write about each day and how fishing went, so we can remember for next time."

Next time? He was already thinking of coming back here with me another time? My heart fluttered, and I smiled when he said that. All I said back was, "Yeah."

"I think we're almost at our campsite," Adam said.

"Ten minutes out!" Mato called from the driver's seat.

"I'll help you convert the table to a bed," Adam offered.

"Give me a minute, and then I'll be ready," I said. Adam nodded and got up to get a drink out of the mini fridge. I wanted to finish writing before arriving at our campsite. Once Adam was out of view, I opened the journal to the page I was on. I only had to finish the last sentence.

But sometimes I still wonder if that could change in the future.

Around 10:30 p.m., Mato pulled into our campsite. A couple of other campers were parked in other campsites, but many campsites were still empty. The only people I saw were an older couple sitting in lawn chairs near their camper, gazing at the stars and holding hands. Otherwise, I heard no sounds, and saw no other people.

After Mato parked the RV, he asked if we wanted to go on a short walk with him. He had been sitting all day and needed to stretch his legs. I wanted to see Montana for myself, and not through a car window, before going to bed. I stepped onto the grass and took in my surroundings. There was a fire pit at our campsite. I could smell smoke, so someone else must have made a fire tonight. It was cooler outside than I expected, so I ran back to the RV and grabbed a hoodie. When I returned, Mato already started walking, but Adam had waited for me.

"So, first impressions of Montana?" he asked.

"Well, right now it's cold," I answered. "But it seems incredibly beautiful here."

"We're higher in elevation, so you'll notice that it feels warmer during the day, but cools off a lot at night," Adam explained. "We're probably around 5,000 feet elevation. And when we drive toward Big Sky, that gets closer to 7,000 feet. Layers are key." We walked in silence, listening to the crunch of our footsteps under the gravel path and the occasional chirp of a grasshopper and croak of a frog. It reminded me of my first run in Rapid City–even though it seemed quiet here at first, there were more noises than I realized once I stopped to listen.

"What's our plan for tomorrow?" I asked.

"We'll wake up pretty early, make some breakfast, and take the Jeep to our first fishing spot," Adam said. "There are some sweet stretches of the Gallatin up this way, but we'll definitely fish some stretches closer to Big Sky on Saturday. It's unbelievable. Be prepared for water like you've never seen before." Adam continued to tell me about fast currents, difficult hiking and wading, and cold water temps. It didn't sound too scary from his explanation, but he kept saying over and over again not to underestimate Montana. I guess I would see for myself in the morning.

Before I forgot, I texted Mom and Dad to let them know we arrived. Less than a minute after I sent that text, Mom replied.

`Great! Thank you for letting me know! Love you!`

Then I texted Grandma. I typed, `You were right about the stars. It's even prettier here than you described.`

A few minutes later, she sent back a smiling emoji. Just another thing that made her the coolest grandma around.

After our short walk around the RV park, I was ready to rest up for our first full day in Montana. Adam took the back bed, Mato took the lofted bed, and I slept where there used to be a table. I fell asleep as soon as my head hit the pillow, and dreamt of wild, blue rivers and colorful, healthy trout.

Chapter 22

"Crap! Nat, wake up!"

I rubbed my eyes, caked with gunk from a deep slumber. Considering my bed could be converted to a table, I slept like a baby. But I couldn't ease myself awake, because Adam was running around the RV like a chicken with his head cut off.

"I set an alarm, but I forgot to plug my phone in last night." Adam was brushing his teeth and frantically looking for something. "My phone obviously died," he said after he spit his toothpaste down the sink. While he was flinging open cabinets, I was still wondering what he was looking for. "And Dad didn't set an alarm, so we're running late. Throw on some clothes and let's go." Before Adam ran out to the Jeep, he said, "If you find a red hat, grab it before you get off the RV." I noticed he was already wearing a red hat, but I knew better than to say anything at that moment.

I scooted out of bed and looked at my phone. It was just after 8 a.m. I threw on some clothes and got ready in under five minutes, moving as fast as I could so I didn't make us any more late. When I stepped out of the RV, I had to shield my eyes. I wasn't prepared for how sunny it already was.

"Come on!" Adam shouted. I ran to the Jeep, and Adam darted past me to make sure the RV was locked. Mato had the car running, so I hopped in the back seat, and once Adam got back to the car, we took off.

"Well, we are certainly well-rested for today. Natalie, you hungry?" Mato asked.

I didn't have to say anything, because as if on cue, I heard my stomach rumble.

"In the cooler next to you, there should be water and bagels. Can you grab some for us, too?" I opened the cooler and grabbed a bottle of water and Asiago cheese bagels smeared with cream cheese for everyone. The next few minutes were silent as we devoured our breakfasts. Once I ate, I looked out the window and was immediately stunned by our surroundings. I did my best to take in all the majestic details. In front of us and to my left, I saw tall mountain peaks. To my right, I caught a quick glimpse of a river before it disappeared behind the pine trees. Even though I only saw the water for a second, I now realized what Adam meant about Montana water differing from South Dakota water.

This water in this river moved faster than the slow streams I was accustomed to in Rapid City. Although it wasn't treacherous or filled with white-water rapids, it looked intimidating. I unlocked my phone and looked at a map to see if I could identify what river it was. I wanted to figure things out on my own without constantly relying on Adam and Mato for information. In some ways, I felt like I had something to prove on this trip. I was the guest this weekend and didn't want to be the needy girl who couldn't do anything on her own. And as much as I wanted to believe I was completely over the mean comments from those fishermen and their sons earlier this summer, I wasn't. Adam was right: Montana was no joke. I wanted to look like I knew what I was doing here.

I pinpointed our location and learned we had just passed a creek that was a tributary of the Gallatin River. It looked like a peaceful place to fish, but I knew Adam and Mato had other plans for this weekend.

I put my phone down and continued to take in the scenery. If I lived here, my screen time report would be so low each week. How could someone be glued to their phone if they lived somewhere as magnificent as this? No perfectly curated Instagram feed or clever TikTok could beat what this place offered. It was too good to be true.

About thirty minutes later, Mato turned down a side road and pulled into a parking area. Adam looked at me and said, "Welcome to the Gallatin."

We got out of the car and I looked at the mighty Gallatin that I'd heard so much about. It was wide, with many spots that looked deep, but I noticed some shallow pockets, too. Before I could examine it more closely, I grabbed my gear out of the car. Hopefully, Adam remembered to grab everything for me since we were rushing around this morning. I saw my backpack and the forest green waders Mom ordered from Amazon. They weren't as nice as the pair that Mato and…

"Are you kidding me? Where are my waders?" Adam glared at Mato. "I thought you said you put them in the car."

"I thought *you* said you already had them in the car." Mato remained calm as he pulled out our fly rods. "There are plenty of spots to shore fish here. You'll be fine."

"Yeah, until I freeze my feet and ankles off whenever I need to step in the water." Adam grabbed a fly rod and net, slung his backpack over his shoulder, and stomped down toward the river without waiting for either Mato or me.

Mato pulled on his waders and tightened the belt around his waist. "He'll calm down once he catches a fish." I stepped into my waders, realizing how baggy they were compared to Mato's. "Make sure you tighten the belt," he told me. "That's what protects you in case you fall in the water. It will help prevent a lot of water from getting in your waders." I tightened the belt, which made my waders more fitted, but also accentuated my short legs.

Mato laughed. "Those look more like MC Hammer pants. But it's better than nothing. Let's go." Mato locked up the car and we walked down to the river, the roar of the water getting louder and louder with each step I took. To my left, the flow of the water downstream got faster as it crashed over a pile of rocks. Mato and I turned right and walked upriver, staying on land for now. The water maintained a steady flow, and we found Adam throwing casts and looking visibly calmer.

Mato stopped several yards short of Adam's fishing spot, demonstrating respectful fishing etiquette. "Let's start here," he said. "There are some great stretches up ahead, but let's get you comfortable. I'm going to help you tie on a set-up called a dry-dropper. Have you been tying your own flies onto your leader or tippet yet?"

"Not really. Adam has been tying on all my flies for me. And if I've lost a fly in a tree or something, Adam ties on a new one." Mato should be prepping his own gear, not be constantly looking out for me. I felt guilty. My helplessness shouldn't ruin his vacation, and I was more motivated than ever to learn new skills on this trip.

Mato smiled. "That's very nice of him. But I think you're ready to pick out your own flies and set up your rod yourself." Mato first showed me how to tie a clinch knot. I followed his example by securing a small dry fly to my leader with a clinch knot, which was pretty easy to do. Then he took out a roll of clear fishing line. "This is called tippet. You can attach it to your leader if it's getting short, or you can use it to tie flies to one another. I'm going to cut off a piece for you that's a little longer than a foot or so, and then we'll pick out a nymph for you to tie on. Tying the tippet to the dry fly is tricky, so I'll do that for you, but then you can tie on the nymph. Look through my fly box and see what you like."

I looked in the fly box and couldn't believe all the nymphs lined up and organized by color and size. Some of them were so tiny, I couldn't believe a trout would even see it, let alone eat it. The one that caught my attention had a gold bead head, a bright turquoise spot on its back, a copper wire body, and the most miniscule tufts of hair sticking out by the bead head. I took it out of the fly box and held it in my hand, making sure not to drop it in the grass. There was no way I would find it if I dropped it.

"Good choice. That one's called a Copper John."

"How do you remember what every fly is called?" If I was going to stick with fly fishing, I needed to learn the trick to remembering all this stuff.

"Time and experience. But as you do this more, you'll catch some nice fish on all sorts of flies, and you don't forget what you were throwing when you catch your nicest fish. Go ahead and tie it on to your tippet here." I grabbed the end of the tippet and threaded the line through the hole at the top of the nymph. After completing another secure clinch knot, Mato made sure I had some other basic supplies: nail clippers, a roll of tippet, some extra flies, and flotant to put on the dry fly.

"Make sure you don't stray too far from Adam or me for now, since we have the bear spray on us. The last thing I'd want is for you to be unarmed and get in a bear's way."

With all my supplies and my fancy two-fly set-up, I scanned the water, looking for signs of fish and spots to cast. This had become one of my favorite parts of fly fishing, besides catching fish, of course. Fly fishing requires you to be observant–of your surroundings, of the water, of the bugs, of the weather, of everything. Water, as simple as it sounded, was also very complex.

This particular stretch of water maintained a steady flow, with a downed tree that created an eddy. The water just in front of the downed tree looked darker and a little deeper, and I bet there were some big trout holding in that pool. Neither Mato nor Adam were casting near there, so I took a few quiet steps toward the downed tree. I double-checked that there were no overhanging trees or other vegetation that I could get caught in while casting. Feeling secure in my waders, I took my first steps into the Gallatin River. The edge was shallow; the water only went up to my ankles. Thanks to my waders, I didn't feel the temperature at all, just the slight pressure of the water as it flowed around me and past me.

I threw my first cast, watching my dry fly drift back toward me. Nothing rose to take it, and nothing ate the nymph and pulled the dry under to indicate a strike. I took a couple cautious steps forward, closer to the downed tree. I reapplied the flotant on the dry fly, so it would float as naturally as possible. There had to be fish hanging out by the downed tree. My heart was racing, and I felt the anticipation of catching a fish in this spot. I visualized my cast, hoping for a better result than when I visualized catching giant rainbows in the creek by Crazy Horse Lake. I refused to hook a stupid yellow flower again, or get caught in the vegetation. As I visualized my cast, I pictured my fly landing up river from the tree, drifting right to the eddy, and a hungry brown (dreaming big here) surfaced to devour the dry fly. I would set the hook, fight it in seamlessly, and net it myself.

Time to make my dreams a reality.

I put my vision into motion–I took two false casts to make sure I had enough line out, and then I let my line soar through the air and land upriver, right where I wanted it to land. I retrieved just enough line so I didn't have too much slack, while keeping an eye on my drifting fly. Suddenly, the dry fly disappeared beneath the surface. This hadn't happened yet today, so I set the hook, hoping for a trout, but also realizing I could have caught a stick or a rock.

It was a fish.

The trout stayed deep, but cooperated as I fought it in. I glanced upstream and saw Adam was still fishing, and I didn't want to turn around and see where Mato was, but suddenly I heard footsteps coming up behind me, followed by splashing through the water.

"Where is she?" Mato asked, his net out and ready.

"Still near this tree, I think," and on cue, we could make out the shadow of the fish under the surface of the water. I kept pulling in my line by hand, and guiding the fish to Mato the best I could. Luckily, he moved swiftly through the water and netted the fish. I let out a sigh of relief, feeling the tension drop from my shoulders while still feeling overjoyed from an exciting catch.

"Your first Montana trout!" Mato exclaimed. I reeled in the rest of my line and waded over to him. In the net was a rainbow trout. But something about it looked different from other rainbows I'd caught.

"That's actually a cutbow! Copper John got the job done." Mato waded toward land and I followed him. I set my rod on the ground so it would be easier to unhook the fish, and then I saw why this fish was called a cutbow.

When I looked under its jaw near the gills, or where its "neck" would be, there was a distinct bright orange marking, like someone slashed its throat. This trout still had a pink stripe across its body, but it was more faded than the markings on a rainbow trout.

"This one's a cutbow and not a cutthroat because of its fins," Mato said as he got out his cell phone. "Look at the white tips on the fin. That's the big tell if it's a cutbow or a cutthroat. We have to get a picture of your first Montana fish!" Mato positioned himself to take the picture as I wet my hands, and then grabbed the trout out of the net. I made sure the downed tree was behind me, so I would never forget where I caught this fish. Mato took a couple of pictures, and then I released the fish, watching it swim back to the downed tree. I hadn't stopped smiling since I set the hook.

"That was awesome! Thanks for the pictures." Although I wanted to be an independent female angler on this trip, I was thankful to share this catch with Mato. And that he was there quickly to net my first Montana trout!

"Of course. Now let's go catch some more." We waded back into the river and cast for about five more minutes until a loud boom of thunder rattled the trees. I looked up, and dark gray storm clouds replaced the clear blue skies.

"Back to the car, now!" Mato shouted. I reeled in my line and waded out of the water, but Adam continued to cast.

"Adam, come on!" If he wouldn't listen to his dad, he might listen to me.

He took another cast and shouted back, "The bite always picks up when a storm rolls in! I'll catch up to you." Thunder boomed even louder, and the sky lit up from the flash of a nearby lightning strike.

I tried one more time. "Come on, this is stupid!" He ignored me and kept casting. I turned around and got to the car as fast as I could.

Although I was worried about Adam, I needed to prioritize my safety, too. Just as I got to the Jeep, the skies opened up. I threw my gear in the trunk and got in the car in a matter of seconds, but was still soaked.

"Where's Adam?" Mato asked.

"Still fishing. I tried to get him to come back with me, but he wouldn't listen." Mato shook his head and stared out the window. Rain wasn't in today's forecast, but I thought back to Adam's story about how unpredictable the weather could be in the mountains.

I heard constant thunder and lightning for the next ten minutes, but there was one distinct noise that was louder than anything I'd heard in my life. I looked through the windshield, and suddenly, I saw smoke coming up from the trees. Not long after that, Adam was running back to the car. He was drenched, especially since he had no waders to keep his body dry. He looked like he just saw a ghost. After he tossed his stuff in the trunk, he got in the car, panting and catching his breath.

"Holy shit. Lightning struck the tree right next to me."

"What?" Mato and I exclaimed.

"Yeah, and the worst part was I had just hooked up with a really nice fish. I think it might have been a brown, and then I lost it when the lightning struck."

I shot Adam an annoyed look. "THAT'S what you're upset about?"

Mato turned and looked at his son. "Adam, no fish is worth your life. You stayed out there way too long."

Adam rolled his eyes. "Whatever, I'm fine. It was crazy seeing lightning that close, though!"

A few minutes later, the storm moved past, and the skies cleared up like nothing had happened. After our chaotic morning, we agreed to take a mid-morning break at camp, put on some dry clothes, and grab some lunch.

"Dad, can we pick up a few more flies while we're here?" Adam asked.

Mato crossed his arms. "Don't you have enough flies?"

"Actually, I lost my favorite fly, that Parachute Adams, on a tree branch during the storm. And a few fell out of my fly box earlier this morning."

Mato sighed, knowing this was a losing battle. "Fine, we can stop at the fly shop before heading back to the river." I had never been in a fly shop, not even the one in Rapid City, since I always borrowed Adam's gear. I expected it to be super lame. What could be so cool about a store filled with fishing gear?

Chapter 23

The fly shop in town looked like an old cabin from the outside. Two rocking chairs sat on the front porch of the shop, and a sleeping golden retriever woke up from a nap when we walked up the creaking wooden steps. The dog eagerly followed us inside the shop. A boy who looked about my age worked behind the front counter, and an older man came out from a back room.

"Come here, Buster!" the old man called.

"Oh, it's okay. We're all fine with the dog. Right?" Mato looked at Adam and me. Adam calmly nodded, but I couldn't contain my excitement any longer.

"Come here, Buster!" I squealed and knelt to pet him. Buster licked my face and rolled over on his back for a tummy rub. Mountains, fly fishing, and stores with dogs in them? Montana was officially my new favorite state.

Mato and Adam started talking to the fly shop employees about fishing, and I kept petting Buster. I looked around the store, and it kind of reminded me of Grandma's house. There were things everywhere: fishing gear, fly rods, fly reels, waders, wading boots, nets, clothes, hats, and of course, flies. Pictures lined the walls of people holding magnificent trout in locations that didn't look real—they could only exist in movies, or as a staged backdrop. I pulled myself away from

Buster and looked at the pictures. The more I observed, the more I noticed a trend.

Almost every picture was of a guy holding a fish. I only counted two pictures of women in the entire shop. I felt frustrated. Why weren't there more women pictured on these walls?

"What's that?" Adam snapped me back to reality. I realized I must have said that thought out loud.

The older man spoke up. "You're right, I need more pictures of women in the fly shop." He pointed to a particular picture. "Do you see the brown trout that lady is holding?" I nodded, intrigued to hear the story behind the photo. I also noticed another woman next to her, smiling and posing with two thumbs up.

"Well," the man continued, "this was about three years ago, but I remember it like it was yesterday... and I've never been more proud to call her my daughter."

"Who's in the picture with her?" I asked.

"That's her best friend of over twenty years. Two strong women, fishing together and creating memories that will last a lifetime. She would be here now, but she's actually out guiding a couple here on vacation."

"That's so cool." I wondered if I would meet any other girls who liked to fly-fish. It wouldn't be Mom, that's for sure. She would sit along the edge of the river reading a book, maybe, but I couldn't imagine her holding a trout. Maybe Ali, Sarah, or Becca would come with me sometime. Fishing was quickly becoming one of my favorite hobbies, and the thought of having another friend to share it with, especially another girl, was empowering.

The man grinned. "I agree. Have you been fishing long?"

"Only a couple of months. Adam taught me how, and I've been having fun with it."

"Good. Make sure it never stops being fun. And don't let anyone tell you that you can't, or shouldn't, be out there. There's a need for women in this sport, like you and my daughter." I let his words sink in for a moment. This was the validation I needed. I shouldn't have to prove to anyone that I can handle being out there, but that's how the cookie crumbles (Ms. Laker used to say that phrase and I'd been waiting for the perfect time to use it!). No one should be criticized or judged for enjoying the great outdoors.

I asked, "What flies have been catching fish this week?" The old man–Joe was his name–helped me pick out some reliable nymphs and dry flies, and then he showed me something I'd seen in Adam's fly box before, but didn't know a whole lot about.

"Have you thrown streamers at all?"

"No. How do they catch fish?"

Joe explained how streamers mimic crayfish, leeches, and other small baitfish. He said bigger, aggressive trout loved streamers. He recommended a couple of different colors and sizes, so I took a black one, a green one, and a purple one to try.

Mato offered to pay for my flies, but Mom and Dad gave me some money for this trip, and I wanted flies that were my own. I also picked out a fly box to put them all in, so I could finally start collecting my own gear. My excitement from our shopping spree came tumbling down after I heard the price.

"Sixty-one dollars? That much for these tiny things?" I gasped.

Joe laughed. "You have to remember, flies are hand-tied. You're paying for only the best labor and materials." I reluctantly agreed, handing him my Greenlight debit card. After he gave me my card back, he said, "Now you come back here before you head home and let me know how you do out there, got it?"

"Yes, sir." He held out his hand and I shook it. He had a powerful grip that I couldn't match, but I tried my best. I heard whimpering at my feet. Buster wanted to say goodbye, too. I shook his paw and grabbed my new flies.

While driving to our next stretch of river to fish, I couldn't come down from my shopping high, and from the validation Joe gave me. "Can we go back before we head home? I have to give Joe a report. And maybe his daughter will be there, too."

"You got it," Mato promised.

Mato, Adam, and I fished a new stretch of the Gallatin, and it couldn't have been a more perfect afternoon. Fish were rising all around us, and I was catching them non-stop on dry flies. We were doing so well that Mato asked us about having a fish fry tonight.

"Yes!" Adam and I exclaimed. Part of me felt a little bad for keeping and eating the fish I had caught, but then I remembered I bought fish and chicken and beef and pork from the store all the time and never thought twice about it.

We each caught and kept two fish for dinner. While the sun disappeared behind the towering treetops, we made our way back to camp to prepare our fish fry. I watched Mato and Adam filet the trout quickly and flawlessly, feeling relieved that they didn't ask me to help. I didn't know if I was ready to be *that* involved with preparing my food, but I knew I could handle seasoning the fish with lemon juice and pepper. The flaky, fresh, lemony trout was one of the best meals I'd ever had, further perfected by the crackling campfire, lingering sunset, and great company.

When we finished cleaning up after dinner, Adam asked if I wanted to go for a walk. The setting sun created a beautiful canvas of colors in the sky. I was looking forward to a relaxing walk to end a perfect first day of our trip, but Adam had other intentions.

"I need to tell you something. I've been keeping a secret."

Chapter 24

Adam's feet shuffled on the rocky path. He stuffed his hands in his pockets, and he wouldn't look at me. What was this secret? Was there another girl he liked? Was he about to say he changed his mind about being friends? Or would it be something else completely? I had no idea what he was going to tell me.

"My parents are getting divorced."

I didn't know how to respond. Did he want this? Was it a surprise? I was sure no matter what his thoughts were about the situation, this couldn't be easy. I would be devastated if my parents split.

"How are you feeling?" I asked. "And why is it a secret?"

Adam started laughing, which I didn't expect. "What guy wants to talk about their feelings? I found out Monday morning and needed some time to process it. I mean, it sucks. But I also know my parents will be happier. I just can't believe they stuck it out this long." We walked in silence for a bit before he continued. "I don't want people to know, I guess. It's no secret my mom is weird. I mean, look at how she was at your Fourth of July party. It's embarrassing." Even though Adam's statements contradict each other, I understood what he was trying to say. Something could be sad, but also a relief. Both feelings could coexist.

I thought about how Mato had been acting so far; he never seemed sad or angry, or showed any signs something was wrong. "Your dad seems to be okay, at least for now," I said. "And who cares what other people think?" I said.

"My dad needed this trip now more than ever. Being out here is helping him process everything. It's not like he didn't try to fix things with my mom. He wanted it to work out, and he still loves my mom, I think." Adam still hadn't looked at me. He stopped walking, and then said, "You can't force someone to change. You hope they will, but you don't always get what you hope for."

The weight of his words lingered as we continued walking. I didn't know how much more Adam wanted to talk about the divorce, or if he wanted to talk at all. Eventually, I said, "Change is scary and difficult, no matter what it is." I reflected on the changes I'd experienced in less than two months, and what change had taught me. "At first, it's like stepping off a cliff. But then you see what's on the other side of the unknown and realize, even though things are different, different can be good, or sometimes even better." Adam looked up at me, giving the slightest hint of a smile. Then I added, "I just want you to know I'm here if you ever need to talk or vent."

"Thanks." Unexpectedly, Adam reached for my hand. It was warm from being tucked in his pockets. I gave his hand a squeeze, and he squeezed back. We continued walking, hand in hand, under the starlit Montana sky. Grandma was right: the unfiltered sky was better than any picture my phone could capture.

Chapter 25

I slept like a rock and woke up Saturday morning refreshed and ready to fish. Our plan was to hike and fish parts of the Gallatin that went through Big Sky. It would take an hour to drive to our fishing spot, so we hit the road pretty early, picking up breakfast sandwiches and some snacks for the day at a gas station. During the drive, I was going to send my family and friends some pictures, but I lost cell service almost immediately. Oh well, I could send them pictures tonight back at camp. They all knew service would be spotty. It wasn't like I was ignoring them on purpose.

We were literally in the mountains now. The road snaked through and around them. I noticed there were a lot of rapids and boulders in this stretch of river. I'd never seen so much white water in my life. This must be a fun river to raft down because I noticed a couple of white-water rafting groups navigating their way down the rapids and around the rocks. My stomach dropped thinking about how scary it would be if your raft flipped in one of those rapids.

Was the whole river like this? There's no way anyone could wade and fish in water this treacherous. I could hear my mom's voice telling me to be careful. I was turning into more of a risk-taker than she ever would be, but I agreed that water with rapids that strong was NOT for fishing.

Less than a mile down the road, the speed of the river changed. The water had a unique coloring to it—not the vibrant turquoise like Grandma showed me in Glacier National Park, but almost a hint of green. It was beautiful to see in person. It must have been a good fishing spot, too, because several anglers were standing in the water, casting all over the river.

Mato said, "Let's drive a little further down. There are too many people here." Note to self: people like their space when they go fishing.

As quickly as the river calmed down, it filled with fast rapids and big boulders again. My eyes were glued to the river and its ever-changing form. Dangerous rapids in some stretches, and almost stand-still water in others. It reminded me that while nature can be breath-taking for its beauty, it can also be breath-taking for its unpredictability and danger.

Mato drove a little further down and approached a bridge that crossed the river and led to a parking area. As we drove across the bridge, I saw a family sitting on the bank of the river, enjoying a picnic. I didn't see anyone fishing, and I wasn't sure if that was a good thing.

While unloading gear from the car, Adam said, "If this stretch of the river is on, we'll probably stay here all day, except for a lunch break in town."

I double-checked I had everything I would need: waders, fly rod, backpack, net, and bear spray. At the gas station this morning, I bought my own bear spray at the last minute. I doubt I would need it today, but felt safer knowing I had some.

"Should I tie something different on?" I asked Adam. I still had the dry-dropper set-up from yesterday. Just because that set-up caught fish yesterday, didn't mean it would catch a thing today.

He picked up his rod and made sure his net was secure in his wading belt. "Keep it tied on for now and see if anything's interested. You can tie something else on if nothing's eating either of those flies." I trusted him, hoping yesterday's set-up would work today, too.

And with that, we walked down to the edge of the river. The grass and dirt path quickly narrowed and eventually transitioned to all rocks. Before I hiked on further, I stopped to observe the water and my surroundings. It looked like I could wade in from some spots but would have to stay on land in others. I noticed some shallow pools, deeper stretches of water, and some downed timber. Across the river, out of the corner of my eye, I saw a boil on the surface of the river. Fish must be eating off the surface.

"There's a hatch!" Adam exclaimed. My confidence soared through the roof knowing that my instincts were correct. "Start casting!" We spread out and took some casts. But no fish were surfacing by us–the only fish surfacing were on the other side of the river.

I felt a bug land on my hand. It was long, skinny, and golden. I looked down at my dark fly–it didn't match the hatch. Even though Adam told me to keep what I had tied on, I also wanted to catch fish. I sat down on shore and looked through my fly box. I found a few yellow-colored dry flies in my fly box that mimicked what was in the air, and decided I needed to make a switch. It took me a while to remove the old flies from my line and tie on the new fly, but I knew this decision gave me the best shot at catching fish. And if I was wrong, so what? I would tie on a different fly. Trial and error.

Once I knew the fly was tied on well, I was ready to keep exploring. "I'm going to hike further down," I announced. Adam nodded and continued to cast. I would've stayed in the water, but the river kept getting deeper, and I didn't want to spook fish. I hopped back on land–or rocks, I should say. With each step, I carefully tested my footing, making sure each rock was stable and wouldn't shift out of place. It was a slow hike, but a pretty one. Eventually, the rocks disappeared, and I had to wade again. The edge of the river bumped up to an embankment, and I would have to climb up some dirt and tree roots to get to land. Before I started my climb, I took a few casts from my new spot. The water was moving at a good speed all around me. It wasn't too shallow or too deep, and there were downed trees several yards on either side of me. Plenty of holding spots for hungry trout, and I hoped my fly would trick one of them.

I started casting to my right, toward the first downed tree. The fly drifted downstream with no takers. I took another cast, this one right by the downed tree. I was afraid I would cast too far and get caught on the wood, but my cast landed perfectly. Almost instantly, a fish popped out of the water and ate my dry fly. There was no need to set the hook—the trout ate *that* aggressively. Adam and Mato were too far away for me to call for help netting the fish, so this catch was all up to me. I pulled my line in by hand and reeled some in when I could to keep control of the slack. I hadn't gotten a good look at the trout to see what it was, but either way, I was excited about this catch. My heart was racing–I thought the nerves and adrenaline before a race were intense, but it didn't come close to the rush I felt trying to catch this fish. I reached for my net, tucked in the belt loop of my waders. This was one of those moments I wished I had longer arms, but I extended my left arm straight out with the net and lifted my right arm straight up with the rod, and had to bring my right arm *just* behind me to land the fish in the net. It was another healthy cutbow! I recognized the white fins and saw the distinct orange marking under its jaw.

"Yes!" I exclaimed to myself. Such an epic first solo catch! I picked out this spot, made a perfect cast, and fought in that fish. I couldn't wait to tell Adam and Mato about it! And at the end of the weekend, hopefully I could tell Joe and his daughter about it at the fly shop.

In the front pocket of my waders were some small pliers. I grabbed them to help me unhook the fish. With the pliers, the fly popped right out of the trout's mouth. I also had my phone in that pocket, so I snapped some pictures of the fish in the net before releasing it. Knowing I had probably spooked the fish in this area, I hiked up on land and get a better aerial view of the river. I was on cloud nine and couldn't wait to do that again on a new stretch of river.

As I scaled the embankment, I could tell people had made this hike before. There were some footprints in the dirt, and the positioning of the tree roots gave me spots to grab onto, or to place my feet while I climbed. I held my rod vertically, doing my best not to bop it on the tree trunks or drop it in the water. I climbed up onto land without breaking my gear or hurting myself. It was only five to ten feet above the water, but looking down, it seemed a lot further than that. To my right, Adam and Mato looked microscopic, far away and casting on the rocks.

I could see so much more in the water from up above, like shallow pockets and deeper pools. I could even see fish swimming around in shallow areas! There was a school of trout by a different downed tree I hadn't cast yet. Some of them were big, too. I estimated they were eighteen to twenty inches long. I also saw a rafting group float by. They were going slow for now, but they were about to hit a fast rapid. I hiked a little further and found an edge to hike back down to the river when I was ready. At the bottom was a large swirling pool of water, shallow on the edges and deep in the middle, with a massive rock wall looming over it. The rafting group was heading straight for it–they would be pushed out from the pool and down into some fast rapids.

It looked awesome! Maybe Adam and I could go rafting one day. But today was all about fishing.

I wanted to hike down there and take some casts. There had to be some fish in the deep parts of the pool, since I couldn't see any in the shallows. But while I was on land, I wanted to explore a little more. And I already had to pee, so this was a great opportunity to test out the pee funnel in the wild.

Behind me was a dense forest of tall trees. I didn't want to go too far; I already couldn't see Adam or Mato anymore. But the forest seemed so peaceful, and I wanted to explore it. Dead pine needles covered the ground. Grasshoppers jumped as I walked by. I heard something slither past my feet, and I saw the tail of a snake move behind a tree. Was it poisonous? How would I even know if it was or not? Were there rattlesnakes out here?

Suddenly, I felt *very* unprepared to be in the woods alone. But I had bear spray in my backpack, and there weren't people that far away.

Just as I was about to turn around and head back to the river, I heard the trees rustling, followed by big, heavy footsteps. Then, the forest became silent. I looked around to see if I could find where this person was. Hopefully it was a friendly hiker, and not a maniac mountain serial killer waiting for their next victim.

Then I saw where the footsteps came from. This large, dark object wasn't a person.

I was looking directly at a bear.

Chapter 26

A grizzly bear was standing fifty yards from me. It stared at me for what felt like hours, but we were both frozen in place for a few seconds before it took a couple of steps closer to me. I responded with a couple of very slow, cautious steps backwards. What do I do? Should I play dead? Do I scream and run? The bear spray was in my backpack, and I was afraid to make any sudden movements. While my brain scrambled for ideas, I saw a cub walk up behind the grizzly bear.

Shoot. Now I *really* was in trouble.

I couldn't stop sweating. My heart pounded out of my chest, and I couldn't control my breathing. The bear and her cub hadn't moved my way, so I took more slow steps backward. I looked out for the ledge of the embankment the best I could while keeping the bears in my line of sight. They still hadn't moved, so I thought I was okay. I took one more step back, and just when I thought I was in the clear, Momma Bear defended her territory.

She charged at me, and I turned around and ran toward the ledge. There was no time to climb, so I slid down the near ninety-degree drop to get away from the bear as fast as possible. I felt something rough scrape my arm; my butt hit a few tree roots on the way down, and I felt like I was sliding forever. I finally made it to the ground but didn't stick the landing. I stumbled, landed on my knees in the river, feeling the sharp pain in my kneecaps from landing on the rocky bottom. Somehow, I held onto my fly rod this whole time, and I didn't break it. It was a miracle! I wanted to turn around and see if the bear had caught up to me, but I also didn't know if it would jump down, pin me to the ground, and try to drown me. Dramatic, I know, but I couldn't rule anything out. I whipped around, and all I could see was the bear walking away from the upper ledge.

Whether I made the right choices didn't matter. I survived, and I wasn't severely hurt. I called that a win.

"Are you okay?" Adam was making his way toward me. I could hear the panic in his voice, even from down river.

"I think so," I shouted back. Now that it was all over, my knees were throbbing from the fall, and blood was dripping down my right arm. Worst of all, I still had to pee (and somehow, I didn't pee my pants from almost getting attacked by a bear).

"What happened? Do you need to go back to camp?"

"No!" I exclaimed. No way was I giving up a day of fishing just because I almost got attacked by a bear. I filled him in on what happened.

"That bear was pissed if it charged you," Adam explained. "Seeing any bear is scary, but running into a grizzly is the worst-case scenario. Let's go to the car and get your arm cleaned up, and then if you feel up for it, we can keep fishing."

"Of course I'll be up for it." The only reason I followed Adam back to the car was so I could pee in the outhouse near the parking area. Adam had to keep slowing down and waiting for me, because my throbbing knees slowed down my walking. Eventually, he and I made it back to the car. I didn't know Mato kept a first aid kit in the back of his car, but I was sure glad he did. When I walked past Mato, he saw my bloody arm and hurried with us back to the parking lot.

After I told Mato what happened, his eyes looked sad, like he had failed me. "I'm sorry we weren't there to protect you."

"Please don't be sorry; I had my bear spray and was ready to use it," I assured him. "I'm fine. Just a little banged up. It looks worse than it feels."

"Even your knees? It looked like you were limping."

"If I can sit for a minute, maybe that will help." I went to take off my waders, but before I did, I reached into the front pocket of my waders to grab my phone–

Crap. "Oh no," I groaned.

"What?" Adam and Mato asked.

"My phone. It was in this pocket, but now it's not there." My heart raced more than it had when the bear chased me off the ledge. My eyes widened and my stomach dropped, realizing what had happened. "I caught a nice cutbow earlier and grabbed pliers from the front pocket to unhook the fish. When I put the pliers back, I must have forgotten to zip the pocket back up. My phone probably fell out when I stumbled down the ledge." My eyes watered. I was annoyed that I lost my phone, but I was more mad at myself because I lost it over a careless mistake. If I had remembered to zip up that pocket, this wouldn't have happened.

Now I had no way to contact Mom or Grandma. They're going to think I'm dead, or that bears ate me (which almost happened), or that I got kidnapped.

"It's okay, it's just a phone," Mato assured me. "You can get a new one. Did you have your photos saved to the cloud?"

"I think so."

"Good. And your contacts are usually backed up, too. Adam and I will go look around where you fell and see if it's still over there. Grab the ice pack from the first aid kit and ice your knees while we're gone."

"Dad, I think I'll hang out here with Nat if that's cool," Adam offered.

I tried to shoo him away. "You don't have to hang out here with me."

He looked at me and said, "I want to."

"That's fine," Mato answered. "I'll be back soon."

As Mato hiked off in search of my phone, I broke up the blue liquid in the ice pack and shook it up. I placed the cold pack on my right knee first, and it immediately soothed the pain. Adam and I sat in silence while Mato searched for my phone. I was so upset about my phone that I didn't want to talk, and Adam didn't force conversation, which I appreciated. It didn't feel awkward sitting in silence, either. It felt comfortable and safe.

About fifteen minutes later, I saw Mato walking back to the car with slumped shoulders. He wasn't smiling. That told me everything I needed to know.

"Sorry, kid. It must have been swept away by the river."

"That sucks, Nat." Adam put his arm around me. "I'm sorry."

"I have some good news, though," Mato added, pulling his phone out of the front pocket of his waders. "I exchanged numbers with your parents when you all moved in. Just in case. I think this is a great example of 'just in case.'" He handed me his phone. I felt a weight lift off my shoulders—at least I could let Mom know I was alive and well.

I opened up a new message and typed Mom's name. She popped right up.

Hi Mom! It's Natalie. I'm fine, but I wanted to let you know I lost my phone. It's probably floating in the Gallatin River. I'm sorry. I'll do any chore I need to when I get home to pay for a new one. Love you.

I handed the phone back to Mato after pressing send. Mato was so thoughtful, even after all he had been through. If he was upset about the divorce, he definitely hid it well. "Thank you so much."

"Of course. How are you feeling?" Mato asked.

"My knees feel better, and so does my arm."

He responded, "Good. But how are you really feeling?"

I realized what kind of answer he was looking for. "Less upset. I mean, look at where we are. How can I be anxious and sad in a place like this?"

"Damn right," Adam said. "I'm ready to get back out there whenever you're ready."

I picked up my fly rod and put the lukewarm ice pack in the back of the Jeep. "Let's do it." A phone was replaceable, but this experience, this day with these people, was not.

·　　·　　·　　·　　·

We were supposed to take a lunch break, but lost track of time from the events of the morning. The fishing in the afternoon was phenomenal—I didn't need to tie on any new flies all day. I had rainbows and cutbows eat the nymph and the dry fly nonstop. Between the three of us, we caught fifty fish. We didn't stop until the sunset began around 8:30 p.m. As the sunlight disappeared, our hunger grew. Only a few miles from downtown Big Sky, we drove into town to pick up some pizza. Adam called in an order as soon as he got service on his phone, and he called at the right time. If he waited even a minute longer, the kitchen would've been closed.

"Everyone cool with buffalo chicken?" Adam whispered to us while he was on the phone.

"I'll eat literally anything at this point," I snapped. While I was fishing, I didn't notice how hungry I was. I was in the zone. But now, hanger had set in.

When we entered Big Sky, I once again laid eyes on the most amazing scenery. Each view I encountered on this trip was more stunning than the last. Mato turned the car down a long road that drove straight toward a lone, towering mountain. Just like many other sights I'd seen on this trip, the mountain didn't look real. A creek winded through some trees, which eventually disappeared behind luxurious apartments and townhomes.

"Do people *live* here?"

"Yeah, but probably not in these complexes. A lot of these are vacation rentals for skiing and golfing. Dad, can we drive up the mountain?" Adam asked Mato like a little kid asked to go get ice cream.

"After picking up pizza, yes." The pizza place was at the base of the mountain, in an upscale shopping center in town. There were lots of shops, restaurants, and bars. Couples, families, and groups of friends were walking around, enjoying the balmy evening air. Mato parked the car in front of the restaurant, and a few minutes later came out carrying our dinner. I was so hungry that the pizza might have been the best thing I'd seen all day. Even better than the river, the mountains, and all the trout.

Mato handed me the pizza, and I placed it next to me gently, like a newborn baby. The smell of salty cheese and spicy buffalo sauce filled the car, and the scent grew stronger when I opened the box. I handed Mato and Adam each a slice, and then I grabbed one for myself. I didn't know if I was that hungry, or if the pizza was truly that good, but that was the best pizza I'd ever had in my life.

Mato fulfilled his promise to drive us further up the mountain. Even though it was getting dark out, the occasional streetlights, porch lights, and natural light of the starry sky illuminated just how wealthy Big Sky was. We could only see homes from a distance, but each house was massive. The styles ranged from rustic cabins to sleek, modern homes, but they all looked big and expensive. I wondered if one of these was really Justin Timberlake's house, or any other celebrity's house. Probably not—those would be tucked out of view of the public eye. I couldn't even imagine what those homes looked like, or how much land they sat on.

The winding roads led to what was called Mountain Village: hotels, condos, and more restaurants and stores. The mountain looked huge here. I couldn't believe people skied down it! Maybe I would come back here and try to ski down it myself. I had only gone skiing a handful of times, but this looked like the most beautiful place to practice.

After circling the Mountain Village property, it was time to drive back to camp. I wished I had my phone just so I could take pictures of this place. Speaking of phones, I handed Mato and Adam another slice of pizza and asked, "Did my mom ever text back?"

Adam checked Mato's phone in the cup holder. "Doesn't look like it."

Weird, I thought. Mom was so insistent on updates during this trip, and now she wasn't texting me back. Maybe the message didn't go through? Maybe she was just busy with something? Or she could be mad at me about me losing my phone? I tried not to worry about it, and focused on enjoying the time I had left in Montana. Tomorrow morning, we would fish for a few hours before driving back to South Dakota.

I was exhausted by the time we got back to camp, but I had a hard time falling asleep in the RV. Why hadn't I heard from Mom yet? I grabbed my journal, transferring my racing thoughts from my mind to the page as fast as I could.

Chapter 27

Adam's alarm woke me up the next morning. My notebook was wide open on my stomach–I didn't remember what time I fell asleep, but I must have dozed off while journaling. I looked at the open pages, not remembering what I wrote in my half-conscious state. I stared at the pages, trying to piece together what I was thinking last night.

I'm having the best time, but something feels off. Losing my phone was a blessing and a curse. Part of me loves being disconnected from the outside world, not feeling the pressure to know what's going on everywhere, all the time. You don't realize how exhausting it is until it's removed from your routine. But at the same time, I have this nagging feeling something is wrong, and I have no way of knowing.

I still had that pit-in-my-stomach feeling, but I tried to shake it off. We ate breakfast outside and drove the Jeep back to yesterday's fishing spot. Everyone agreed it was too good not to go back, and it was just as productive that morning as it was the day before. I hoped a beautiful morning on the river, surrounded by mountains, would help me calm my anxious thoughts.

Mato fulfilled my promise to go back to the fly shop in Bozeman before picking up our RV and starting the trek home. Whether he did it out of guilt because I almost got mauled by a bear and I had lost my phone, or if he really wanted to go back, I was hoping this visit would include an opportunity to meet Joe's daughter.

We pulled into the parking lot at the same time as another car–a red Ford Bronco. The tires and bottom half of the car were covered in dust, probably from off-roading or driving down some deserted back road. A young woman with blonde hair, a sky blue long-sleeve, and gray pants hopped out of the car and walked into the shop. From what I could tell, she looked very similar to the picture I saw the other day. I followed her into the shop, with Mato and Adam trailing behind me.

Joe was behind the counter, and Buster was playing tug-of-war with the blonde woman. "You're back!" Joe exclaimed. "How's fishing been?"

"It's been great," I answered. I told him all about fishing the Gallatin, my bear encounter, and driving through Big Sky. "I wish we didn't have to leave already."

"I'm sure you'll be back soon. Before you go, there's someone here you should meet." The woman walked over to me, Buster following right behind her. She held out her hand. "I'm Shyloh. So nice to meet you."

I shook her hand, suddenly feeling nervous. "Nice to meet you, too. Your dad told me about the fish in some of these pictures, and I was hoping I'd get to meet you before heading home." Out of the corner of my eye, I saw Adam looking at some flies. For a second, I totally forgot about him and Mato. I introduced them to Shyloh before I forgot, not wanting to be rude.

"I hear you just started fly fishing, and you're already hooked?" Shyloh tucked a strand of wavy hair behind her ear.

"Yeah, Adam and Mato taught me. I still have a lot to learn, but I'm proud of how much I've improved already."

"It just takes practice. There's never a wasted moment on the water. You always learn something new, or see something incredible, or meet a new friend."

"Like the day you caught that brown?" I pointed to her picture hanging on the wall.

Shyloh laughed. "Thank God my best friend Amanda was there to net that fish and take that picture. But not every day is a perfect day on the water." She paused before continuing. "No matter how nice you are, no matter how talented you are or whatever, someone will always find something to criticize. You will never make everyone happy. I worked my ass off to become a trusted guide in this area. I've had to work harder than any other guide around here. All because I'm a woman. I had to build trust. I had to prove my knowledge, skills, and passion. And most people here recognize that and respect that. But not everyone. And you know what? That's okay."

I could tell Shyloh was confident and resilient, but I wondered if that was always the case. She continued, "So if you love fly fishing, don't let anyone stop you. Don't let anyone tell you that you can't do it. Or shouldn't do it. Don't get me wrong, there are certain limits to this, of course. But if you enjoy something, and it doesn't hurt you or others, don't let some negative Nancy tell you otherwise."

"My friends back home don't exactly 'get' my new hobby," I told Shyloh. "It bothers me, even though I know it shouldn't. But it still does." I don't know how this suddenly turned into a therapy session, but it felt good to talk to someone who understood what I'd been feeling this summer.

"Then they aren't your real friends." Shyloh said this matter-of-factly, as if she said the sky was blue. "Real friends accept all of you, including the parts of you that change and grow."

I asked, "Does it bother you that you don't see a lot of women on the water?"

Shyloh smiled. "Not as much as it used to. I'm seeing more girls fishing now. Most of them are with a guy or a group of guys, like you are this weekend, but that doesn't matter. It's a beautiful sport. Everyone should try it at least once in their lifetime. I think it's important to be welcoming of others in this space."

"What do you mean by that?"

Shyloh laughed. "Girl, you ask some tough questions! That's a good thing, though." Shyloh gathered her thoughts before she continued, "I think most people want to try something new. They want to take risks and be challenged. But most people end up not following through for a lot of reasons. They might be afraid to fail. They're worried about what others will think. Some might not feel accepted, because people who look like them don't do that particular thing. For example, women going fishing."

"That happened to me earlier this summer. It sucked. But if it doesn't hurt me or others, why should I care what people think?"

"Exactly. Too many people don't do what makes them happy because they're too worried about what others think." Shyloh pulled out her phone and opened her Instagram page. Her feed was filled with unbelievable fishing pictures. But what she showed me next was even more impressive. She pulled up several other female angler profiles. Some of them also fly-fished for trout, some of them fished salt water, and one of them was holding a ginormous fish. It had to have been at least three feet long.

"What kind of fish is that?"

"That's a musky. I've musky fished a few times in Wisconsin. I haven't caught one yet. It's challenging, but really fun. I can't imagine how fired up I'll be when I finally catch one."

This was the absolute worst time to not have a phone. I wanted to follow these accounts right now. Thankfully, Shyloh wrote a few of the Instagram handles for me to follow, including hers. I tucked the paper in my backpack, ready to follow all those accounts as soon as I had a phone again.

We talked a little longer, and then Mato said it was time to get on the road. "Thanks for all the advice," I said to Shyloh.

Shyloh gave me a hug. "I'm so glad I met you today. Never stop casting."

I wanted one more souvenir from this trip, so I picked out a sticker to put in my notebook. It was in the shape of a trout, with the word

"Gallatin" spelled out in the colors of a brown trout. It would look perfect on the inside cover of the journal.

It was about 1 p.m. when we finally hit the road, so with a couple of stops for food and gas, we would be home closer to 9 p.m.

The time passed slowly. I was sad, but still a little excited to be headed back to South Dakota. At least in my new home, there would still be fly fishing and beautiful places to hike. I would be even more sad if we were driving to Illinois.

How lucky I was to be in proximity to such beautiful places.

•   •   •   •   •

Mato had been checking his phone all morning, and still hadn't received a message from my mom or dad. He kept reassuring me that everything was fine and that they were just busy. I hoped he was right.

We listened to some classic rock and a few podcast episodes to pass the time. The podcast Mato picked out was about someone called 'The Feather Thief.' Some guy who was a fly-tier stole these rare feathers from a museum so he could create the most beautiful flies. The flies weren't even supposed to be used for fishing; they were made for art. Adam looked up some photos and showed me, and then we searched for pictures of crazy flies people have tied. My favorite was a fly someone made that looked like a hot dog.

The podcast made the drive go by fast, and before I knew it, I saw the welcome sign for Rapid City. We pulled into the driveway just before 9 p.m. I told Adam and Mato that I wanted to say hi to my parents first, and then I would grab my bags and help unpack the RV. I was looking forward to seeing my parents and telling them all about my trip, while hoping they wouldn't be too upset about me losing my phone. Maybe Grandma would even be here, so I could tell her all about the trip tonight, too.

I walked into the house through the garage and found Mom and Dad sitting at the kitchen table. Mom's face was red and blotchy, and Dad was holding her hand.

"Welcome home, Nat," Mom said as she wiped her eyes.

"Hi, hon." Dad forced a smile.

I set my bags down. My heart sank, and I immediately knew things weren't okay. "What's wrong?"

They both stared at me. Mom shook her head. "Something happened to Grandma while you were gone."

Chapter 28

Before I conjured up every possible catastrophe in my mind, Dad filled me in. "Saturday morning, Grandma was supposed to come over here. She was going to help Mom with some yard work, and then go grab lunch in town. She didn't show up when she said she would. After waiting fifteen minutes, your mom tried calling her, and she didn't answer."

Mom continued, wiping away more tears. "I got worried. She's always on time. So Dad and I drove over to her house to make sure she was okay." She started crying again. Dad squeezed her hand.

"There was an ambulance on the street in front of her house. When we pulled up, she was being taken out on a stretcher. The paramedic told us she had a stroke, so we followed the ambulance to the hospital." I was frozen in place, stunned by the shocking news. Mom and Dad were crying, but for some reason, I wasn't. I was in a state of shock, overwhelmed by questions and emotions.

How bad was the stroke?

Was Grandma okay?

Why didn't anyone tell me until now?

Would she make a full recovery?

I was sad for Grandma, scared about what I would hear next, and mad that I was just finding out about the stroke thirty-six hours after it happened.

"When we got to the hospital," Mom spoke quietly, "the paramedics told us that Grandma called nine-one-one. She was getting ready to drive over, but she got dizzy and felt weak. As she was on the phone with the dispatcher, the left side of her face started going numb." Mom couldn't stop crying. "The ambulance took longer than it should have to get to her house. Plus, once the paramedics got there, her doors were locked, even though they told her to unlock them."

"How is she now?" I interrupted. Mom was rambling. They could tell me all the little details later. She was putting off the inevitable.

"Grandma's still at the hospital," Dad answered. "She's doing better today, but she suffered a lot of damage from the stroke."

"What kind of damage?" These two were killing me. They were treating me like I was five, not fifteen.

"The stroke affected her speech and mobility."

This wasn't enough detail for me. "So, she can't talk or walk?"

"She can talk a little. The doctors think her speech will mostly come back. Same with her walking."

"But she'll be okay?" That was all I wanted to know.

Mom and Dad nodded. Dad said, "She won't get worse, and she isn't going to die. She just has a long road of recovery ahead of her."

"Why didn't you tell me until now?" Mom and Dad looked at each other, silently debating who would answer that question.

"We were at the hospital when I got your text from Mato's phone. We were busy talking to doctors, waiting for updates, and making sure Grandma was okay. And we didn't want to worry you while you were gone."

"But that's my grandma!" I shouted. "She could have died. I wouldn't have been able to say goodbye."

"You're right," Mom agreed. "I'm sorry. But even if you knew, she wasn't allowed any visitors until very late last night. They were running tests and trying to get her comfortable in her room. Even today, Dad and I could only visit for a bit. Doctors keep checking on her and are working on a rehabilitation plan for her."

"So, when can I see her?"

"We'll go tomorrow."

"Okay. What about my phone? You aren't mad?"

"No, honey," Mom said. "It's just a phone. It was under insurance, so one of us can take you to the store tomorrow to get a new one."

I was worried about my phone while Grandma suffered a stroke. I felt stupid for worrying about something so trivial.

"Thanks."

"So, how was your trip?" Dad finally asked.

"Fine." I stood up and walked outside to get my bags.

"Where are you going?" Mom asked.

"To get my stuff and unpack." I just wanted to be alone to process everything.

My bags were outside the RV; Adam and Mato must have put everything away already and were in their house. I grabbed my bags and dashed up the stairs to my room. I pulled my journal out of my backpack, flopped onto my bed, and started writing. My hand could barely keep up with my mind.

This is NOT fair. Grandma was perfectly healthy when I left. We were training together. She gave the best gifts. We had plans for this week.

I'm mad at Mom and Dad for not telling me right when it happened.

I'm still mad at Mom and Dad for keeping Grandma from me for so long.

I'm sad that this amazing person, who I was getting to know so well, is really sick.

I don't know why bad things happen to good people. Grandma doesn't deserve this.

I don't understand how a perfectly healthy person can have a severe stroke.

Tears splattered on the page slowly, and I couldn't stop them from falling. I closed my notebook and cried myself to sleep.

Chapter 29

Sun poured in through the windows when I woke up the next morning. I rolled over and looked at the time on my phone: 8:55 a.m.

Crap! I should be at cross country! I forgot to set an alarm! Why didn't Mom or Dad wake me up? I rushed downstairs to find Mom finishing her coffee and Dad straightening up the kitchen.

"Good morning," Mom said, as if nothing was wrong.

"I overslept!" My family didn't believe in being late for anything. Why weren't they also in a state of panic like I was?

"Relax," Dad said. "I called your coach and told them about Grandma. She understands, and she knows you'll get your workouts done this week."

"But the season starts next week!" I needed to be with my team. Every day of training counted. I already took off some days while I was in Montana–I couldn't risk any more time off now.

Mom walked over and put her hands on my shoulders. She gave them a squeeze–my shoulders were tight with tension and stress. "You can take one day off. Taking time off to rest is just as important as staying disciplined in your training."

I didn't want to admit it, but she was right. I nodded and sat down at the kitchen table. Dad brought me a plate of scrambled eggs, fruit, and toast. While I ate breakfast, I finally told Mom and Dad all about the weekend, even about the bear.

"Well, it sounds like you did everything right. I'm also glad you didn't need to use your bear spray." Mom was calmer about the bear incident than I thought she would be.

"At least you have a good story about how you lost your phone," Dad chuckled. It felt good to laugh. I didn't realize how important it was to feel happiness and joy after hearing the news about Grandma; wallowing in sadness wouldn't make the situation better. Eventually, we made a plan for the day: Dad and I would go get a new phone, and then meet Mom at the hospital to visit Grandma.

First stop: getting a new phone. I was expecting this to be a painstakingly slow process, but I had a new phone (not the newest iPhone, because Dad was cheap) less than thirty minutes after arriving at the store. Part of me was glad to be back on the grid, mostly so I could follow those Instagram accounts Shyloh shared with me.

Next stop: the hospital. My heart rate spiked as we walked inside and went up to Grandma's floor. I wasn't sure what to expect. What would she look like? Would she be awake? I felt scared, even though I had nothing to be afraid of.

"You should show Grandma pictures you took on your trip," Dad suggested. I spent the car ride to the hospital getting logged back into all my accounts and syncing my photos from the cloud. "Grandma would love to see those. Maybe hold off on telling her about the bear, though."

"You don't think she would love that story?"

Dad laughed. "She probably would, but wait until she's at least transferred to a rehab facility." As we got closer to Grandma's room, I heard Mom talking to Grandma—something about how Mom would make sure Grandma's flowers were watered and her plants wouldn't die while she was in the hospital. Grandma had a strict gardening routine, and not even a stroke could affect her watering schedule. Dad and I paused outside her door before walking in. I took a deep breath, and

Dad rubbed my back. "Remember, she's going to be so happy to see you."

My eyes teared up, and I wiped them away before entering the room. I needed to be brave for Grandma. When I walked in, she was sitting up in bed. The right side of her face could form a smile, but the left side of her face was slacked. "Hi, Nat."

Mom's jaw dropped. "Those are the first words she's said since she got here."

I walked over to Grandma's bed and held her hand. I didn't know what to say. 'Sorry that you had a stroke, that sucks' didn't seem like a good option. I went with, "How are you feeling?" Grandma nodded. I was happy she could communicate with me in different ways. She lifted her other hand and pointed to the necklace she gave me.

"I'm wearing it every day."

Mom updated us on Grandma's progress. The right side of her body hardly had any effects from the stroke, but her left side suffered significant damage. She had some nerve pain in her hand and foot, but something in her IV made her more comfortable for the time being. She had physical therapy that morning, and she would have speech therapy in the afternoon. The doctors were planning on moving her to a rehab facility tomorrow, and she would be there for a while as she recovered.

"Nat, show Grandma some of the pictures from your trip," Mom said. I pulled up the pictures I had taken before I lost my phone. Thank God iCloud back-up worked even in the remote areas of Montana. I showed Grandma the trout pictures I had taken, our campsite, the RV, and the mountains. Even though I didn't have pictures of Lone Mountain and downtown Big Sky, I described everything in as much detail as I could. I also told her about the fly shop, and Shyloh. Grandma looked at me the whole time while I was talking. She was still there, still Grandma, even though she couldn't talk and move the way she could a few short days ago.

"I remember you told me to pay attention to the stars," I said to Grandma. "I tried taking pictures, but it didn't do it justice. You were right. They were the brightest stars I've ever seen." Even though Grandma had limited mobility, I could see her trying to smile as I told her about my trip, but especially when I mentioned the stars.

We visited for an hour. Between showing Grandma pictures, telling her about my trip, Mom talking about work, and Dad talking about new grilling recipes he wanted to try, the time flew by. Her speech therapist walked in as we were leaving. She wore bright pink scrubs and looked very nice.

"You must be Diane's family," the nurse said. "I'm Annie."

"Thank you for taking such good care of my mom," Mom said.

"I'm not supposed to say this, but Diane is my favorite patient," Annie said. "She's stubborn, but in the best way. I've never had a patient so motivated in therapy."

Typical Grandma. I was happy she had great people taking care of her, and even in the hospital days after having a stroke, she was still acting like herself.

I hugged Grandma before I left.

"Love you," I whispered in her ear. "Keep working hard; we've got a 5K to run in a couple of months!" The 5K was probably adding fuel to her recovery fire.

"Love you," she mumbled to us as she left. She was a tough cookie who wouldn't let a stroke slow her down.

Chapter 30

The next morning, Mom got a call from the hospital that Grandma would be moved to a physical rehabilitation facility much closer to our house. I was relieved her recovery was going well, and she was moving to rehab so quickly. When I wasn't visiting Grandma, I continued running, preparing for the start of the cross country season next week, hanging out with my teammates, and spending as much time with Adam as I could.

Adam and I fished a stretch of Rapid Creek one Thursday afternoon. Being on the water felt therapeutic. As we cast and drifted a simple dry-dropper pattern, I filled Adam in on everything going on with Grandma.

"You know the best thing you can do for her?"

"What?"

Adam said, "Keep living your life. Keep doing the things you love. That's how she lives her life, and when she recovers, she'll get right back to doing all her favorite things. Shyloh gave you similar advice. Do what you love, because it's a gift."

I thought about the simple act of running. Of casting this fly rod. How I had taken those movements, my physical abilities, for granted. It could be taken away in an instant.

That gave me an idea.

"What are you doing tomorrow?" I asked.

"Nothing planned. Why?"

"Want to try Hidden Creek again?"

Adam thought about it for a minute. "As long as you're up for it. I know it isn't easy hiking or casting. But I think fishing will be good. The rain Monday and Tuesday brought water levels back up a bit."

"Then let's do it. We can pack lunches and make a day out of it. School starts soon anyway, so there aren't many more opportunities for fishing days like this."

"And then you can tell your grandma all about it next time you see her." We continued fishing for most of the afternoon. Adam ended up coming over for dinner, and then we hung out in the basement to put together a plan for tomorrow.

We pulled up some maps of Custer State Park and the Hidden Creek. Looking at a map helped me feel more prepared for what was in store tomorrow–no surprise hikes; I knew exactly what to expect. Adam had a spot in mind that he wanted us to hike to, which was this tall canyon wall with a cut-out right above the water. Big trout sat under the cut-out. He made the hike there once before; he showed me a picture on his phone. It looked unbelievable. I wanted to see it for myself.

"You should tie on one of those streamers you got at the fly shop in Montana," Adam suggested as he put his phone away. "Big trout love streamers."

"Good idea. I'll make sure I have one tied on before the hike."

Then Adam looked me in the eyes and said, "I should have told you this earlier, but I was impressed with how you handled Montana last weekend."

I smiled, surprised at the timing of the compliment, but happy to hear him acknowledge me stepping out of my comfort zone yet again. "What makes you say that?"

"You escaped a bear, caught some awesome fish, and didn't complain once. Montana is no joke."

"I loved being there," I said. "I can't wait to go back."

"You're officially a mountain girl." He winked at me. My heart fluttered and my cheeks were on fire.

Before the moment became more flirty than it already was, I grabbed my phone to snap us out of the moment. "You gotta see these fishing pictures Shyloh posts." I opened my Instagram account, typing in Shyloh's handle. When I clicked on her page, her feed was filled with trout pictures that she and her clients caught. Adam and I viewed her stories from today, and she was floating down a river with some clients she took out for a guide trip.

What a life!

"Let's look at the other accounts she recommended," Adam said. I typed in the next handle Shyloh recommended: Jolie Outdoors. Jolie's bio said she lived in Alaska, and her pictures showed wilderness even more rugged and untouched than in Montana. If I thought Montana was next-level, Alaska was on steroids.

"Did she kill that bear?!" Adam exclaimed. I clicked on a picture of her next to a dead bear and read the caption. Sure enough, she hunted that bear. She also hunted deer and elk. Along with trout, she had caught lots of different species of salmon.

"She seems really cool. Let's look at the next one." I typed in the next handle, and it brought me to a much different-looking feed. This woman named Trisha lived in Florida and fished in salt water. The fish she caught looked unreal. One picture showed her holding a Mahi-Mahi, and another one showed her holding a fish called a tarpon. Adam knew nothing about saltwater fishing, either. We started looking up the fish Trisha had caught and then looked up some saltwater fly fishing videos on YouTube. People took boats out to flats, fishing with giant flies to catch these fish.

"That looks so fun," I said, watching someone hook into a saltwater fish.

"Let's try that next summer," Adam said casually. I looked at him, shocked, but happy at the same time. I had known the guy for two months, and he was talking about planning a trip for next summer, and a far-away trip at that. But I also loved the idea of planning adventures for next summer with him.

The look on my face must have matched my mixed thoughts, because Adam frowned at me. "Do you not want to?"

I immediately felt bad, worried that I hurt his feelings. I had to make up for it somehow. It was my turn to be brave, so I scooted closer to him. "I think it's a great idea. I just wasn't expecting you to say any of that."

"Any of what?"

Boys. You had to spell out everything for them. "Planning next summer already, including a cross-country trip."

"We could make a big vacation out of it, and hire a guide since we know nothing about saltwater fishing. My dad would probably love it. Maybe your parents would want to try it, too."

"I like that idea. But let's plan for one thing at a time. I want to get through tomorrow before planning a fishing trip in Florida."

Adam laughed. "Sounds good." Then we spent the rest of the night watching more fishing videos on YouTube to get mentally prepared for the Hidden Creek.

Chapter 31

As I got ready for the Hidden Creek adventure Friday morning, I was more excited than nervous. I was ready to prove to Adam and myself that I could handle this treacherous hike. And no matter what happened, I would learn things along the way and make the most out of it.

When I got to Adam's house, I picked out a streamer to tie onto my fly line: a black-bodied fly with some olive-green accents and a gold bead head. Once my streamer was tied on, we loaded up the car and started our adventure.

The drive over was pretty quiet. I thought about the last time I was here—I panicked and gave up. I told myself I wasn't ready for that rugged of a hike. But was that true? Did I give up on the hike? Or did I give up on myself?

I thought about Grandma, recovering from her stroke. She was slowly gaining her speech back, and she had to learn how to walk again.

My Grandma: the sky-diving, running, gardening, daring woman that she was, could now barely walk.

I looked down at my legs: they were strong, and they were capable of so much. I looked at my arms and hands. They could cast a fly rod, they could hold fish, they could write.

I could do so much that I took for granted.

Today's adventure wasn't for me. It was for Grandma.

Adam drove through Custer State Park much faster this time. I still searched for animals and took in our surroundings, but Adam and I were on a mission today. We got to the parking area for the Hidden Creek and prepared for our hike.

Physically, I was ready. I put on my waders, packed the pee funnel, and ensured we had enough food to give us energy throughout the day. I was also in the best shape since the end of last track season, thanks to all my cross country training.

Mentally, I was working on it, but felt much more ready than last time. I needed to remember today's adventure was for Grandma.

Adam locked the car, and we headed down the trail. This was the easy part: a dusty trail, some tall grass, and the occasional sounds from insects and small animals. I was more aware of my surroundings this time, too. We had good cloud cover, which would help with fishing. I heard the water getting louder, which meant the hike was about to get more challenging.

The water was already higher in the creek than it was last time we were here; it was up to my knees, but mid-calf for Adam. Thanks to our waders, we easily waded across the creek to continue along the trail. I smiled after I stepped foot on land. I'd already made it farther than I did last time!

As the hike continued, I smelled something rancid. I knew what it could be, and the gigantic pile of poop on the trail confirmed my suspicions.

"Ugh, what animal did that?" I gasped.

Adam started laughing. "That's from a horse. Sometimes people ride horses along this trail."

"If that's from a horse, I can't imagine what bison poop looks like."

We laughed and kept hiking. So far, this voyage through the Hidden Creek felt more lighthearted and fun. After a few minutes, we reached another part of the creek, and then the trail disappeared. Adam turned back to face me. "We're going to have to wade upstream for a while. Are you ready?"

At first, I looked at him like he had three heads. But then I remembered who I was hiking for. Grandma would've been pumped for this challenge. I took a deep breath and said, "Let's do it."

The creek started shallow, no deeper than my ankles. It was like I was splashing through some puddles. But the creek got deeper, and suddenly the water was almost up to my knees. I wondered how many fish I had spooked. Casting wasn't an option because the trees were hanging so low over us. Even though I wasn't that tall, I had to duck under branches and dodge spiderwebs. We were holding our fly rods straight out in front of us, like they were nine-foot magic wands.

I wished I could cast a spell to get rid of these trees and get through this stretch of the hike.

"How does it look up ahead?" I shouted to Adam, who was several yards ahead of me. The silence only made my anxiety worse.

He turned around and saw I had fallen behind and waited for me to catch up. "It opens up soon, but the creek will get a little quicker. The rocks get slippery up ahead, too, so you'll have to be careful with your footing."

"How much longer until we get to that canyon wall?"

"It's still a ways away. There will be some spots to fish until we get there, though."

So we kept moving, one foot in front of the other. Because sometimes, that's the only thing you can control.

Eventually, the trees cleared, and I didn't have to worry about breaking my fly rods on low-hanging branches. But soon enough, the current picked up, and the search began for pockets of slower water to wade through. I followed Adam's lead, but still fell and banged my knees on a couple of rocks. As the pain subsided, I wondered if we would ever get to fish.

It was as if Adam had read my mind. "Up ahead is a good place to take some casts."

"Great!" I shouted back, a little too eagerly. I looked ahead and saw some boulders sticking up out of the creek, and slow pools of water tucked around the boulders. We waded as fast as we could to that spot and began casting.

Fishing with a streamer was different than using a worm, a dry fly, or a nymph. Streamer fishing was much more active. Once I cast the streamer, I let it drift for a bit, and then I began stripping line so the fly looked like it was moving. Adam reminded me that a streamer imitated a leech or a crayfish or a minnow, so the point was to make it look like it was live bait, or something dying or weak, so the trout had an easy meal. After a few casts and no strikes, I suddenly felt something. I set the hook, only to feel my fly get caught on something.

"Crap. I think I'm snagged."

"See if you can get it out from here before getting closer. That pool is pretty deep."

I yanked my rod to the left, and then to the right. The fly didn't budge. I took a couple of steps closer and reeled in some line and did the same thing. No luck. The water was up to my hips now. Reluctantly, I took a few more steps, and the water rose to my waist. The fly didn't want to unhook from whatever it was stuck on. All I knew was I didn't want the water to come up any higher on me; I was trying my best to fight the pressure of the water rushing past, and around me. It was becoming more challenging to keep my feet planted on the ground. What if I got swept away? What would I do?

Before I tried anything else, I glanced down at my waders. My belt was tightened, and the front pocket was zippered. There was no way I was losing my phone again, and I certainly didn't want to lose this streamer before I caught a fish with it.

I took another small step forward. The water came up a couple more inches, and I had to keep my arms lifted so they weren't submerged. I gave my fly rod one good yank, and the streamer came flying out of the water. Relieved, I worked my way back to shallow water. Since I spooked any fish that were in this area, we continued our way upstream.

The hike took us back on land, through more dense trees, and eventually into the creek again until I finally saw it. The canyon wall. It looked even more magnificent in person—probably because I was tired and hungry and had to pee, but still. We made it.

Adam and I high-fived, and then he pulled me in for a hug. I relaxed in his embrace, letting go of the tension I held in my body. I let out a breath I didn't know I was holding. All of a sudden, I started crying.

"What's wrong?" he asked.

Nothing was wrong, but a wave of emotions came crashing down out of nowhere. I was proud that I made the strenuous hike out here. I was thankful I had Adam to do it with. I was grateful for my strong body and mind to push through the tough parts. But then I was sad, thinking about Grandma, and how her physical strength was taken away so quickly. Which made me feel guilty for being out here when I could be visiting her.

"Nothing," I whimpered. I didn't want to turn this moment into a therapy session. I could journal or talk to Adam about it later, but not now.

Adam squeezed me a little tighter. "You were great on the way out here. That was the hard part. Now let's see if we can get a fish or two to cap off an already great day."

"I need to pee first." I handed Adam my fly rod, then waited until he turned around and covered his eyes before I did what I needed to do. As I was putting the funnel away in my backpack, I told him he could open his eyes. We carefully waded closer to the canyon wall to scope out the area for fishing.

There was still decent cloud coverage, thankfully, but this was where polarized sunglasses helped tremendously. I lifted them to wipe away dried water marks from my tears, and when I put them back on, I saw a dark shadow dart through the water, underneath the rock wall. There was maybe a two-foot clearance between the surface of the water and the overhang of the canyon wall. I bet there were some big trout hiding under there, and I would have to coax them to come out and eat.

"Do you want me to go first? Or do you want to?" Adam asked.

"I'll go first." I didn't hike all this way to stand around and watch Adam fish.

The water was shallow, but I only took a couple of tentative steps forward, being careful not to spook any trout. I looked behind me and saw there weren't any trees, giving me plenty of space to cast without getting caught on anything. I felt confident as we put ourselves in a position to go for some big trout.

No puny fish would go for this streamer unless they were really hungry or really stupid. I also knew my first casts would be my best opportunities. I wound up with three false casts to make sure I had enough line out, and to make sure my streamer would land exactly where I wanted it to. My eyes focused right underneath the canyon wall. If my streamer could land there before drifting downstream a bit, then I could strip line and hopefully trick a hungry trout.

After my third false cast, I let the next cast soar. I wished I was wearing a GoPro and filming this because that cast was picture perfect. I let out the right amount of line, and my streamer landed exactly where I wanted it to. When my fly drifted to where the line made a forty-five degree angle with my rod, I began stripping line. I pulled in about a foot of line, and let the streamer pause in the water for a second. When I stripped line again, I felt a powerful tug at the end of my line.

I set the hook. It was game on.

"Hell yeah!" Adam exclaimed before I could say anything. He quickly put his rod down behind him and grabbed his net. As I brought in more line and got the fish in more shallow water, I could tell it was a bigger fish. Adam scooped the net under the trout, and I could finally relax and celebrate this catch.

I took the net from Adam. "Hidden Creek brown!" I exclaimed. It was a male, based on how long and pointed its jaw was. What I loved about brown trout was how different each one looked, even though they had the same characteristics. This brown trout had seven or eight big, pink spots right above its belly, and then some slightly smaller brown spots. In the sunlight, I saw a flash of blue on its cheek. I popped the streamer out of its mouth and set my fly rod down by Adam's. He took a few pictures of me holding the trout. Next to the Montana backdrops, me holding this brown trout with the canyon wall in the background had to be one of the coolest trout pictures I'd taken. I released the fish and watched it swim back to the canyon wall, feeling overwhelmed with emotions again. I couldn't wait to tell Grandma about this fish and this day, and I was still in awe that this was my life. A few short months ago, I knew nothing about fly fishing. I didn't stray out of my comfortable bubble of friends, hobbies, or places.

I didn't know how much I had been missing out on.

I opened my arms for another hug from Adam. "Thanks for the net."

"Thanks for being such a badass."

Adam and I took a few more casts in this spot. He caught a brown that was a little smaller than mine, and then we hiked upstream a little further. The rapids picked up, and the wading got more difficult the further we went. We stumbled over rocks and navigated pockets of deep water. As the day went on, I became more comfortable wading through the water.

We reached a part of the creek that had some fast rapids and big rocks in the middle, and up ahead was another patch of medium speed water, which would be great for fishing. Adam said if we made it to that point and took some casts, we could have a snack there, then hike back and fish along the way. I agreed—I didn't know how far we had hiked, and I knew the journey back would take a decent amount of time. Adam took the lead, since this was tricky water to navigate. I watched the path he took to wade around the rapids, up over the boulders, and into the slower water. He turned to make sure I had a solid start, and then he continued wading upstream. The water looked fast, and some parts looked deep, but it wasn't anything I couldn't handle. I took a couple of steps forward, feeling my way for steady rocks to stand on. As the water got faster, it was harder to see what I was stepping on. I took another step forward and planted my right foot on a rock that felt steady when I initially put my foot on it, but suddenly, the rock moved.

And then a head popped out of the water.

It was chaos after that. I screamed and lost my balance, falling backward into the fast rapids. I let go of my fly rod when I fell and couldn't see where it went. And to top it all off, not one, but two giant snapping turtles were coming right toward me.

Chapter 32

Now is NOT the time to freeze up! I thought to myself. It wasn't the best pep talk, but I knew I had to do something, and fast. Angry, territorial animals were swimming at my face, I potentially lost or broke an expensive fly rod, and I didn't want to get totally submerged in the creek.

I took some deep breaths and thought through my escape route, one step at a time. My top priority was to get out of the water. One detail I remembered from some YouTube videos Adam and I watched is that you should never fight the rapids if you get swept away. Let the water push and pull you out instead of fighting it. So that's what I did. Luckily, the fast water pushed me into slow, shallow water. I stood up as soon as I could and got on land. The snapping turtles still had their sights on me, and eventually, they made their way to the shallows. That's when I finally got a look at how big they were. Their shells were over a foot long in diameter, like they were giant, round dinner plates with legs. Their eyes looked angry, and their mouths were wide open like they wanted to eat me. At that point, I did what any sensible human would do.

I hid behind a tree.

Yes, I hid from two turtles. And it worked! Once I was out of their line of sight, I saw them walk away, and eventually get back into the water and start swimming. Now I knew to be even more careful about what I was stepping on when wading. Relieved that my snapping turtle encounter was over, I checked my waders to see if I had lost anything. Luckily, the front pocket stayed zipped, and so did my backpack. Besides my backpack getting soaked, nothing inside got damaged. All my flies were protected. The sandwich I packed was soggy, but the rest of my food was fine. I took a sip of water, then pulled out my phone (safe in its new waterproof pouch) from my waders. My first instinct was to call Adam and let him know what happened since we got split up, but I had no service.

I put my phone back and looked around. I had to find my fly rod. Technically, it was Adam's, so I would feel horrible if anything happened to it. I didn't see it in the immediate area, so I walked downstream a bit. I didn't see it in the creek, stuck in rocks, or on land. Now I was panicking. I didn't want to go too far, because I wanted to make my way back to Adam as safely as possible. I crossed my fingers that I would find it on the hike back and braced myself for him to be mad at me. That set-up cost hundreds of dollars, and I would be pissed, too, if that was my expensive rod and reel. I don't even have a good reason for losing it. This all happened because I got scared of some turtles.

I stayed on land as long as I could before getting back in the water. I was anxious about stepping on any rocks because they could all be turtles waiting to attack me, as ridiculous as that sounded. But after watching those beady eyes glare at me, and those angry mouths gaping at me (even though their mouths looked like an old person's who forgot their dentures), I was extra careful.

"Nat!" I heard a deep voice shout faintly. "Nat!" This time, it was a little louder.

"Adam!" I called back. We were playing a real-life game of Marco Polo.

"Nat!" The voice was more distinct this time. I stayed put and finally saw Adam around the curve of the creek. I waved my arms around so he could see me and continued to call out to him. Eventually, his eyes found me, and I could tell how relieved he was. He waded back to me as fast as he could. The closer he got, the more confused he appeared.

"Um," his eyes scanned my body up and down. "Where did your hat go? Why is your hair covered in leaves, and why are you soaked?"

My hands flew to my hair, and sure enough, there were leaves and a couple of small twigs stuck in my hair. That must have happened when I was hiding from the turtles. I hoped I could find my hat on the hike back, too.

I explained what happened and Adam's jaw dropped before he burst out into laughter. "Wait, you hid from the turtles?"

"Yes!" I exclaimed. "It's not funny!"

"You have to admit, now that you're okay, it is kind of funny."

I put my hands on my hips. "Well, I'm not ready to laugh yet. Mostly because I still need to find my hat and your fly rod." I thought if I casually slipped that detail in there, Adam wouldn't be as mad.

"My fly rod is gone?" His tone sounded angry, and his eyes grew wide. I was afraid smoke would start coming out of his ears. I knew I had to calm him down to prevent the situation from getting any worse.

I tried reassuring him. "I bet we will find it."

He nodded, calming down. "You're probably right. And the most important thing is that you're safe. Let's head back and hopefully we come across it."

Adam handled that better than I thought he would. I thought he would leave me out here, stranded with the turtles. We backtracked, and I found my hat right away by the tree I hid behind. Adam enjoyed laughing again about how I hid from some turtles. He then told me about other times he'd come across snapping turtles. One time, he saw one crossing the road. He stopped to pick it up and put it on the shoulder of the road since most people would end up running it over. There was another time he was fishing, and he hooked a snapping turtle in the neck. I bet it was as angry as the turtle I stepped on. He ended up cutting the leader, and the turtle got away with one of his favorite flies.

While I was listening to Adam tell these stories, I kept scanning our surroundings for his fly rod. My eyes noticed something long and green glistening under some shallow water up ahead. Upon closer investigation, it was the fly rod!

"I wonder what other things we could find in this creek if we looked close enough," Adam said as he picked his rod out of the water. "That reminds me of another story my dad told me about when he fished in Idaho one summer." I reached out my hand, offering to carry the rod back. Adam gave me a reluctant look.

"I promise I won't drop it this time!"

"Here you go, butterfingers." I took the rod, gripping it tightly in my hand while we walked and waded toward the car. "My dad was fishing this river known for having huge trout, but they aren't easy to catch. You catch all of them on dry flies, even though you don't see the fish rising often. Anyway, one morning when my dad was fishing, he hooked into something. He assumed it was a fish, because he saw his fly go below the surface, and he felt pressure on his line." Adam paused his story while crossing another fast stretch of water.

Once we got to calmer water, he continued. "So he set the hook and started fighting in this fish. But he said it felt like he was dragging something lifeless. Eventually, he saw a long and skinny object come out of the water. He caught someone's fly rod!"

"What?! So it was floating by and your dad's fly hooked into the rod?"

"Correct. He got out of the water, unhooked the fly from the rod, and inspected it. It was engraved with someone's initials, and the plastic wrap was still on the cork handle of the rod. Dad didn't know what to do, so he set it down safely along the bank, hoping he would find the owner eventually."

"Did he ever find the owner? Or did he end up keeping the rod?"

"Not long after he caught the fly rod, my dad saw some guy running along the bank of the river, frantically looking for something. He had a hunch that the guy had lost his fly rod. So as the guy ran by, my dad asked what he was looking for. The man said he lost his fly rod. Then my dad asked the man to describe the rod to him, and his description matched the rod he found."

"I bet he was so relieved that your dad found the rod!"

"For sure. The guy, his name was Rich, was visiting from Colorado. He had recently gotten that fly rod. He was taking a picture of a fish his cousin caught, and the fly rod slipped between his legs and started floating down the river. I think my dad and Rich even exchanged numbers."

I was so engrossed in Adam's stories that when I looked up, I realized we made it back to the last stretch of trail that led to Adam's car. Just like earlier, a rush of emotions came over me: relieved, happy, proud, tired, and hungry. We hadn't eaten all day, despite packing an overabundance of snacks, so we devoured all the snacks while watching the sunset. As I polished off a bag of pretzels, I asked Adam a question.

"Any updates on the divorce?" Adam looked at me, slightly annoyed, and I felt bad for asking. "Sorry," I sputtered.

"No, it's fine," he sighed. "They're in the middle of custody, which is dumb since I have less than two years until I'm an adult. Once they get past that, then it should go quickly."

My heart dropped. Would Adam be moving? Would he have to spend days or weeks with his mom? Adam must have read my mind. "I'm not moving, don't worry. My dad wants full custody, but my mom is being difficult and wants me to spend weekends with her, even though she is still couch-hopping."

"If she doesn't have her own place yet, a judge can't allow that, right?"

"Doubt it. I think she's just dragging things out to be difficult. We can talk more about this later. Let's hit the road before it gets dark."

I was glad Adam shared that with me, but it forced us to end an eventful day on a low note. Adam hid his struggles so well; I didn't know everything that was going on. I hoped he could keep trusting me wherever our friendship took us.

Chapter 33

The start of the school year was quickly approaching. My days were crammed with cross country practices, school supply shopping, and visits with Grandma when I could. I started school on a Tuesday, so on the last full day of summer, my family and I pretended to be tourists in our own state. I was finally going to visit Mount Rushmore.

Between moving, Mom starting her new job, my schedule, and now Grandma's recovery, we hadn't been able to go out a lot as a family. Even though I'm going to be a sophomore and prefer to hang out with my friends and Adam, I do (deep down) still appreciate spending time with my parents.

We left around 8 a.m., since I had to get back in time for cross country practice at 3 p.m. Coach wanted us to adjust to afternoon practices with school starting. On our way to Mount Rushmore, Dad took the most scenic drive, going past Pactola Lake and Sheridan Lake. The mountains leading up to Mount Rushmore were beautiful–not as beautiful as the mountains I saw in Montana, but pretty close. As we got closer to Mount Rushmore, every sign had some sort of reference to this historic landmark. Clearly, this was the tourist capital of the state.

Welcome to Keystone! Home of Mount Rushmore

Stop in for a burger before going to Mount Rushmore!

Lodging less than 5 miles from Mount Rushmore!

As we entered Mount Rushmore National Park, I understood why Mom and Dad wanted to visit on a Monday morning. I saw plenty of cars in the parking lot, but there were a lot less than if we arrived later in the day, or if we visited on the weekend.

The three of us walked down the Avenue of Flags–a long path lined with all the state flags–toward Mount Rushmore. I spotted the Illinois flag, white with an eagle in the center. For so long, Illinois was all I knew. That was my home. But in only three months, South Dakota felt more like home than Illinois ever did. I admired the other forty-nine state flags billowing in the breeze, wondering where else I'd like to visit. Maybe I could even convince Mom to take a trip with me.

Then I directed my gaze toward Mount Rushmore itself. My eyes focused on Abraham Lincoln, and my mind flashed back to the overnight field trip I took in seventh grade to Springfield, Illinois. I remembered visiting Lincoln's tomb and rubbing the nose on an Abe Lincoln statue for good luck. I also remembered dinner at a local buffet, where Syd and I ate way too many pieces of pizza, followed by three bowls of soft-serve ice cream. Then we stayed up way too late in our hotel room, playing MASH and laughing until our abs hurt.

I missed what our friendship used to be.

"You alright, kiddo?" Dad asked. "You're pretty quiet."

"Yeah," I responded. "I'm just admiring the scenery. It's incredible."

Mom stood between us, wrapping her arms around Dad and me. "I'm so glad we moved here," she said.

I smiled, looking up at the hand-carved mountain. "Me too."

We took some pictures and read some signs with interesting facts about the scenery leading up to Mount Rushmore. I learned there used to be resident mountain goats on Mount Rushmore, but they ended up escaping. On the drive home, I admired the mountains and confirmed they were more breathtaking than Mount Rushmore itself. I mean, it was still an amazing landmark, and I was glad I got to see it, but I don't need to go back there anytime soon.

I made it home just in time for practice. Mom and Dad dropped me off at school, and I joined my team at the athletic entrance. Everyone was groaning about school starting tomorrow and talking about how they spent their last day of summer doing absolutely nothing.

"We went to Mount Rushmore today," I shared.

"You haven't seen it yet?" Ali asked.

"Not until today."

"And?" Becca asked.

"I mean, it was cool," I responded. "Cooler than I thought it would be, actually."

"It's just a mountain. What's cool about that?" another girl on the team, Clara, chimed in.

"That's exactly how I feel about Chicago when people go on and on about the Willis Tower and the Bean."

"I LOVED taking pictures by the Bean when I visited Chicago!" Sarah exclaimed.

"Same!" Clara added.

"And what about those fountains?! People's faces appear and it looks like they're spitting water at you," Sarah said.

"Yes! Did you go to Navy Pier?" Clara asked.

"See," I interjected, "now you get how I feel. Those places are cool to me, but so overrated since I live right there. Exactly how you all feel about Mount Rushmore."

Sarah shrugged. "Touché." Coach rounded us up for dynamic stretches and then went over the workout. As I was listening to Coach, I got an alert on my watch. It was a text from Mom.

`Grandma's rehab called. She is doing well and gets to come home soon!`

I grinned from ear to ear, but at the wrong time.

Coach June said, "What are you smiling about, Nat? I've never seen anyone so happy about hill repeats followed by a forty-minute run."

"Oh," my face dropped immediately. Talk about bad timing! "I just found out my grandma gets to come home from her rehab center."

"Yay!" Ali leaned over to hug me. The rest of the team started clapping and cheering, too. I wasn't expecting that response, but I appreciated their support and celebratory cheers.

The workout was grueling, but it flew by with thoughts of Grandma's homecoming and the startling reality of the first day of school tomorrow.

After practice was over, Ali's parents drove me back home. When I got out of the car, I smelled food on the grill—barbecue chicken, maybe? Even if Dad was grilling a piece of cardboard, I would eat it. I was starving. I went inside and saw Mom and Dad in the kitchen, and someone else sitting at the table.

"Grandma!" I exclaimed. She couldn't smile fully yet, but her smile was almost back to normal. She gave me a gentle hug. "Sorry, I'm all sweaty from my run."

"It's okay, dear," she mumbled. I ran upstairs to take a quick shower, and when I came back down, dinner was ready. I loved when that happened.

Even though Grandma was out of rehab, she wasn't completely back to her old self. Dad grilled barbecue chicken, as predicted, and made coleslaw and corn on the cob to go with it. I watched Grandma pick up her fork and knife to cut into the chicken. Since her left side was most affected by the stroke, she struggled to maintain a steady grip on her fork. Her hand was shaky as she slowly cut one tiny piece of chicken. We all watched her before digging into our food. Grandma didn't like that.

"I'm not some handicapped freak. Stop staring at me like one." She began cutting a second piece of chicken but lost her grip on the fork. The fork clattered on her plate, and she winced in frustration.

"Here, Mom, let me finish cutting your chicken for you." Mom reached over to pick up Grandma's fork and knife. Grandma swatted her away like a gnat, but Mom persisted.

"I can help, too." When I reached over to pick up her utensils, Grandma swatted at me, too. But unlike Mom, I wouldn't take it.

"Why won't you let us help you?"

Grandma exclaimed, "I don't need help! I–"

"You left rehab two hours ago," Mom interrupted. "You've recovered a lot, but you still have to keep going to physical therapy and doing your exercises." Grandma rolled her eyes. If Grandma wouldn't listen to Mom, maybe she would listen to me.

"Remember when we went for one of our first runs earlier this summer?"

Grandma glared, "Yeah, when I was a perfectly able-bodied person. Unlike now."

"You ARE still able-bodied." Mom said.

"No, I'm not."

"Will you listen for a minute?" I said, my tone sounding sharper than I intended. "You told me something that morning I haven't forgotten. You told me to embrace change because it can be good. You told me don't be afraid of being uncomfortable. I bet things have been pretty uncomfortable lately, am I right?"

Grandma nodded. She looked weak in this moment of vulnerability.

I continued, "So this is your time to be uncomfortable. To slow down. To focus on getting as much strength back as possible. And things may look a little different for now, or even in the weeks and months to come. That's okay."

Dad raised his eyebrows and asked, "When did you get so wise?"

I laughed. "I learned a thing or two from all of you. Especially you, Captain Stubborn." I looked at Grandma and she smiled.

"You're right. I just feel like my life is over because of this stroke. And I hate asking for help."

"Aren't you glad we're here, though? Only ten minutes away? Isn't it nice to have family close by to help you?" Mom asked.

Grandma replied, "I should be asking *you* that, since you moved away from me all those years ago."

Mom sighed, and it was silent for a minute before she answered. "Yes. Taking this job was the best thing I could have done. It brought us back to you, and it brought you into Natalie's life, and I shouldn't have kept that from either of you."

Mom looked Grandma in the eyes, and then me. "I'm sorry." Mom looked back at Grandma and said, "Mom, you weren't around growing up. That really hurt. It felt like you loved traveling and being away from me more than you loved me. And once we had Natalie, I didn't want her to get hurt the way I did. I didn't want her to get to know you, only for you go be gone more than you were around."

"You didn't even give me a chance," Grandma said. I could hear in her voice how hurt she was. It made me tear up.

"And that was wrong of me. Just because that was my childhood experience, didn't mean that was how you would treat your grandchildren. I love the relationship you two have, and I just hope we can all make up for lost time now."

Before I knew it, everyone was crying. Even Dad shed a tear. It was a monumental family moment–everyone had let their guard down, including Dad, who sat back and listened, instead of fighting Mom's battles and cracking jokes to ease the tension. A lot of changes this summer had been physical or geographical. This one was emotional and personal.

After getting up to hug Grandma and each other, we had to reheat our dinner because it had gotten cold. During dinner, the conversation shifted to high school, and Mom told me some funny stories about her high school years–school dances, senior pranks, and volleyball. I enjoyed hearing more of Mom's high school stories. The older I got, the more I enjoyed getting to know my mom as a person, despite how different we were when it came to certain things. I was still nervous about tomorrow, but I knew it would all be okay.

When my dad drove Grandma home, Mom and I went upstairs and made sure I was all set for tomorrow: I picked out a killer first-day outfit, I packed my cross country bag, and I put my journal from Grandma in my backpack. It's not every day you're the new kid, so I wanted to be ready to document the day.

I set an alarm on my phone before going to bed. Just as I was about to set my phone on my nightstand, I got a text from Adam.

`Too bad we have to go to school tomorrow instead of spending the day fishing`

I laughed, agreeing with Adam's text. Even though I would still be the new kid tomorrow, I didn't take it for granted that I was already surrounded by the best of friends.

Chapter 34

Even though I set my alarm for 6 a.m., I woke up at 5:30 a.m. It's impossible to sleep well the night before the first day of school.

I groggily put on the outfit I picked out, grabbed my bags, and went downstairs. The smell of bacon and egg breakfast sandwiches greeted me as I entered the kitchen. Mom and Dad were finishing their breakfast and coffee as I sat down at the table.

"Happy first day of sophomore year!" They both exclaimed.

"You're going to have to give me some of that energy for today," I yawned. "Or better yet, you can finally let me drink coffee."

"Nice try, kiddo." Dad assembled my breakfast sandwich: scrambled eggs, pepper jack cheese, bacon, drizzled with sriracha, all on an Asiago cheese bagel. Instead of coffee, I got a coffee mug full of orange juice. I scarfed down my breakfast, and Mom headed out a few minutes before Dad and I were going to leave.

"Have a great day, honey. Can't wait to hear about it later." I gave her a hug, still feeling nervous about the day. Before Dad and I left, I double-checked that I applied deodorant, confirmed there was no food stuck in my teeth, and made sure nothing looked weird about my outfit–I was doing everything in my power to get through the day unscathed. Once Dad pulled out of the driveway, I felt more and more jittery. I texted the girls to see where they would be before classes started, and then I texted Adam. Becca responded right away, saying they would be at the bottom of the main staircase. That made me feel better. I had a place to go, and people to meet. Nothing back from Adam, yet. I hadn't heard from Syd in weeks, but sent one final Hail Mary text.

First day of school here today. Hoping it doesn't suck.

"You're awfully quiet, kiddo." Dad commented as we got closer to school.

"I'm worried about how today is going to go."

"You'll have a great day. You already have friends, and I'm sure you'll meet more people who want to be your friend, too. And if today ends up sucking, you can let it out at cross country."

"True," I agreed.

We pulled up to the school, and there was a line of cars and buses pulling into the roundabout. This was the familiar part–I'd come up this way plenty of times during the summer. Everything else was a mystery. Luckily, I spotted Ali walking into the school. I hoped she would be at the bottom of the main stairs like she and the girls promised.

Dad knew better than to hug or kiss me before he dropped me off for my first day at a new school, but when I looked at him, I could tell he was getting emotional, which was rare for him. "I'm proud of you, kid. Have a great first day."

"Thanks, Dad. Love you."

"Love you, too." I got out of the car and waved as he drove away. I adjusted my backpack on my shoulders and took a deep breath. No turning back now.

·   ·   ·   ·   ·

Ali, Becca, and Sarah were at the bottom of the main staircase, as promised. I had first period English with Sarah, so she and I walked to that class together. Our English teacher, Mrs. Pine, seemed cool. She had a bunch of books scattered around the room. Our first assignment was to look around and pick out the ones that interested us the most. While many girls gravitated to *The Summer I Turned Pretty* and *One of Us Is Lying* (I had read and loved both books), I was drawn to a book with a dusty hiking boot on the cover. *Wild.* Something about the simplicity of the title and cover drew me in, and that it was a memoir. I hadn't read a lot of memoirs before and wanted to try something different. Maybe I would like it–I picked it up and brought it back to my desk. At least it was a better first day activity than two truths and a lie.

The rest of the morning flew by. Everyone was super nice, and I realized I had nothing to worry about after all. By the time lunch rolled around, I was starving. I planned to sit at lunch with Ali, Becca, and Sarah, but I wanted to see Adam during lunch, too. As I walked to the cafeteria, I pulled my phone out of my backpack. No new messages from Adam, but there were a bunch of messages in our cross country group chat. Some texts were complaints about already getting homework, and there were some messages about where we would all sit during lunch.

I looked for Adam in front of the cafeteria. There were no signs of him, but it was also hard to tell. I refused to waste my lunch looking for him, so I joined my teammates at their table. They were in the middle of a conversation about how some boys ripped a soap dispenser off the wall in one of the bathrooms this morning.

"Idiots," Becca commented. "Why do people try everything they see on TikTok?"

"Hold up, some things you see on TikTok are actually good ideas," Trish, another girl on the team, said. "Have you seen that TikTok about making grilled cheese in the air fryer? Game. Changer."

Lunch was over before we knew it, and it was on to our next class. Walking to my math class, I asked the girls if anyone had seen Adam. I thought it was weird that I hadn't seen him or heard from him all day.

"Nope," most of them answered.

"I think I saw him heading to the office earlier," Ali said.

"I'm sure I'll run into him at some point today." Once I got to math, I sent a quick text to Adam before class started. *First day going well?*

I checked my phone when I could during class; still no response from him or Syd. Now I was getting annoyed. This was a perfectly good day up until now. Adam was ghosting me, and Syd was still being a lousy friend.

The rest of the day was a blur because I couldn't stop thinking about why Adam was ignoring me. Even Coach had to tell me to chill because I was running extra hard, releasing all my frustration toward Adam during interval reps.

When Dad picked me up from practice, I was short and snippy with his questions.

"How was your day?"

"Fine."

"Are your teachers nice?"

"Yep."

When we pulled into the driveway, I saw Adam get out of his car.

"I'll meet you inside," I told Dad as I exited the car. I walked toward Adam–he couldn't ignore me all day.

"Oh, hey," he said, as if nothing was wrong. "How did today go?"

"Well, I wanted to tell you earlier, and I would've told you in person if you didn't ignore me."

"I didn't ignore you," he countered. "Cell service is poor. I didn't get your messages until now."

"I call BS. Unlock your phone."

"Huh?"

"You heard me. Unlock your phone and open your messages." He did. I looked at our text thread, and he read my last message at 11:46 a.m., right before lunch. "Great. So you ignored me, AND you lied to me." I shoved the phone back at him and stormed into the house.

"Wait! I can explain."

But I ignored Adam and went straight to my room. I opened my journal and started scribbling down my thoughts from the day. My hand couldn't keep up with my mind. Pretty soon, I had filled up three pages of writing with unfiltered thoughts about my Grandma's stroke, my lost friendship with Syd, and my frustrations toward Adam. I only stopped when my hand seized up from a cramp. I took a deep breath, suddenly feeling lighter and less angry. The first day of school was like the day Adam and I went back to the Hidden Creek. For whatever reason, it brought out a lot of emotions. Like the day I was out on the Hidden Creek, I had some decisions to make.

Moving here was supposed to be an opportunity for a new beginning. A fresh start. Instead of being mad about how others acted, I needed to focus on *my* actions. What did I want to do? What was the next right step?

On a new page, I jotted a few ideas. And I would start two of them tomorrow.

Chapter 35

The next day, before school started, I walked down to the P.E. offices before I could change my mind and back out of my grand idea.

"Hey Coach June, do you have a minute?"

Coach June looked surprised to see me. "How's it going, Nat? Sit down." She waved her hand out to the chair in front of her desk.

"I wanted to talk to you about an idea I had."

"I'm listening." I could tell she was, too. She closed her laptop, ready to listen to my crazy request. Ever since I met Coach June at the start of cross country camp, I knew she would be my favorite coach I ever had. She pushed us to see our potential, even when we struggled to see it ourselves. She challenged us to dream bigger for our own goals, and for our team. I hoped her optimistic and supportive mindset would pay off now.

"I know our first race is the week after Labor Day, and I'm not supposed to be running other races during the season," I started.

"But you want to run a road race during the season," Coach June finished my sentence. It was like she heard this request before.

"Yes, but I have a good reason. You see, my grandma and I were going to run this 5K together. But because of her stroke, she obviously can't run. She's in a wheelchair now, and I was thinking of offering to push her through the 5K."

Coach stared at me for a minute before responding. Her silence was deafening. This idea was so stupid; why did I come to her in the first place? I went from feeling brave and proud of my idea to instantly regretting everything.

Finally, she said, "I hope you've been doing a lot of push-ups." I was relieved, and thankful, that my coach trusted me enough to make this exception to her in-season racing rule. "You have about two weeks until the race, right?"

"Yeah. I'm going to suggest the idea to my grandma after practice. I didn't want to say anything to her until I knew it was okay with you."

"Normally, I wouldn't make this exception. The team's best interest is my top priority, and I don't need you getting injured or pushing yourself too much too soon. But family always comes first, and it will be a phenomenal workout. Let me know if there's anything I or the team can do to help."

"Will do. Thanks, Coach."

"You bet. Glad to have you on the team, kid."

With that confidence boost under my belt, I was on Cloud Nine the rest of the day. I couldn't wait to visit Grandma that evening. Mom, Dad, and I were picking up Chinese and bringing dinner to her house after practice, and that's when I would ask her about the new 5K plan.

At practice that afternoon, I told some girls on the team what I was planning to do during the Labor Day race.

"That's amazing!" Ali said.

"It won't be easy, but if anyone can do it, it's you," Sarah said.

"Can we come watch?" Becca asked.

"If you want," I said. "If you're going to be around, it could be fun. Maybe I'll suggest that to the whole team."

"You should!" Becca agreed. "We could make posters and be your cheering squad. Let's talk to Coach after practice." I loved how encouraging this team was. It reminded me what true friendship was all about: wanting the best for each other and supporting each other's goals.

The team ran the idea by Coach after practice, and she was in favor of it, too. Coach told us she would email the team that evening, so people had time to plan. Becca said she would coordinate poster-making.

"Wait until I ask Grandma tonight! She could still say no."

Ali side-eyed me. "Have you met your grandma? She's going to say yes." Becca and Sarah nodded in agreement.

They weren't wrong. "Okay. Can you wait to send the email out until tomorrow though, just in case?"

"Sure thing," Coach June said.

Sarah's mom was going to drive me home after practice, but as I walked with Sarah toward her mom's red F150, I saw another familiar car in the parking lot. Adam was leaning against the side of his car, and he waved me over. I still needed to know why he ignored me and then lied to my face yesterday, but I was in no mood for it then.

I tried to ignore Adam, but he couldn't take a hint. He walked toward Sarah and me.

"Hey, can we talk? I'll give you a ride home."

I looked at Sarah, who responded for me. "She doesn't want to talk to you now."

Even though that was true, and I appreciated her being mad at Adam for my sake, I needed to be the bigger person here. "I'll ride home with him. I'll text you later."

Sarah glared at Adam before she got in her mom's truck. Adam and I walked back to his car in silence, and no one spoke until we pulled out of the parking lot.

"Look, I shouldn't have lied to you the other day. I got your text at school, but just when I was about to reply, some of the baseball guys came over to talk to me. I literally just forgot to text you back."

"Then why did you lie?"

Adam didn't respond immediately, and I hoped he wasn't crafting another lie. He finally said, "I don't have a good reason at all. I was flustered when I saw you."

"Why?" None of this was making any sense.

"Do you know how much more I talk about my feelings since I've met you?" Adam laughed. "It's weird. Anyway, some guys I used to play baseball with asked me about coming back to play fall ball with them."

"Do you want to?"

"I thought about it. So when I got home, I brought it up to my dad, and he got pissed."

"Why? Does he not want you playing baseball?"

"No, he doesn't want to pay for it. I guess the divorce is draining my dad's bank account, and he's stressing out. And then I felt bad for adding to his stress, so I stepped outside to give him some space, and that's when I saw you."

My heart sank, realizing I had caught him at a bad time yesterday. Now I felt bad for getting mad at him. "I'm sorry."

Note to self: you never fully know what someone is going through.

"You have nothing to apologize for. I'm sorry I took my shit out on you." He let out a deep breath, visibly relieved to get that secret off his chest.

"So your dad's that stressed?"

"Yeah." Adam said, eyes focused on the road. "He isn't talking about it a lot, but yesterday showed me how much he's keeping from me. I won't ask about baseball again, and just make up some excuse to the guys about not playing this fall." Adam pulled into my driveway. "So are we cool?"

"Yeah, we're cool."

"Want to hang out later?"

"I'm actually going to my grandma's house for dinner, but does tomorrow work?"

"Sure does." Adam smiled.

I smiled back and got out of the car. "I'll text you later."

"And I'll respond this time!"

•   •   •   •   •

I told my parents about my 5K idea on the way over to Grandma's. Surprisingly, they were both on board. Mom didn't ask me a million logistical, anxiety-ridden questions, and Dad even offered to do push-ups with me each night. We pulled up to Grandma's house, Chinese food in hand, and found Grandma relaxing on the couch. A rare sight indeed! She grabbed her walker, pulled herself up, and shuffled toward the kitchen.

"Smells delicious! I'm starving!" Grandma's speech was still slurred, but it was good to see her returning to her old self. Dad put our takeout in the middle of the dining room table, and we dug into the egg rolls, Kung Pao chicken, and Mongolian beef. Grandma could scoop her own servings of chicken and rice without our help. I was so proud of her and couldn't believe the progress she had made since her stroke.

"Grandma, I have an idea I want to run by you." Grandma looked at me, waiting to hear what I had to say. "You know how we were supposed to run that 5K about two weeks from now?" She nodded, and her eyes looked sad.

Dad chimed in. "You'll love Natalie's idea. It's brilliant!"

I looked at Grandma and said, "What if I run the 5K while pushing you in a wheelchair during the race?"

I thought Grandma was going to choke. She coughed, then sipped her water through her straw. "I refuse to be seen out in public like that!"

"Like what?" I was confused–I thought she would like this idea.

Grandma answered so quietly I could barely hear her. "Like a weak, old woman."

My mom sighed. "Mom, you are not weak at all. You're the strongest person I know."

"Exactly," I agreed. "I asked my coach about it and told my teammates. They all think it's a great idea."

Grandma gave me an angry look. "I can't believe you told your team I can't run."

"Well, it's the truth," I said. "It's nothing for you to be embarrassed about."

She stared at me, not wanting to accept my words. If she could be stubborn, so could I. Finally, she said, "I'll ask my doctor about those running wheelchairs. I'll make sure they get my insurance to cover it. You really think you can push me for three point one miles?"

"I'm going to try. It won't be the easiest race I've ever run. But it would be a lot worse if you weren't running it with me."

That was the clincher. Grandma attempted a smile, and even the left side of her face started showing expression again. "If you all think it's a good idea, and your team does too, then why not? I'm not gonna start being a quitter now."

"Cheers to that." Everyone raised their glasses. Even Grandma could lift hers for a quick cheers. I did ten push-ups right after dinner and another twenty before bed that night, and my arms already felt like Jello. It was going to take way more than hundreds of push-ups to get me through this 5K. I hoped I wasn't in over my head.

Chapter 36

The weekend before the 5K, Ali, Sarah, and Becca came over after practice to hang out. I texted Adam to join us after dinner. We were chilling in the backyard when he came over, preparing to start a bonfire.

"Nat, did you see Shyloh's newest post?" Adam pulled out his phone and showed us. On Shyloh's Instagram page, her newest post was a reel of her catching some monster brown trout on a picturesque river.

My jaw dropped. I was simultaneously happy for her and envious of her life. "Not until now, but that looks amazing! Did she say where she is?"

"The caption said she's in Montana, but not specifically where. This spot looks insane; there's no way she would reveal her exact location. Then it would be ruined."

My friends were looking at us, clearly intrigued by the conversation. "Are you gonna show us this picture or what?" Sarah asked.

I waved them over. "This is the girl I met in Montana this summer." We all watched the reel a couple more times, and then Ali gasped.

"I just had the BEST idea. Nat, you should totally post your own outdoor content. Maybe even make a YouTube channel!"

Sarah agreed. "You and Adam are always exploring, and lots of other girls our age would love to see that!"

"What if," Becca wondered, "you started with your big 5K next weekend?"

"Like, make a video of me running the 5K with my grandma?"

"Yes!" the group exclaimed. Now, everyone was talking over one another about content ideas and which platforms I should be on.

"Hold up, this sounds like *a lot* of work." I needed to process this idea. Did I really want to post more of my life online? Was my life *that* interesting for people to follow and pay attention to? Did I have a message worth sharing?

But it could be fun. I already enjoyed taking lots of pictures. It wouldn't be that difficult to put together videos of the beautiful places I've explored. Even if no one cared about my page, I would have all those memories documented to look back on for years to come.

Maybe it was worth a shot.

We spent the rest of the night brainstorming names for my account. We started with Natalie in Nature, but then were torn between two names: SoDak Nat, and Ryba Outdoors. I liked how both names were short and catchy. The only thing I didn't like was that Ryba Outdoors used my last name. The internet could be a weird, creepy place, and I didn't want any psycho internet stalkers knowing more about me than they needed to.

In the middle of our heated debate, Mom came outside with some marshmallows and roasting sticks. "What are you all chatting about?"

"Natalie is going to start an outdoor social media channel!" Becca exclaimed.

"You're going to *what?*" The shrill tone in her voice foreshadowed at least a dozen more questions to follow. I calmly filled her in, showed her Shyloh's page, explained how my adventures could empower people to get outdoors, and promised not to post anything that could compromise my safety and privacy.

And with that, I created an Instagram and YouTube channel for SoDak Nat (with Mom having access to both accounts, of course).

Chapter 37

My English class started the year with a novel-in-verse of our choice. My teacher wanted us to begin the year with a book we wouldn't hate, and something easy to get us reading again, since she assumed most of us didn't read over the summer. For the record, I read four books this summer, thank you very much.

The novel-in-verse I chose was *The Canyon's Edge,* by Dusti Bowling. Even though I didn't relate to some specifics of the story (no spoilers, but the main character Nora has been through A LOT), I could relate to her in other ways. Nora and I both had to deal with things in our family. We both love the outdoors. We both persevered through unfortunate situations to realize how capable we were.

And most importantly, through transformative experiences (I knew moving across the country wasn't the same as being stranded in a slot canyon), we've come out stronger and more self-assured than ever before.

While I should've been spending more time reading and not waiting until the last minute to get my homework done, my new priority was creating fun content for my SoDak Nat pages. As I posted my first few pictures and stories to my new Instagram, I couldn't deny the confidence boost of getting some positive comments on my feed. It started with my teammates, but then I noticed comments from people outside of South Dakota.

`Sick catch!`

`My dad fly fishes, but maybe I'll go with him next time. This looks fun!`

Shyloh commented, `You're an inspiration. Tight lines!` How cool was that?

But not all the comments were supportive. During lunch one day, I received a notification that someone commented on my most recent picture. It was a profile I recognized.

`@syd_sparkles: who are you trying to fool? Fishing is stupid. Get a life. No girl wants to do this.`

The cafeteria was buzzing with noise, but my world suddenly went silent. Someone who was one of my best friends became not just a stranger overnight, but also a bully. I quickly deleted the comment and texted her.

`What was that comment about?`

I watched the three dots appear under my message, and a few seconds later, they disappeared. No response. Syd had no problem posting a nasty comment on my page, but didn't have the courage to speak to me about it.

Some friend she was.

"Nat, are you okay?" Sarah broke my trance. "You've been quiet and on your phone for a while."

I wanted to respond with "I'm fine," but that would make me feel worse. So I told my friends what happened.

"What the hell? Who does she think she is?" Ali asked.

"What's her problem?" Becca said.

"She's jealous," Sarah commented. "You're out here living your best life and inspiring others, and she doesn't like that. Real friends will cheer you on, not knock you down."

That made me feel a lot better. I won't lie; it still hurt that my former best friend was now a bully and a coward. But I looked around the table at my teammates. Girls that supported me, encouraged me, and challenged me to be my best self. Of all the things I gained from this move, new (and better) friends were at the top of that list.

Although I felt reassured by my new friendships, I couldn't let Syd's comment go. When I got home from cross country that evening, I went up to my room to Facetime Syd. This wasn't a texting conversation, or even a phone conversation. I didn't want to hide behind a screen like she did.

After a few rings, she answered. Syd was in her room, a familiar spot I knew so well. "Nat?" Syd sounded shocked that I called, which was understandable.

"Hey," I said. "We need to talk."

Syd rolled her eyes. "No 'It's so good to see you!' or 'How's it going?'" Her body language was irritating, but made me feel better about what I needed to say.

"I saw your comment on my post. It really hurt me, because I'm sad that we've drifted apart. I missed you a lot when I moved out here, and I really tried to share parts of my new life with you." Syd didn't respond. She stared at the fuzzy blankets on her bed, avoiding eye contact, waiting for me to continue. "When you stopped responding to my messages, I just kind of gave up."

"It's like I don't know you anymore," Syd said. "You're basically dating this guy I know nothing about, you have a new team, and now you fly-fish? You've never cared about fishing."

"You're hanging out with Kennedy now," I started, realizing how defensive I sounded. I took a deep breath, remembering the reason I called her in the first place. "First, I'm not dating that guy. We're just friends. And it's okay that we have different friends and hobbies. But your comment was mean. That sucked, Syd. I didn't think you were like that."

Syd shook her head. "I thought we could make our friendship work long-distance, but you've completely changed. I miss the old Nat."

I thought back to my life in Illinois. There was nothing wrong with the old Natalie, but I really liked the new Natalie better.

"And that's fine," I said. "But I don't. I love my life here, which surprised me as much as it's surprised you. But change can be a good thing. I'm sorry you can't support that."

Syd looked away from the phone, like her attention was elsewhere and not on our crumbling friendship. "K, good luck with your fishing and stuff." Then she hung up. I tossed my phone on my bed and sighed. That brief conversation was surprisingly exhausting. I'm bummed Syd didn't apologize for her hurtful comments, but it also confirmed that she's not a true friend. Ali, Sarah, and Becca would never talk to me the way Syd just did. And even though Adam had made his fair share of mistakes, he could apologize and own up when he was wrong.

That call wasn't the closure I wanted, but it was the closure I needed. Now I could really focus on the people and things that mattered.

Chapter 38

The Tuesday before our 5K, I still had not practiced running with Grandma in her running wheelchair because she hadn't received it yet from her doctor. After cross country, my parents and I drove over to Grandma's for dinner and some wheelchair running practice. I had worked my way up to at least fifty push-ups a day: ten in the morning, thirty at practice, and ten before bed. Physically, I felt prepared. But mentally, could I do it?

I was surprised to see Grandma sitting in her wheelchair on the sidewalk in front of her house. She didn't look happy to be in a wheelchair, but she didn't look embarrassed about it either, like she was at dinner a couple of weeks ago. We were making progress.

As soon as I stepped out of the car, Grandma shouted, "Let's get this over with! I'm getting hungry." Mom and Dad went inside to prepare dinner, and I jogged over to Grandma. Today was an easy run day at practice, but I had a tough hill workout yesterday. My legs were still sore, so I was worried about how our jog would go.

"Alright, we're going to run for one mile today," I explained. "There's a loop around your neighborhood that's just about that distance. I'll run as much of it as I can without stopping for breaks."

"And you better not let me fall out of this thing. Or hit any bumps or cracks."

"I won't let you fall out," I promised. "But I can't guarantee no bumps or cracks. Just hold on tight!" I set my Garmin on running mode. I needed to get an idea of how fast I could run while pushing a wheelchair with a person in it. Even though I would never say it out loud, I was worried how much this would slow me down. I was used to running fast. But now, speed wasn't the primary goal.

As soon as I started running and pushing, I realized how challenging this was going to be. Typically, I had more movement in my arms. They helped me maintain my pace when I got tired. Now, pushing this wheelchair, that's taken away from me. I also had to think about something I hadn't considered yet: turns. Normally, I could hug a tight curve when I turned in a race or during a regular jog. As I approached our first left turn, I had to think about when to turn Grandma's chair and how easy it would be to do so. Luckily, turning the chair and keeping the pace consistent wasn't hard.

"How are you feeling?" I checked in with Grandma. She turned her head to look at me with a wide grin on her face.

"This is so fun! Can you go any faster?"

"I'm trying!" I glanced down at my watch. We had barely gone a tenth of a mile, and my pace was not impressive at all. Still, I kept going, one foot in front of the other. Pretty soon, another unforeseen obstacle appeared: a hill. What if I couldn't get Grandma up the hill? What if I got tired and lost my grip, and she rolled backward down the hill and crashed? There was no way I could let that happen.

I stopped thinking of worst-case scenarios and focused on my usual techniques as I approached the hill: I lifted my knees more with each stride and focused my eyes on the top of the hill. Any other time, my arms would pump back and forth, but now my priority was to keep us moving forward. Grandma seemed nervous, too. This was the first time I noticed her grab onto the arms of her wheelchair since I started running. I controlled my breathing and got to the top of the hill as soon as I could. Once we made it to the top, I steadied my jog and kept going.

My lungs felt like they were going to burst. My legs turned into Jello *and* lead simultaneously. Honestly, I didn't know how I would get through another three quarters of a mile.

And then a race this weekend that was a little over three miles. What was I thinking?

"You're doing great dear—oh! Watch out for cracks!" Grandma steadied herself as the wheelchair bumped over a crack in the pavement. I nodded, even though Grandma couldn't see me, but I was too winded to respond. I concentrated on getting this done as soon as possible.

Time moved in slow motion, and I zoned out as much as I could. I shifted my thoughts between my breathing, looking up and not down at the wheelchair, and not letting my form get sloppy. I remembered that first run with Grandma months ago, and how she just kept pushing herself, even at the end of the workout. Once she put her mind to something, she refused to quit.

It only made sense to take on the same mindset.

Suddenly, I felt like I was pushing a feather, not a wheelchair. My stride felt natural, and we were cruising along the neighborhood streets. There was another small incline, which felt like nothing compared to the first hill. The setting sun greeted us as I turned us down the homestretch and finished the one-mile loop in front of Grandma's house. My watch beeped once it hit the mile mark, and I brought Grandma's wheelchair to a stop in the garage. I looked down at my watch—11:05. That was nowhere near my personal best mile time, but I did it all without stopping.

Grandma stood up and shuffled over to her walker. "Not bad, sweetheart. Think you're ready for three point one miles this weekend?"

"I hope so!" If I said it enough times, I might start believing I would be ready. "Hey, can you sit back down in your wheelchair for a minute?"

"Why?"

"I want to take a selfie for my Instagram. We gotta let people know we're getting ready for the big race this weekend! My teammates are coming, and one of them is going to help put together a YouTube video of the race."

Grandma stared at me, not responding for a while. Then, she asked, "Why?"

I explained how I started an Instagram page and YouTube channel to show how anyone can get outside and try new things, and that our race would be a great example of that. Grandma cheered at that comment–she was all for female empowerment. She agreed to a few pictures of us training with the wheelchair before heading in for dinner.

I posted a selfie of Grandma and me on Instagram (with Mom's approval of the picture and caption. Hopefully she'll stop doing this on *every* post). I was nervous about what others would think. This wasn't a fly fishing post, or my typical outdoors post, so would people be supportive? Would people even care?

Luckily, the support came flooding in, with dozens of likes and comments in a matter of minutes. And the best part was, there were NO negative comments! So many people thought it was cool that we were running the 5K together, and that I was pushing Grandma the whole time.

So many people believed in me. My team believed in me. My family believed in me. I just needed to believe in myself.

Chapter 39

Friday afternoon couldn't get here soon enough. All I could think about was the long weekend. I had the 5K on Saturday, and on Monday, Adam and I were going fly fishing before having a barbecue with our families. The school day dragged on, but thanks to a short practice, I was home by 4:30 p.m. When I got home, I found a long, wrapped tube on the kitchen table.

"What's this?" I asked as I dropped my bags on the floor.

"Just a little something," Dad smirked as he walked in behind me. Mom was in the kitchen getting dinner ready.

"Go ahead and open it. There's a card, too." I removed the card from the envelope, and on the front of it was a picture of me holding the first trout I ever caught. Inside was a note from my parents:

Dear Natalie,

We don't tell you enough, but we are so proud of the person you are becoming. Moving across the country was no easy feat, but you have handled it so well. You are making wonderful friends, and we love that you are so close to your grandma by choice. We are sorry for not giving you the opportunity to know her sooner, and thank you for helping us rebuild our relationship with her. We love our little family here in South Dakota.

Even though your birthday isn't until next month, we figured you would want this gift now. Actually, we wish we could've given you this sooner, but at least you can use it for some fall fishing.

Love, Mom and Dad

I had a good idea about what the gift was, but I ripped off the wrapping paper as fast as I could to confirm my suspicions. Sure enough, I now had a fly rod of my own. Inside the gun-metal gray case were the four pieces of the rod. I took them out and carefully pieced them together to assemble my dark green four-weight fly rod. I also got an electric blue reel. It was the coolest rod and reel combo I'd ever seen.

"Well?" Mom asked.

I was so excited and shocked that I forgot to say thank you! I hugged my parents and thanked them before I forgot again.

"Adam gave us some recommendations. We're clearly not fly fishing experts," Dad said.

"You did great. This is perfect. I can't wait to try it out this weekend."

I brought my assembled rod into the backyard to take some practice casts. After a few casts, I heard a familiar voice ask, "How do you like the new rod?" I looked toward the fence, and Adam's head popped over it.

"It's perfect! I heard you helped my parents pick it out. That was really nice of you to do."

"To be honest, I'm getting sick of you borrowing all of my stuff," he teased.

"I'm still going to borrow flies from you until I get more of my own," I said as Adam hopped the fence. While I continued to practice my casting, we talked about our plan for Monday: hit a few stretches of Rapid Creek to maximize fishing time before our Labor Day barbecue. We had a few spots in mind and were talking about flies to use when Mom called me in for dinner.

Adam gave me a hug before he left. "Good luck at the 5K tomorrow. I can't wait to watch you crush it." The hug and his words helped me believe I could do this.

I didn't stay up too late that night. After dinner, I got out my clothes for the morning, did some stretches, and journaled before going to bed.

I can't fall asleep, even though I know a good night's sleep is what I need to run my best race tomorrow, especially for Grandma. There's so many things that could go wrong. Oh my God, I just had the most horrific vision: what if a wheel fell off Grandma's wheelchair mid-race? What if—

A realization struck me like a bolt of lightning. Before I finished that sentence, I put my pen down. Why do I think about all the things that could go wrong, when I should think about everything that could go right?

My grandma was alive, and we could still run this race together, even if it wasn't exactly like the original plan. All my favorite people would be at the race, cheering me on. I would be able to make a YouTube video out of the whole experience. And it would be one of the more beautiful races I'd ever run, because let's face it: the Black Hills were a little more scenic than the flat, industrial Illinois suburbs. I drifted to sleep as I visualized Grandma and I crossing the finish line, with my family and friends cheering us on.

•　　　•　　　•　　　•　　　•

The next morning, my alarm woke me up at 5:45 a.m. The race started at 8 a.m. After quickly changing and eating breakfast, my parents and I went and picked up Grandma. In true Grandma fashion, she was ready to go. She wore her Labor Day weekend best: a blue t-shirt, red leggings, and aviator sunglasses. She was standing with her walker; her running wheelchair was folded up and ready to put in the car.

I looked down at my white tank top and black spandex shorts. Note to self: buy cooler running clothes.

"Beautiful morning, isn't it!" Grandma said as we helped her get in the car. Once Dad put Grandma's wheelchair in the trunk, we drove to the course. The 5K course went around Rapid City. Although it wasn't somewhere scenic, like closer to Mount Rushmore or through Spearfish Canyon, this 5K would be a fun way to see a little more of my new town. But I probably wouldn't be focused on sightseeing. I was here to run as fast as I could while pushing Grandma in her wheelchair.

Some runners were already here and warming up by the time we pulled into the parking area for the 5K. People were stretching and jogging, pinning on their bibs, and lining up at the port-a-potties. Up until now, I didn't have the pre-race jitters. But once I saw the start line and the people I'd be racing against, I felt very jittery.

Grandma didn't want to get into her wheelchair until right before the race started, but Dad made sure it was correctly assembled and working. The last thing we needed was a wheelchair malfunction in the middle of the race. While Dad worked on the wheelchair, Grandma and I pinned on our bibs. About thirty minutes out from the start of the race, I did a shake-out jog. I wanted to get warmed up before pushing the wheelchair around, and I needed to get out some of my excess energy.

Coach June taught us this week about trying a grounding trick when we felt nervous or anxious, not just in cross country, but any time. With my mind so uncentered, I thought this would be the perfect time to try this new technique.

I looked for five things I could see: other runners, the start line, a blue Subaru Outback, Mom taking pictures of Grandma, and my watch.

Then, four things I could touch: my watch, the nearby port-a-potty door (but I REALLY didn't want to touch that), the trunk of a tree, and the concrete sidewalk under my feet.

Then, three things I could hear: people talking, birds chirping, and cars turning into the parking lot.

Then, two things I could smell: the crisp, clean air, and the sugary donuts waiting for us at the finish line.

And when I finished my shake-out run, I took a sip of orange Gatorade, which was the one thing I could taste.

It worked! I was calm, back in the present, and ready to run our race. Grandma got in her wheelchair, and I jogged over to the start line with her. Many people looked at us, and I don't blame them. We were a sight to see. Grandma's racing wheelchair was as compact as it could be, but it still took up plenty of room. I accidentally bumped into someone's foot and received a mean glare from that person. Luckily, we came across more kind people than critical ones, and someone offered for us to start at the very front of the race. I kindly declined, knowing that I wouldn't be running that fast. It was easier for us to start toward the back, instead of slowing everyone down from the beginning.

I looked down at my watch: 7:55 a.m. Five minutes until the start of the race. Grandma reached up and grabbed my sweaty hand–even though we hadn't started running yet, I already broke a sweat from the adrenaline and nerves. People were lined up along the streets, ready to cheer us all on. I hadn't seen my teammates yet, or Adam. I knew Mom and Dad would try to see us at one or two spots on the course before watching the finish, but I didn't know where they would be.

"You've prepared so well for this day," Grandma reassured me. "Go run your race and don't forget to have fun. And definitely don't forget about the donuts at the end."

"Thanks for still running this race with me, even though it wasn't like you originally planned," I said.

"It's one of my favorite adventures so far."

"Runners, the race will begin in one minute," a voice boomed over a megaphone. The chatter of the crowd quickly died down, anticipating the sound of the gun and the thousands of feet about to pound the pavement. Grandma gripped the arms of her wheelchair, yet still looked as relaxed as that day we cruised through the park. I steadied my gaze toward the start line, ready to leave it all on the course.

"Runners, take your marks…"

A few seconds later, I heard the pop of the starter's pistol, and we were off.

Chapter 40

I started my watch once we crossed the start line, which was about thirty seconds after the gun went off. I often have a time goal when I run, but today was all about effort and having fun.

I heard lots of cheers, cowbells, and clapping in the first minutes of the race. As I picked up speed, I heard someone yell, "Go Natalie! Go Grandma Diane!" I scanned the crowd and found Mom, Dad, my teammates, and Coach June. Sarah was filming the start of the race. I grinned but didn't wave–there was no way could I push this wheelchair one-handed yet! Grandma waved both of her hands and started cheering as we passed by our fan club.

After the first third of a mile or so, the pack thinned out. Everyone was finding their pace, including us. I felt strong, and Grandma's wheelchair was cruising right along. Maybe it was the adrenaline, or maybe it was all the push-ups, but everything felt effortless so far.

The first challenge was almost half a mile into the race: our first hill. It was a steady incline, and I could tell it slowed people down. After a fast start, now everyone was running an honest race.

"No hill is too big for us!" Grandma exclaimed. Easy for her to say; she wasn't the one running up it. But I appreciated having a personal cheerleader. I visualized the hills we practiced leading up to this moment. If I made it up those hills, I could make it up this one, no problem. I brought my attention to my breathing: inhale through my nose, exhale through my mouth. I lifted my knees and charged up the hill. Even while pushing Grandma, we passed people going up the hill.

Once we crested the top, the one-mile marker was in sight. What I liked about this race was how there was a clock at the one and two-mile markers, so runners could keep track of their pace.

"Go Natalie!"

"You're doing amazing!"

"Looking strong!"

I scanned the crowd as we approached the mile marker. Sarah was there with the camera, and someone else I hadn't seen until now–Adam. Mato also came with to cheer us on. I couldn't believe how many people were here to support Grandma and me.

"Don't slow down, Nat! Keep up the pace!" Sarah's feedback snapped me back to reality, right when we crossed the one-mile mark. 9:08. Not impressive on a normal day, but it was the fastest mile I had run while pushing someone in a wheelchair.

Now I wanted to see how much faster I could go. After the mile mark, there was a short downhill stretch, which was great for gaining speed. We turned into an older neighborhood in Rapid City, and this stretch was pretty flat. This part of the course was furthest away from the start and finish line, so not too many spectators were out here cheering us on. It was nice to run part of the race in a more quiet and less chaotic stretch, but that only made the voices in my head grow louder.

There's no way you can keep this pace for two more miles.

You should slow down.

You're not as strong as you think.

You're crazy for even thinking you could do this.

As the thoughts crept in, my legs felt heavier, and so did Grandma's wheelchair. Funny how your mind affects your body so quickly.

"Don't slow down, Nat. You're doing great," Grandma encouraged.

"I'm getting tired," I panted.

"You're over halfway done. Remember the donuts at the end. Your mind is your most powerful muscle. Think positive thoughts."

I forgot about the donuts at the end of the race, so I'm glad Grandma reminded me. I also thought about some words of wisdom Coach June shared the other day at practice: when you're feeling tired, that's when it's time to dig deep. You have more to give than you ever thought possible. Don't sell yourself short.

With a shift in mindset (and my new goal to get to the donuts ASAP), I picked it back up. I felt like I was exaggerating my running form, but that's what it took to bring my pace back up, and even faster than before. We turned out of the neighborhood and ran past the two-mile marker: 17:21. I definitely shaved time off that second mile, even as tired as I felt. There were 1.1 miles left in the race, and it was time to leave it all on the course.

As I was thinking about leaving it all out on the course, somebody was doing just that. A runner was puking on the side of the road. I felt bad for that person, but couldn't afford to stop and check on them. Hopefully they would be able to finish, but I had to stay focused on my race. I saw Mom and Dad again, cheering us on.

"How are you feeling?" Mom called out. I needed to remind her (again) to not ask me questions during any of my races.

"Great!" I lied. I knew I would feel great when we crossed the finish line, but right now, this sucked.

"Amazing!" Grandma exclaimed. "Natalie is doing amazing!"

Those were the words that jinxed us. At that moment, my left shoe came untied, even though both my shoes were double knotted, and I confirmed they were double knotted, right before the race started. I could feel my shoe getting looser and looser, and heard the aglets of my laces slap the concrete with each step. I couldn't stop to tie my shoe, and I couldn't let Grandma roll away while I re-tied my shoes. And I didn't want to stop her wheelchair since our pace was picking up, and only getting faster.

"Um, Grandma," I said.

"Yes?"

"My shoe's untied."

"Want to stop and tie it?"

"Not really."

"Try to run with it untied as long as you can, and then do what you need to do."

She made it sound so simple. I did exactly what she said. We made it less than a quarter of a mile before my untied shoe became too annoying. I had to decide: run a slower time because I stopped to tie my shoe? Lose my shoe and keep our momentum going? Or deal with it until we finished the race? I knew this race wasn't about running a certain time, but if I stopped to tie my shoe, I was afraid of losing our speed and momentum.

Screw it. I saw my teammates again, cheering us through this part of the race. "Someone grab my shoe!" I yelled as I kicked off my left shoe. Every step on my right foot felt springy, and every step on my left foot felt like I was being stabbed by hundreds of miniscule pebbles. It took everything in me to ignore the discomfort and keep my stride as natural as possible.

"You sure you're okay?" Grandma asked. I appreciated her concern, but also didn't want to think about my situation. I needed to keep a one-track mind to finish this race with negative splits.

"Yep." Back to the basics. I focused on my breathing. I focused on steering the wheelchair and weaving it around finishers as we were less than a half mile from the finish line. As we got closer to the end of the race, the pack became more crowded again. I didn't want anyone slowing us down.

"On your left!" Or, "On your right!" I would call out. The person in front of us would turn around, look shocked to see a wheelchair barreling toward them, and jump out of the way.

I wished I could use this trick during cross country season! So many people got out of our way–they just moved to the side while maintaining their pace.

I glanced down at my watch to see what my time and pace were. My watch said I had run 2.8 miles, I was 23:20 into the race, and my current pace was eight minutes per mile.

Woah! We were flying compared to earlier! And as much as everything hurt in this moment, I felt like I could give even more. I found another gear in me and ran even faster.

One foot in front of the other.

Inhale, exhale.

Tired? Run even harder.

Pretty soon, we were in the final stretches of the race. Hundreds of people lined the course near the finish line, taking pictures and cheering on the runners. I saw our entire cheer squad filming, rooting for us, and waiting to celebrate our achievement.

"Almost there, Nat!" Grandma encouraged me. "Last tenth of a mile!" I sprinted as hard as I could. If I wasn't holding onto a wheelchair, I might have collapsed right then and there. My lungs were burning, my legs were as heavy as lead, and my foot was throbbing from running barefoot for almost a mile. But I was so close, and I couldn't give up now.

"Let's go, Nat! Almost there!"

"Donuts at the finish line!"

"You're running a great pace!"

As the finish line grew closer, so did the clock. I shaved off a bunch of time the second half of the race, even after losing a shoe. Grandma and I crossed the finish line at 25:37. I was immediately disappointed by the time. But my foggy brain remembered we crossed the start line late, so I looked down at my watch and saw 25:07. Knowing my time was closer to twenty-five minutes even, I was more content with the results. A good time is a bonus. The most important thing was Grandma and I still raced this 5K together, even if it didn't happen as originally planned.

I hobbled over toward my family and friends. Thankfully, Adam met us and took Grandma's wheelchair for me. I was so used to pushing it for over three miles; it felt weird not having to push anything.

Adam said, "You crushed it, Nat! A bunch of us got pictures and videos. You're going to love them."

"Amazing job, Nat!" Dad said, giving me a hug.

Mom walked over with donuts for Grandma and me. "I'm so proud of you."

I had never been so happy to see a donut. I was thirsty, but I was even more hungry. Even though it wasn't the most healthy post-race meal, I definitely earned it. The sugary, glazed donut melted in my mouth and I barely thought about the taste as I scarfed it down, focused only on satisfying my hunger.

Grandma stood up from her wheelchair as Mom unfolded her walker. "That was amazing," Grandma said. "I had a blast, and I'm glad we did this." I nodded in response, since I was still chewing the donut. As Grandma gave me a hug, tears welled up in my eyes. Grandma pulled away after a couple of tears fell on her shoulder.

"What's wrong?" she asked.

Pretty soon, I couldn't contain my emotions. More tears streamed down my face, but I also started laughing and smiling. My family and friends probably thought I was crazy.

"I can't believe I just did that. I ran over three miles, pushing my grandma in a wheelchair. Four months ago, this isn't even an idea I would've had."

"I barely knew you four months ago," Grandma reminded us.

"Four months ago," Adam chimed in, "I didn't know you either. And you didn't know how to fly-fish."

"You barely knew South Dakota was a state four months ago," Dad joked.

"You've grown so much in such a short amount of time," Mom said.

"And we all have the best new friend and teammate," Ali added.

Looking back at the past four months, I left everything I knew (or thought I knew) in Illinois, moved across the country where I knew no one, finally got to know my grandma, met Adam, learned how to fly fish, consistently pushed myself out of my comfort zone, and finally learned what I love, who I am, and the person I wanted to be. I gained so much more than I lost.

I thought about the old Natalie: following along with the crowd, doing what others want me to do, not always thinking for myself, and scared to take risks.

I didn't recognize that girl anymore. Like, at all.

I looked at all these people who were here for me today, who supported me no matter what, and who challenged me to be the best version of myself. People who were confident in who they were, knew what they wanted, and went after it.

"Thank you," I said to everyone. Those two simple words summed up how I was feeling. Thankful for the unexpected move, friendships, and discoveries that gave me the best summer ever.

Chapter 41

Even though everything was still sore Monday morning, Adam and I needed to take advantage of our day off to go fishing. My cross country races started next weekend, and Adam got a part-time job at the local fly shop.

We headed out a little after 6 a.m., for a full morning of fishing, since the afternoon would be spent at my house with our family and friends for a Labor Day cookout. Illinois Natalie wouldn't wake up before 8 a.m. on a day from school, but now, I would get up at any hour to spend time on the water. I also couldn't wait to test out my new fly rod on Rapid Creek. Adam and I went back to where it all started; the exact same spot where I caught my first rainbow a few months ago. We also packed Go Pros to film more fishing content for my social media pages.

Once we got to our fishing spot, we tied on the flies we wanted to throw, put the Go Pros on our hats, and scoped out the water. The sun was still rising, but the overcast skies would definitely help the bite. Fish were rising to eat, and I was excited about the potential for a dry fly bite. I slowly walked upriver, staying on land, still scouting the water. I found a stretch of the creek with a deeper pool near a downed tree. A perfect hiding spot for trout. Adam wasn't too far away, fishing some faster rapids. I knew if I needed him, I could holler. But I also wanted to see how much I could do on my own.

I had a dry-dropper rig tied up. I applied flotant to the dry fly and double-checked that my knots were secured. Now that I was using my rod, I took more pride in my casts and wanted to prevent careless mistakes.

I threw the perfect first cast on my new rod, and I felt like I was in the movie *A River Runs Through It.* The only things missing were the Montana mountains, and Brad Pitt. I watched my flies land naturally in the water, with no bunched up line and leader. The flies drifted downstream with no eaters, so I took another cast. Still no interest. I decided a longer cast could help, with more drift time downstream. I took a couple of false casts to make sure my aim was spot-on, and I had enough line out to cover the distance. On the third time around, I let the line go, and my cast landed right where I wanted it to. There had to be a hungry trout here that wanted to eat one of these flies!

Sure enough, I watched the dry fly go under the surface. I set the hook, and it was game on. I watched the rod bend as I started fighting in this fish. Right away, it tried to dart away from me. After catching many fish this summer, I knew by now that I needed to be patient. I couldn't always force the fish in my direction without risking a break-off, so I let out a little line while still keeping plenty of tension.

After the trout took a power run, it paused for a moment. I took this chance to reel in some line. I still hadn't had a good look at the fish. Since it hadn't gone airborne at all yet, it made me think this might be a brown trout. I pulled and reeled in more line and made sure I had access to my net. I was still on land, so I stepped into the creek to make netting the fish a little easier. Then I grabbed my net from my belt loop. This would be a challenging fish to land solo, but I knew it could be done. I couldn't lose my first fish on my new rod, and I felt the pressure to not mess this up. I knew what I had to do; it was just a matter of executing each step perfectly.

I could see the dark shadow of the fish in the water beginning to tire out from its fight. I lifted my right arm as high as I could, so I could pull the fish in using the strength from my rod. With the net in my left hand, I scooped up a beautiful brown trout. It wasn't a giant by any means, but I estimated it was around fourteen or fifteen inches.

"You caught one?" Adam walked my way.

"Yep. A nice brown." Then my stomach dropped. "Do I have the hat cam on?"

When Adam's smile faded, that said it all. I sighed, disappointed and frustrated that I didn't film my first fish on my new rod.

"Don't worry about it. That won't be the last one you catch today." He high-fived me. Sometimes, I still wondered what the future of our friendship looked like. Honestly, I was happy with how things were now. We've flirted and tested the waters and were there for each other through big family changes. Even though Adam could annoy the crap out of me, I don't know where I would be today if I hadn't met him at the beginning of summer.

"Can we get a picture before I let him go? Especially since I forgot to film that entire catch?"

"You bet." I unhooked the trout and admired its beauty before lifting it out of the net. I didn't think I would ever get tired of looking at trout. Each one has its own unique markings and coloring, and it didn't hurt that they lived in the most beautiful waters in the world.

"Ready when you are," Adam said. I wet my hands and lifted the trout out of the net. This one was photogenic–he didn't squirm at all for the pictures. "These don't need to be edited or anything. Perfect lighting!"

I didn't want to keep the trout out of the water much longer. As soon as he was in the water, he took off. "Let's catch some more!" Before taking another cast, I turned on my hat cam, making sure I didn't forget to capture another moment.

•　　•　　•　　•　　•

The first couple of hours were full of action. Fish ate the dry flies and the nymphs. It was a feeding frenzy! By 10 a.m., the fishing slowed down. We stayed out for another hour before calling it a day and driving back.

After organizing our gear and taking a quick shower, it was time for our Labor Day barbecue. I could already smell all the food Dad was grilling: corn, brats and hot dogs, burgers, and chicken. It was the last of Dad's favorite holidays: Memorial Day, Fourth of July, and Labor Day. All summer holidays, and all involving grilled food.

I made my first plate of food as people arrived. Grandma, Adam, and Mato were already in the backyard with Mom and Dad. Ali, Becca, Sarah, and a few other teammates arrived shortly after. Two of Adam's friends from the fly shop, Brandon and Derek, joined us, too.

"Can I have everyone's attention?" Sarah announced as people finished making their plates. I was already on seconds–fishing made me hungry today!

"As many of you know," Sarah began, "Our girl Natalie completed a 5K this weekend. But not just any ordinary 5K. She was supposed to run this race with her grandma. Natalie's grandma suffered a stroke earlier this summer and has made an amazing recovery." Everyone clapped for Grandma. She smiled and waved, like she just won a big award.

"Unfortunately, that meant they couldn't run the race together like they had planned. But Natalie made sure they could still participate in this race together and ran a 5K while pushing her grandma in a wheelchair."

"You may also know," Becca stood up next to Sarah, "that Natalie has started an Instagram page to promote fly fishing and the outdoors, especially for girls our age. The next step is to start a YouTube channel, so we took the liberty to create your first video for your page."

I knew a bunch of people were filming parts of the race this weekend, but I couldn't believe they already had the video edited and ready to go.

"If you could all come inside, let's watch Natalie's highlight video from the Labor Day 5K!" Everyone piled into the family room. The video was already cued up and ready to play on our big-screen TV.

The opening clip showed me warming up before the race and helping Grandma get situated in her wheelchair. Becca and Sarah filmed an intro at the start line, explaining to viewers what I was doing and why. Then, the camera panned to us on the start line. I looked focused, and quite frankly, pretty badass. I wouldn't mess with me!

Then the gun went off, and we were on our way. This is when I finally waved at everyone while crossing the start line. The rest of the video included everyone cheering, several shots of me running throughout the race, and even the moment I kicked off my shoe. The other best part of the video was the music. It was the perfect soundtrack made up of instrumental versions of songs by AC/DC, Queen, The Rolling Stones, Billie Eilish, and Taylor Swift.

It's like Adam read my mind. "I helped with the music," he announced proudly to the group.

The video ended with us crossing the finish line. I was sprinting; I looked tired, and my ponytail was frizzy and falling out. Note to self: figure out a better hair situation for cross country races. But I stopped picking apart the little details and appreciated what my friends did for me. Once the video was over, everyone cheered and clapped.

"That was so cool. Thank you for putting that together!" How lucky was I that I had such supportive, encouraging friends who genuinely wanted me to succeed? I thought I knew what true friendship was like, but what I had with Syd wasn't that. Looking around the room at Adam, Becca, Sarah, and Ali, *that* was what real friendship looked like.

"If this doesn't inspire people, I don't know what will," Mom said, drying her eyes.

"Is the video public on YouTube yet?" I asked.

"Not yet," Becca answered. "We wanted you to see it first."

I was relieved the video wasn't public yet. I didn't know how people would respond. Would they be supportive? Would they somehow find mean things to say about running a race with my grandma?

But just like everything else this summer, I had to take a risk and believe in myself to learn how much I was capable of, and to discover what truly makes me happy. And putting this positive, inspiring video into the world and sharing mine and Grandma's story was absolutely worth the risk.

"Can I hit publish?" Grandma asked. "I'm not as good with this technology stuff as you kids are, but I think I can handle this!"

"Of course," I said. Grandma went over to Sarah's computer and pushed the publish button. Our story was officially on YouTube for everyone to see, and my YouTube channel officially had its first video.

As scary as it was, I also felt a sense of peace. The same peace I feel when I'm fly fishing, or running, or spending time with people who care about me and believe in me.

This summer was a journey to find myself, and I did—in South Dakota, of all places. South Dakota didn't just have a mountain with some dead guys' heads on it. South Dakota was the place where I finally felt like me.

Epilogue

Late September

I held my phone up, making sure I had the perfect view of the creek and fall foliage without giving my location away. When I could tell our background wouldn't reveal our spot, I pressed the record button.

"What's up? SoDak Nat here, enjoying an incredible day on the water with Adam." Adam wrapped his arm around my shoulder and smiled, revealing his charming left dimple.

"We're crushing it out here, with five trout each within the first hour of fishing! Couldn't ask for a better start to the fall fishing season," Adam said.

"Stay tuned for a vlog on my YouTube channel of today's adventure, and tips on how to fish with streamers," I added before signing off with the signature close to all my videos. "Tight lines, and remember, life is best lived outside of your comfort zone."

I pressed the record button again and quickly posted the video to my Instagram stories."You're such a pro now," Adam said. "It's like you've been doing this your whole life."

I laughed, knowing that couldn't be further from the truth. "Fake it 'till you make it, right?" Walking back to the edge of the creek, I double-checked that the black streamer bait with flecks of blue metallic thread was still tied on well. I glanced toward Adam, watching him take casts around a downed tree. There was a strong probability of big trout hanging out in that spot. I pulled out my phone and took a picture of him mid-cast. Action shots received a lot of engagement on my

Instagram page. Right after I took that picture, Adam's rod doubled over.

"Big fish," he said. I ran toward him, net in one hand, phone in the other.

Sure enough, Adam was hooked up with a chunky brown trout. I could see the olive-green streamer out of the corner of the trout's mouth, and its buttery brown tail splashing out of the water during the fight.

"Take your time," I said, my heart racing like I was catching the fish myself. The adrenaline rush of fly fishing never got old. I filmed the fight while waiting for the perfect opportunity to net the fish. I could hear Adam's ragged breath. It was a delicate dance between wanting to net the fish as soon as possible and trying not to rush the fight with the risk of losing the fish. Just then, the fish stopped splashing around. This was our chance. Adam pulled the fish toward me, and I scooped the net under the trout. Touchdown!

"Yes!" we both hollered.

"That has to be at least an eighteen-incher," Adam estimated. "Is the hat cam rolling?" When I confirmed it was, he fist-pumped the air. The trout measured eighteen inches on-the-dot. I took a few pictures of Adam holding the brown trout, keeping our location discreet. A true angler never revealed her fishing spots.

"Video release," Adam said. When I was ready, I pressed record on my phone and nodded at Adam. "Adam here with SoDak Nat. Just landed this beautiful brown trout thanks to Natalie's help with the net. Don't be afraid to cast around downed timber. That's where the big fish like to hide. Gonna let this guy get bigger." As Adam lowered the trout back into the water, it splashed and swam directly toward the downed tree. "Time to catch some more!" He said before I stopped filming.

"I can't wait to edit this later. Are you able to come by and help?" I asked.

"You bet," Adam said.

While I had service, I sent pictures of Adam's brown trout to my parents, my grandma, and my cross country group chat. Without fail, my grandma was the first to reply.

That's quite a catch! Both the fish and Adam Grandma sent with a winky face emoji.

I laughed, shook my head, and put my phone in the front pocket of my waders.

If you told me not even six months ago that I would have a social media platform for fly fishing, I would've laughed in your face. I would have also laughed if you told me that my grandma would be one of my best friends, and that the cute boy-next-door wasn't just a cliché in the movies. Life has been a wild adventure since moving to South Dakota, and I can't wait to see where the next adventure takes me.

Acknowledgements

First, I thank God for the answered prayer of becoming a published novelist. It is an honor to share this story with you, the reader.

Since I was in elementary school, I knew I wanted to be an author, but had no idea where to even begin. After frantic Google searches trying to figure out how to learn about writing and publishing a novel, I found The Book Incubator. Thank you, Mary Adkins, for believing in my potential. I would not be the writer or person I am today without your support and guidance. Thank you to the members of The Book Incubator team who encouraged me and believed in me when I didn't believe in myself, especially Harrison Gale, Liz Pickart, and Ashley Strosnider. And to all the current members and alumni of The Book Incubator, I learn so much from you and am inspired by you every day. Writers are the most kind and supportive people out there, and I have the best of the best in my corner!

To my early readers: Gayle Brown, Jen Eberle, Kristine Kramer, and Liz Pickart. Your love for reading, your insights, and your thoughtful attention to detail made this story so much better. Asking for feedback is terrifying, and I thank you for being so gracious and honest with your feedback.

To Reagan Rothe and the team at Black Rose Writing: thank you for believing in this story, and for believing in me. I couldn't ask for a better partner to bring this book into the world!

When I started drafting *Rapid City Summer,* I was (and still am) dead-set on filling a void in the market. We need more books to fill the gap between middle grade and young adult. Not every middle schooler wants to read younger middle grade stories, and not every young teen is ready for more mature young adult stories, and that's okay. I wrote this book with my 7th grade students in mind. To my students, both past and current, thank you for making Ms. Spy's classroom the best place to be. Thank you for asking tough questions, doing (most of) your work, and having fun along the way.

To my colleagues: teaching is a wild, wild world right now. I don't know what I would do without seeing your faces each day. To my LZMSS family, especially Noreen, Maggie, Heather, Jenn, and Sara-thank you for all the jokes, the cookies, and your endless support.

To my mom: I am in awe of you and all you've done for me, our family, and your students. You instilled in me the importance of hard work and respecting others. Most importantly, you've taught me to never give up and always believe in myself. You're the best mom a kid could get!

Finally, to Mike: this book literally wouldn't exist if we never met. We learned to fly fish together years ago (which is truly a miracle, considering my fishing skills were nonexistent when we first met), and it's taken us to some of the most beautiful places in the country where we've created the best memories. Thank you for showing me that life is best lived outside your comfort zone. I love you and can't wait for a lifetime of adventures together.

About the Author

Connie Richardson's debut novel was influenced by her own love of fly fishing and her favorite locations out west. She teaches middle school English and language arts and coaches cross country in the Chicago suburbs. Connie has published articles, short stories, and blog posts for the National Council of Teachers of English (NCTE) and Scribbler, and she is a writing mentor in Mary Adkin's MFA-alternate program, The Book Incubator. When she is not teaching, writing, or fly fishing, she enjoys running and cooking, trying out new recipes for her family and friends.

Note from Connie Richardson

Word-of-mouth is crucial for any author to succeed. If you enjoyed *Rapid City Summer*, please leave a review online—anywhere you are able. Even if it's just a sentence or two. It would make all the difference and would be very much appreciated.

Thanks!
Connie Richardson

www.ingramcontent.com/pod-product-compliance
Lightning Source LLC
Chambersburg PA
CBHW030819210726
48290CB00002B/659